"I need your help, Ray."

"You name it."

"I want you to take my boys and keep them safe," Jodie said.

His eyebrows shot up. "I'll fight a madman for you, two if necessary…but take care of year-old little boys…? I'm not the man for that." He stepped backward, a hand up as if to ward off blows.

"This time you don't get a choice, Ray."

"But the boys need *you*. And they need their father, not some stranger they've never seen before this week. No matter what happened between you and their father, you have to let him know his sons are in danger."

"I agree," she said, her voice dead level now that she'd made up her mind to do what she had to in order to keep her boys safe. "The boys' father does deserve to know the truth. That's why I just told him."

ABOUT THE AUTHOR

Joanna Wayne lives with her husband just a few miles from steamy, exciting New Orleans, but her home is the perfect writer's hideaway. A lazy bayou, complete with graceful herons, colorful wood ducks and an occasional alligator, winds just below her back garden. When not creating tales of spine-tingling suspense and heartwarming romance, she enjoys reading, golfing or playing with her grandchildren, and, of course, researching and plotting out her next novel. Taking the heroine and hero from danger to enduring love and happy-ever-after is all in a day's work for her, and who could complain about a day like that?

Books by Joanna Wayne

HARLEQUIN INTRIGUE
288—DEEP IN THE BAYOU
339—BEHIND THE MASK
389—EXTREME HEAT
444—FAMILY TIES

Don't miss any of our special offers. Write to us at the following address for information on our newest releases.

Harlequin Reader Service
U.S.: 3010 Walden Ave., P.O. Box 1325, Buffalo, NY 14269
Canadian: P.O. Box 609, Fort Erie, Ont. L2A 5X3

Jodie's
Little Secrets
Joanna Wayne

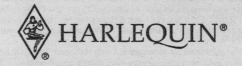

TORONTO • NEW YORK • LONDON
AMSTERDAM • PARIS • SYDNEY • HAMBURG
STOCKHOLM • ATHENS • TOKYO • MILAN • MADRID
PRAGUE • WARSAW • BUDAPEST • AUCKLAND

With special thanks to my wonderful editor whose encouragement and insight help me make each book special, and to my hardworking agent who keeps me on task. And to Wayne, always.

ISBN 0-373-22471-0

JODIE'S LITTLE SECRETS

Copyright © 1998 by Jo Ann Vest

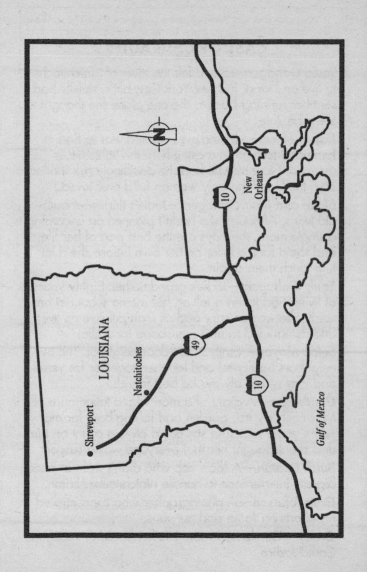

CAST OF CHARACTERS

Jodie Gahagen—She'd left the town of Natchitoches to live and work in New York City, but a stalker had sent her running back to the one place she thought she'd be safe.

Ray Kostner—All he'd ever wanted was to find fame and fortune in a city where the lights never dimmed. Now that he had, he'd willingly risk it all to save the life of the only woman he'd ever loved.

Blake and Blair Gahagen—Jodie's thirteen-month-old twins. Although she hadn't planned on becoming a single mom, the boys are the best part of her life, and she'd face a killer on her own before she'd let him touch them again.

Emily Gahagen—Jodie's grandmother. Eighty years of living had taken a toll on her memory but not her spirit. She was as spry and as manipulative as ever and determined to find a husband for Jodie.

Selda Mayan—Emily's next-door neighbor. The two neighbors had cried and laughed together for years and they would always be best friends.

Gentle Ben—A giant of a man who'd taken care of Miss Emily's yard, garden and fishing boat for many years. Jodie was sure she could always count on him until events taught her that everyone was a suspect.

Butch Deaton—A local cop who didn't want or need big-city interference to handle Natchitoches crime.

Greg Johnson—A photographer who concentrated his efforts on Jodie and her sons.

Grady—Gentle Ben's son. His father didn't trust him. Could Jodie?

Prologue

There was no mistaking the signs. Jodie Gahagen had run away from him.

Hands trembling, the man reached down and picked up a pillow from her bed. He hugged it to his chest, burying his nose in the folds of cotton and goose down. The smell of her hit him in the gut, heightening his anger.

He dropped to his knees and rested his head on the pale pink sheets, sucking in the intoxicating fragrance. Two nights ago, the thought of Jodie Gahagen had woke him in the middle of the night. So strong, he hadn't been able to fight his need for her. He'd crawled from his bed and driven through the night to come to her.

Luckily, he'd found her that night, here in her bed. Alone. Her cotton gown had skimmed her flesh, waves of red hair spilling over her pillow, haloing her beautiful face and fanning her creamy shoulders.

The images crawled through his brain, like a video in slow motion. He knotted his hands in the bedsheet. That night he had watched while she slept, her breasts rising and falling, maybe against this very sheet. He could have taken her then, but he was a gentleman. He could wait until she wanted him the way he wanted her.

The only sign he had left of his presence was the note, carefully tucked inside the crib of one of the twins. A reminder that he had been there again and that he would return.

After all, he was in love with Jodie Gahagen. She would love him, too, once she got to know him, the way she had loved the others.

And there had been others. So many men. No. The memories were running together. His mother, his unfaithful wife, the waitress who'd flirted and then laughed in his face when he'd asked her for a date. They had used men. They were not ladies, not sweet and honest the way Jodie was.

Familiar feelings washed over him, clawing at his insides, burning in his chest. Later, he would be strong enough to fight them into submission. Then his brain could take over, his cunning, logical brain that let him outsmart everyone, especially the stupid New York City cops. But for now, he pressed his head deeper in the pillow and longed for the day Jodie would be his.

A few minutes later he slipped out the door and into the darkness, a faceless blur in the maddening masses that was Manhattan.

Chapter One

Jodie Gahagen completed her hamstring stretches as the first sounds of a southern morning began their wake-up chorus. A bird's call, the splash as a turtle slipped from the bank into the Cane River. The sound of her own feet as they crunched into a pile of dry leaves. She and her sons had invaded a world that had been isolated from human contact.

Her nerves grew shaky at the thought. She'd never expected to be the only jogger on the trail this morning. But she shouldn't be surprised. After all, it was also six o'clock on Sunday morning, and the majority of the town's inhabitants were still snuggled in their beds.

Jodie yawned widely at the thought and stretched to touch her toes. Obviously, the sleepers hadn't been blessed with the dual alarm system she possessed. At thirteen months, her twin dynamos showed neither religious nor humane considerations for Sunday as a day of rest.

She tugged at her shorts and walked to the front of the stroller to check on them. Blair offered a smile, but Blake just stared at her over the plump thumb that was stuck in his mouth. "Are you early birds ready to roll?" she asked, brushing a wisp of red hair from Blair's forehead and dabbing at a spot of drool that dribbled down Blake's cute little chin.

Blair cooed a response and waved his hand like a frustrated traffic cop.

"Then let's get this show on the road," she said, giving the safety buckles of the double jogging stroller a final check. Movement behind her jerked her to attention and she spun around. A gray kitten stared up at her.

"A cat, just a cat," she whispered, steadying her breath and reaching down to run long fingers through his thick coat. Nothing to worry about, not here in the haven of hometown familiarity. Natchitoches, Louisiana, was a world away from New York.

Squaring her shoulders, she wrapped her hands around the handle of the stroller and started off at a brisk pace. In seconds, the world seemed to slide into order. The morning exercise ritual rejuvenated her, got her blood pumping and forced her mind into gear. The boys liked it, too, although the exercise for them consisted of swinging their pudgy arms and craning their necks to see any and every bit of action along the river route.

Trees, birds, tail-wagging dogs. They liked everything about their new hometown. Why not? Their unemployed mom was now home all day instead of only for rushed breakfasts in the morning and hurried dinners, baths and hugs at night. Besides, on the rare occasions she strayed from sight now, they had a doting great-grandmother jumping to supply their every want or need.

She was glad for this time with Grams. That was the one good thing that had come from the bizarre web that entangled her. Still, running away from trouble was not her style. If she'd had only herself to think about, she would have never given up, not as long as she'd had a heartbeat. But the night the lunatic had laid his murdering hands on her sons, the stakes had soared.

Now she and her boys were safe, but the man who'd turned her life into a house of horrors still walked the streets of New York City, and sooner or later his sick games would entrap another innocent victim.

An icy tremor shivered along her nerve endings, and she reined in her thoughts. Forcing body over mind, she picked up her pace, concentrating on the gentle strain to her muscles, the surge of pulse and power. The first mile rolled past, and the sun climbed over the tops of the brick storefronts, layering the town in heat and humidity.

A drop of perspiration slid down her forehead, and she whisked it away with her wristband. It was already November, but you'd never know it by the temperature. The weather was one of the fickle charms of north Louisiana.

Summer lingered into fall, then shocked the system with frigid cold fronts that swooped down from the northwest and plunged the temperature into the teens in a matter of hours. But until the icy winds blew in, she was going to enjoy exercising in the great outdoors.

A pickup truck rattled by on the street that wound up the hill from the river, and the driver honked and waved. Jodie waved back. She didn't recognize the man or the vehicle, but he undoubtedly knew who she was. *Miss Emily's granddaughter, visiting from the big city. The girl was married finally, with adorable twins. She was visiting for quite a long spell, too, already heading into the fourth week. And without her husband. Jodie Gahagen was the talk of the town.*

Fortunately, the hometown folks relied on speculation and their own imaginations to fill in the details. Jodie intended to keep it that way. Secrets secured the foundation of her new life, erected the barriers that kept her and her sons safe. As if in agreement, Blair waved his hand and giggled.

"You got it, tiger. Mommy won't let anything or anybody get to her boys."

Her boys. Hers and hers alone. The familiar tightness

settled in her chest. Hers alone because she'd never told their father they existed. Until a few months ago, she'd been sure she'd made the right decision. Now she only prayed she had.

She rounded a curve, and her breath quickened. A man stood a good fifty yards ahead of them, half hidden in the shadows and overhang of a weeping willow. His shoulders were stooped, and an old jacket was pulled tight around him in spite of the rising temperature. Jodie's hand slid to the whistle in her pocket.

Head high, she gulped in huge helpings of air. This was exactly the kind of crazy, senseless fear she was forced to fight. But there was no reason for her heart to race here, in the middle of Natchitoches.

Still, she had jogged far enough for one morning. She slowed, steering the stroller into a 180 degree turn. Safely headed in the opposite direction, she twisted her head and stole a glance behind her. The man had disappeared.

Her feet flew now, eager to return to the homey warmth of Grams's house. Grams's world was timeless, slow and safe. Tall, white columns greeted you there, like protecting sentinels, ushering you into a world of cushioned couches, lacy curtains and dark, rich woods.

Grams and her unchanging world had sheltered and comforted Jodie when she had lost both her parents in a plane crash. She'd been only ten years old, frightened and alone, and wishing she had died with the people she loved most in the world. Somehow, Grams had convinced her that what her parents would want most was that she embrace life the way they had.

Now Jodie had returned to Grams's world, this time seeking safety for herself and her sons.

She jerked around as the sound of footsteps at her heels roared into her consciousness. The back left wheel of the stroller ran off the edge of the asphalt trail with a grinding bump.

"You better teach your mom to drive, kid." The voice was thick and husky. And shockingly familiar.

She kept her head down, praying to go unrecognized as the hulk of a sweating body dodged the stroller.

"Jodie Gahagen, is that you?" He stopped on a dime and changed directions.

She tried to answer. The words died in her throat, and all she managed was a nod.

"I can't believe you're out here at the crack of dawn." he said, matching his pace to hers. "Mind if I jog along with you and the kiddos?" he asked, after the fact.

Did she mind? Oh, yeah. So much so she could feel the cold sweat popping out on her body. In fact, next to the madman she was here to escape and the reincarnation of Jack the Ripper, she didn't know of anyone's company she minded more than Ray Kostner's.

"You can run wherever you like," she panted, her gaze straight ahead so that he couldn't see the anxiety he created. "It's a free country."

"I need to meet your tax man."

She felt his gaze all over her body, from the top of her clinging T-shirt to the bottom of her brief running shorts. Déjà vu? No. Everything had changed since she'd seen him last.

"You're looking great," he said. "Motherhood must agree with you."

Small talk. Nice and easy, give nothing away, not until she was in full control and calling the shots. "Thanks," she managed to reply. "It does. The same way bachelor-hood agrees with you."

A puff of wind whipped a tuft of hair loose from her ponytail. She brushed the flying strands from her face, all the while aware of Ray's nearness and the fact that she couldn't afford to let down her barriers for even a second.

Two men had the power to hurt her, in different ways, but no less destructive. Ray Kostner was one of them.

"What are you doing back in Natchitoches?" she asked, determined to play his game of cordiality at the same level of perfection he managed. "Don't tell me you've given up the Big Easy quest for fame and fortune."

"No way. But Dad had a bypass last week."

"Oh, no." This time her response was genuine. Parker Kostner was a dear. He'd helped half the town out of one jam or another, whether they could afford him or not. His son was *not* a chip off the old block.

"Grams must have forgotten to mention it. Is he okay?" she asked, panting.

"Yeah. He's mending well, just ornery as ever. He's determined to get back to the office and take care of business. Mom is just as determined he's going to follow the doctor's orders."

"And she's recruited you for backup."

"That's about the size of it. I've settled into the spare office in Dad's suite while I help him out with a pressing case. If he comes near the office, I'm required to throw him out."

"I can't imagine anybody throwing your dad anywhere."

"I didn't say I was always successful."

"That's not what I hear about you."

"So, have you been asking about me, Jodie Gahagen?" His voice was low and teasing.

A sudden tingling feathered her skin, caressing her face and neck like a summer rain. Her grip tightened on the stroller handle until pain skittered her nerve endings and jolted her to her senses.

"No," she said, her voice shaky in spite of her resolve.

"But you know how my grandmother likes to talk. Your name came up."

She slowed her pace to a near crawl, hoping Kostner would rebel at the lack of challenge and leave her behind. She was in no condition to one-up him in conversation or speed. The truth was she never had been.

Apparently the lack of physical exertion didn't faze him anymore than her cool responses to his small talk had. He stayed at her side, stopping when she did at the corner where she'd parked her car.

"Do you need a ride back to Miss Emily's?"

"No, I have my car."

"Then how about a cup of coffee? We could—"

"I'm afraid not. The boys are ready for their cereal."

Ray stooped beside the stroller. "Cute kids," he said. "Bright red hair, just like their Mom."

"We have to go now," she insisted.

He didn't budge. He took Blair's hand, and the small pudgy fingers wound around Ray's. "Those dark eyes must have come from his lucky dad, though."

"No, neither of the boys looks anything like their dad." Her words were too caustic. If she kept this up, he would pounce on her inconsistent responses like the expert lawyer he was. But he had no right to do this to her. She wasn't a book he could pick up and put down whenever time or interest swayed him.

"Did I say something wrong?"

"No." She backed the stroller a few inches and maneuvered around him.

Undaunted, he followed her up the hill. "How long are you going to be in town?"

She looked up and faced his penetrating gaze, and her determination plummeted to the soles of her running shoes. "I'm not sure. Probably another week or so."

"Their dad must miss the boys." His gaze slid over her

again, his eyes saying way more than she wanted to hear. "And if he doesn't miss their mom, he must be crazy."

She stepped to the side of the car and unlocked the door. "He can handle it," she said, picking up a wriggling child and buckling him into the car seat.

"Since we're both in town for a while, how about dinner tomorrow night? For old times' sake."

He smiled down at her, the same boyish grin that had devastated her at fourteen and seduced her much later.

"I'm busy," she answered, turning away from him while her mind was still ruling.

"The next night then?"

"I'm busy tomorrow night and the night after and the week after that."

"I'd hoped we were still friends."

Friends? *A man who drove you wild with passion and then walked away as casually as if the week you thought was heaven had been a date for burgers and fries?*

"Friends usually return other friend's phone calls," she answered, her eyes on the stroller. "But I'm not mad, I'm busy, just like I'm sure you were. Besides, I'm not interested in reviving old times."

She quieted Blair with Cheerios as Ray bent and rescued Blake from the stroller. Wrapping his large hands about the small boy, he swept him into the air above his head. Blake, her usually slow-to-bond child, rewarded Ray's efforts with soft baby chuckles. He'd apparently inherited her weakness for bad choices in his bonding habits.

"The kid likes me," he boasted.

"He likes anyone who pays attention to him," she lied, all but yanking him from Ray's arms. Her fingers fumbled with the buckle on his car seat.

"No, I think he just has his mother's good taste. I can remember when she liked me."

"I still like you. Why shouldn't I?"

"Then why is a friendly dinner out of the question?"

"You have a short memory. I just told you that I'm very busy these days. I'm also married."

"Even busy, married women eat. Dinner and conversation. That's all. I promise I won't let you seduce me into any feelings unsuitable for dinner with a married woman."

"I don't think so, Ray."

His tone swung from light to deadly serious. "It never hurts to have someone to talk to when times are rough. Free legal advice is hard to come by."

"So that's what this is about. You didn't just happen to be out running at daybreak, did you? My grandmother put you up to this."

"Your grandmother cares about you."

"I'm fine. Just fine. But if I need your services as a friend or a lawyer, I'll let you know."

"Good. You call, and I'll come running. Just like always."

Exactly. Just like always. Ray Kostner and the NYPD. If a few meaningless words and halfhearted efforts could solve her problems, they'd take care of her.

"See you around," she said, with a quick wave of her hand. Seconds later, she jerked the car into gear and sped out of his sight.

JODIE WAS JUST beginning to relax again by the time Tuesday evening rolled around. There had been no visits or phone calls from Ray. Apparently he had taken her at her word that she had nothing to say to him.

At least not now.

One month ago, the story would have been different. She'd called him then, in the middle of the night, her hands shaking so badly she could barely dial the number that she knew as well as her own.

A woman had answered, her voice heavy with sleep, but

still soft and syrupy. And Jodie had hung up and dialed Detective Cappan instead. The lanky, gum-chewing cop had rushed right over, but that time he hadn't been able to mask the anxiety that coated his empty reassurances.

She'd told him her plan, and he'd agreed to help, all but guaranteeing her she wouldn't be followed to Natchitoches if she covered her tracks the way he instructed. By all accounts, she was in California now, lost in the Wild, Wild West, a suitable backdrop for her world of lies.

First, a mad stalker in New York. Now Ray Kostner in Louisiana. A trip down the Amazon was beginning to sound easy.

Stooping, she rescued the last dripping, rubber duck from the tub. The twins were already bathed and fed and in the kitchen doing their final bit of entertaining for the night.

"What would you like for dinner tonight, dear?" Grams's voice echoed down the long hall.

"Whatever you'd like." A salad would have been fine with Jodie, but that would not be one of the choices. Full-course dinners were the way of the old South, and Grams was a bonafide follower of tradition. Words like *calories, fat content, fiber* and *cholesterol* were not in her vocabulary. Maybe at eighty-three, Jodie would drop them from hers, too.

Eighty-three. What a nice age. There had been several long nights during the last few weeks when her chance at winning the lottery had seemed a safer bet than reaching her next birthday. A sudden prickle of gooseflesh dotted her arms, and she massaged it away. The nightmare was behind her.

With quick steps she joined Grams and the boys in the kitchen.

"Okay, Grams, what can I help you do?" she asked, grabbing a flowered apron from the hook by the door.

"You could you get that bowl of purple hull peas from the refrigerator."

"Will do." She settled in for what was sure to be a monumental task.

Her grandmother saved everything, ladling spoonfuls of leftovers into plastic containers with colorful tops and tucking them haphazardly into every available corner of the fridge. Locating a particular item was similar to finding your size at an end-of-year clearance. You usually settled for close and were glad to get it.

The nearest thing to close this time was corn, cabbage or yellow squash. "Could you give me a clue, like what day you cooked these peas?"

"Don't you remember? We had peas and pork chops." Grams rubbed her temple, streaking it with flour. "It must have been Saturday. No, let me see, was it Friday?"

Jodie gave up the search. They'd had pork chops on Tuesday a week ago, with green beans and sweet potatoes. The cleaning woman had undoubtedly trashed the remains on Wednesday, but no use to burden Grams with details.

She never seemed to remember them in their exact state anyway. Her memory was fading with her eyes, in contrast to her desire to manipulate, which was keener than ever. The incident with Ray at the jogging trail had proven that.

"I must have accidentally thrown the peas out, but I'll open a jar of the ones you and Selda canned this summer," Jodie offered. She opened the perfectly preserved legumes, dumped them into a saucepan and placed them on a back burner.

"How was your run this morning?" Grams asked, patting out a doughy biscuit.

"Fast, hot and tiring, like always."

"Then why do you do it?"

"It's good for me."

"It's bad for your knees. I heard that on 'Oprah,' or was

it that new show with Rosie something?'' She flipped a biscuit into a baking pan. ''I guess you didn't see that Kostner boy again.''

The question was thrown out as if it had just popped into her grandmother's mind. Jodie wasn't fooled. Grams had probably been searching all day for a way to bring Ray into the conversation.

But *boy?* The man was four years older than Jodie's twenty-seven, at least six foot two and reeked of power and manhood. ''I didn't see him,'' she said, shaking a quick dash of salt and pepper into the peas. ''I guess it was my lucky day.''

''I reckon it was. You don't want to go getting mixed up with the likes of him. Confounded, money-grubbing lawyers. I don't trust a one of them.''

''Ray's dad's a lawyer, and you like him.''

''That's different. Ray's too big for his britches, running off to New Orleans when there's plenty of work for decent folks right here at home.''

''You said the same thing about me when I moved to New York.''

''Hmmph. I was right about that, too.'' She muttered the words under her breath, but not so low she didn't mean for Jodie to hear them.

''So is that why you had Ray look me up Sunday, so he could tell me I should move back to Natchitoches for good?''

''I didn't do any such of a thing. You know I gave up trying to mind your business for you years ago.''

''Yeah, right.'' Jodie reached an arm around the bent and bony shoulders and gave her grandmother a quick hug. ''I know you mean well, Grams, but I don't want or need Ray's help. I just have a few issues I need to work through.''

Grams kept right on working. ''Well, you're welcome to

stay here as long as you want. That's what families are for. The fact is, I'm going to miss you and the boys like crazy when you leave. But don't let that influence you.''

''We'll miss you, too. Next time we won't wait so long between visits.''

''That's just why I'm concerned about you.'' She slapped a biscuit into the baking pan and wagged a finger at Jodie. ''First, you don't visit me for nigh to two years, putting me off with all kinds of flimsy excuses, even with me begging to see my new great-grandsons. Then you show up on my doorstep unannounced and tell me you're going to be here for a while. And as far as I can tell, you haven't had one phone call from that husband of yours.''

''I told you. We've agreed to an amicable separation until we decide what to do.''

''It doesn't sound too amicable to me. Doesn't sound a bit natural, either. You didn't take his name when you married him, and what kind of father don't give a gosh darn about two wonderful sons?''

What kind indeed? The kind who didn't want a wife or children to start with. ''You don't have to worry about me, Grams. This is the nineties. The boys and I will be just fine on our own.'' Jodie grabbed two stoneware plates from the shelf and started toward the kitchen table, praying she was telling the truth.

''I thought we might sit at the dining room table tonight,'' Grams said, taking the plates from her. ''It'll be a pleasant change. And we'll use the good china, the crystal, too. No use to let it go to ruin just keeping the shelf occupied.'' Her words were almost drowned in the melodic chime of the doorbell.

''Are you expecting someone, Grams?''

''Didn't I tell you? Ray Kostner's joining us for dinner.''

''You most certainly did not tell me. I would have made

plans to be somewhere else. I just told you, I don't need his advice.''

''Well, then it doesn't matter that I forgot to mention it. He's coming over to give *me* a little advice tonight.''

''How convenient. You need help from the confounded money grubber. Sometimes you'll have to share with me how you choose your dinner guests and your advisors.''

The doorbell jangled persistently this time, and both Blair and Blake joined in the excitement, one clapping, the other swinging his pudgy fists and babbling.

''Now are you going to get that or do I have to do it myself?'' Grams said, dusting her flour-covered hands over the sink.

Shaking her head in surrender, Jodie answered the bell and ushered Ray inside.

''What a pleasant surprise,'' he said, stepping over the threshold. ''I was afraid you might already be away doing whatever it is that keeps you so busy.''

She shot him an icy stare. ''My plans changed.''

''Good, I'm looking forward to catching up on your life. You've apparently been making a few changes since I saw you last. A new husband, twin boys.''

''It's been a long time.''

''Yeah. I guess it has.'' He leaned closer. ''But that was one thing about us. We could go months, years even, without seeing each other, and still fall back into each other's lives like we'd never been apart.''

''We're older now, I've changed. I don't fall into things anymore.'' Especially things like strong arms that belonged to a man who had the power to tear the heart right out of her if she gave him half a chance.

Ray started to follow her back to the kitchen. They both stopped when the doorbell rang again. ''More guests?'' he asked. ''I didn't dress for a party.''

''I don't know. I wasn't on the guest list committee.''

"Lucky for me." He sniffed appreciatively. "And that smells like Miss Emily's pot roast. I'd have driven up from New Orleans for that."

Jodie walked back to the front door and peeked through the peephole. Roses, yellow ones, tucked in and between baby's breath and asparagus fern stared back at her. Her stomach took an unexpected lurch. Shaking, she eased the door open.

"Delivery for Jodie Gahagen." The teenager stepped from the shadows into the illumination of the porch light.

"Who sent them?" she demanded.

He backed up half a step and gave her a sideways glance. Frowning, he slipped the acknowledgment card from the pronged holder and placed it in her hands.

She ripped the envelope open and yanked out the card. *An admirer.* The words jumped at her like a vampire, sinking sharp teeth into the jugular and draining the blood from her body.

"Is something wrong?" Ray moved to her side and wrapped an arm around her shoulder. She didn't pull away. Trembling, she stared at the card, turning it over in her hand.

"See, I told you they were for you." The delivery boy stuck the flowers at her.

"I can't accept them unless I know who sent them."

"Well, ma'am, if you're Jodie Gahagen, they're for you, no matter who sent them. But I guess I could take them back to the shop if you don't want 'em." He flashed Ray a pleading look. "Miss Gloria won't like my bringing the delivery back though, not after she made me work overtime to get it to you tonight."

Ray fished in his pocket and pressed a couple of bills into the teenager's hand. "We'll keep the flowers," he said, taking the bouquet from him, "but tell Miss Gloria that in the future, Miss Gahagen likes her admirers identified."

Jodie heard the voices, heard the door close, heard Ray asking her what was wrong. She couldn't respond. The fear was overpowering, churning inside her with hurricane force, choking her breath away. Weak and disoriented she slumped against the wall.

"Hey, they're only flowers. We can toss them in the trash if they're going to upset you like that."

"No, I'm okay."

"Then you're a damn good actress. You're white as a ghost and trembling like a kid on his first Halloween."

Still shaking, Jodie continued to stare at the card, letting one finger trace the row of red hearts peeking from a border of roses. Red hearts, the unmistakable signature of a man who'd vowed to have her for himself or see her dead.

"Is someone harassing you, Jodie? Is that what this is about?"

"Yes." The whispered response worked its way through the cottony dryness that clogged her throat and lungs. Her mind swirled in fear and confusion. Still, one truth hammered through the whirlwind. She couldn't protect her boys by herself, not now that the stalker had found her.

Ray wrapped his hands about her waist and pulled her to him. "Just tell me who's bothering you. If it's your husband—" His face pulled into hard lines, and his muscles strained at the sleeves of his shirt.

"No. It's not my husband. But I didn't come to Natchitoches just to visit."

"Your grandmother told me you were having marital problems. It's none of my business, but if the man is threatening you, I can make it my business."

"Just listen, Ray. My grandmother doesn't know the real story, and I don't want her finding out. Promise me you won't tell her a thing about this."

"You have my word. Now, what is it I'm not telling?"

"Someone was stalking me in New York. I've never met

him, at least not that I know of. But he left me flowers and gifts and frightening notes.''

''You surely must have some idea who it is.''

''No. I only know he knows *me* too well. He knows the color of the towels in my bathroom, the pattern of the sheets on my bed, the label in my nightgown.''

''That son of a…'' Ray's words trailed off and he gathered Jodie in his arms, gently rocking her against his chest. ''No wonder the flowers frightened you. But chances are they aren't even from him. And even if they are, he'll never follow you to Louisiana. Stalkers are almost always cowards who—''

Jodie's nerves tightened into frayed knots, and she jerked away from him. ''Don't give me statistics. I know them all, and none of them apply in this case. This is no ordinary stalker.''

''Ordinary or not, he won't get away with his perverted tricks in Natchitoches. The police will have him behind bars before his feet get southern dirt between his toes. You couldn't be safer.''

''Don't humor me, and don't fool yourself. I know better than anyone what the police can and can't do. It's myself I have to depend on now, but I need your help.''

''You name it.''

''I want you to take Blake and Blair and keep them safe.''

His eyebrows shot up. ''What did you say?''

''You heard me right.''

''I'll fight a madman for you, two if necessary, but no kids. I'm not the man for that.'' He stepped backward, a hand up as if to ward off blows.

''I know. You're a no-ties kind of guy. That's the way you've always wanted things, but this time you don't get a choice.''

''There's always choices. The boys need *you*. And they

need their father, not some stranger they've never seen before this week. No matter how you feel about your husband, no matter what's happened between the two of you, you have to let him know his sons are in danger.''

''I agree,'' she said, her voice strong and dead level now that she'd made up her mind to do what she had to in order to keep her boys safe. ''The boys' father does deserve to know the truth. That's why I just told him.''

His gaze fastened on hers, his eyes demanding. ''Don't play this kind of game with me, Jodie. I don't understand it.''

''Think about it, and you will. A chance meeting between old friends. Chinese takeout and champagne. A rainy night that stretched into seven.'' The truth tore at her heart, shredding it into little pieces.

''No, if you'd gotten pregnant by me, you would have called and told me. And you would never have married another man while you were carrying my children. I know you better than that.''

''So you do.'' She tilted her head to face him head-on. ''There never was a husband, Ray. There was only you.'' She watched as every muscle in his body hardened to the consistency of solid steel.

His reaction didn't surprise her at all. He'd made it plain from the beginning, a wife and kids were not part of his game plan. It wasn't his fault her heart had refused to accept the truth. Or that the protection they'd used had failed.

''When this is over, you can ride off into the sunset in your flashy sports car, and I'll never try to stop you or ask anything of you. But right now Blair and Blake need you. And, whether you like it or not, *you* are the boys' father.''

Chapter Two

No! No way in the world! The protest, silent but deafening, echoed in every corner of Ray's brain. He wasn't a father. He couldn't be. Fathers were nurturing. They read bedtime stories, changed dirty diapers, shoveled green, slimy baby food into yelling mouths.

Fathers were gentle, loving, caring. All of the things he wasn't, the things he couldn't be.

"There must be some—" One look at Jodie and the challenge stopped in midsentence. Fear clouded her eyes and powdered her delicate skin with a chalky whiteness that tore at his heart. He reached a hand toward her, his own doubts crushed with a sudden and suffocating desire to cradle her trembling body in his arms. His arms encircled her waist and he pulled her against his chest.

She stayed there less than a heartbeat before pushing away from him.

"I know you're afraid, Jodie, and I want to help you, but…" He trailed his fingers down her arm.

"Sure you do. About as much as you want to be run over by an eighteen wheeler. But, let's not make anything more of this than what it is."

"What's that supposed to mean?"

"It means you can wipe the panic from your face and cut the patronizing routine. This is not some ploy to catch a husband. When this is over, my sons and I will fly back to New York and you can run back to your life of Porsches and parties, and—"

She tossed her head back, swinging her shiny red mane into a tangle of curls that resettled reluctantly about her face and shoulders. "And whatever else it is that you do in New Orleans."

"I'd say what I do is my business."

"And it can stay that way. I don't give a damn about your choice of entertainment or your conquests. But like it or not, you are a father, and right now, your sons need you."

His sons. There it was again. But the accusation was only words, and saying them didn't make them true. Jodie was running scared, steeped in fear as thick and tangible as the worn Persian rug beneath their feet. She might claim anything to get protection for her boys. He didn't blame her a bit.

A shudder of relief coursed his body. That was it, of course. She was making up the whole paternity issue out of desperation. His brain reveled in the solution his frantic reasoning offered. Fatherhood was inconceivable. Defending beautiful women he could handle. Hell, he'd practically made a career of it.

"Why don't we step into the living room?" he offered, taking her arm. "That way you can fill me in on the details about your stalker."

"Does that mean you'll take the boys and keep them safe?"

"It means I'll do what I can to keep all of you safe. Me and the police and half the parish if need be. You're in Natchitoches now, not the Big Bad Apple. Killers don't wander around the streets unnoticed. The truth is, nobody wanders around here after 7:00 p.m."

"A new criminal in town might not know that."

"He'll turn into a believer if he shows up here."

"Will he, Ray? I guess we'll find out soon enough. He's either here now or on his way. The flowers are proof of that."

With an arm around her shoulders, Ray led her to a Victorian sofa made for delicate ladies half his size. He eased down beside her, his long legs fitting awkwardly in front of the low-slung coffee table. Careful not to topple the collection of crystal pieces that glared at him threateningly, he scooted the curved cherry legs of the table back a couple of inches, catching a crocheted doily on the edge of his watch.

Jodie unhooked the fragile threads with shaking fingers, and once again he felt the overpowering urge to hold her close. He grabbed her hand and encased it in his. It was cold as ice.

"This man really has you spooked."

"A man. Only a man," she said, her eyes cast downward. "I keep telling myself that, but in my heart I know he's a monster."

"He's a man." The assurance sounded good, but Ray wasn't sure he believed that himself now. Not after seeing Jodie like this. He struggled to assimilate the fear in her eyes with the images of her that lived in his mind.

Jodie in faded cutoffs, shimmying up the highest oak in Miss Emily's yard and dangling from a half-dead branch to save a wild-haired tomcat. Jodie in her first year of college, taking on the dean and finally the governor to right the injustices of campus housing policies.

Pain stabbed him in the gut as his mind considered the possibilities of just what it had taken to reduce her to this state of desperation. "Has this man touched you, Jodie? If he's laid a hand on you..."

"He's never touched me. He left packages and letters. I

found them outside the door of my apartment or on my desk in the advertising firm where I worked."

"But he has been in your apartment in New York?"

"Yes, but only once while I was there. That night he picked up Blake and moved him into the crib with Blair. He left a note, a promise that he would return."

Ray felt the involuntary tightening of his muscles, and his hands knotted into fists. "The guy's a sicko."

"Exactly. And for some reason he's picked me to be the receiver of his morbid attentions."

"No wonder you were so afraid of him. It's just a damn shame a guy like that could get by with forcing you to give up a job you loved and make you run the length of the country to escape him."

"To *try* to escape him. Apparently I failed." Resignation tugged at the corners of her mouth.

"Not necessarily. Even though he hasn't identified himself, there's a good chance you know him, at least casually, or he knows someone you know. Either way he could have heard that you have a grandmother who lives in Natchitoches. He may have wired the flowers here on a hunch. Especially since Miss Emily is the only family you have."

"Then he's as good at hunches as he is at terrorizing."

"It looks that way. But I still don't think you need to panic. Wiring flowers from New York is a far cry from traveling a couple of thousand miles just to torment you for no good reason. There are millions of victims in New York he can switch his sick attentions to."

Jodie stiffened her shoulders and sucked in a deep breath.

"That's my girl," he whispered, giving her hand a squeeze. "You'll lick this thing."

"I'm not your girl." She yanked her hand from his. "I'm not anyone's girl. I'm a woman. And believe me, Ray Kostner, I've heard enough empty reassurances. I'm only asking one thing of you."

"I'll do whatever I can."

"Take the boys. I want them away from me entirely until this mess is over."

He swallowed, but the choking lump in his throat didn't disappear. Getting involved with Jodie Gahagen again would mean breaking every promise he'd made to himself over the last two years. The woman was pure, unadulterated trouble to a man like him. And she was asking the impossible. But, she needed him, and he didn't have a chance in hell of convincing his heart to walk away and leave her alone and frightened.

"I'll help you find the lunatic who's stalking you. Count on it."

"That's not good enough, Ray. It's not me I'm worried about."

"I'll do everything I can."

"I don't want everything. I've given up on expecting that a long time ago. I'm only asking one thing of you now. Either do it or stay out of my life." A lone tear escaped and slid down her pale cheek.

Ray brushed it away, his finger lingering on her skin, his gaze locked with hers. "I can't take the boys. I haven't the slightest idea how to tend to kids. Even if they were mine—"

"*If* they were yours?" Accusatory fire leapt to her eyes. "If they were yours, you'd deny them to keep your precious freedom intact. Old good-time Ray Kostner. Free and easy." She met his gaze head-on, her lips drawn into thin, straight lines, the color returning to her face in shades of livid red.

"Well, don't worry, you're off the hook. You're right. They're *not* yours, and they don't need you."

"Take it easy, Jodie. I know you're upset, but we need to look at this stalker issue rationally."

"*We* don't need to do anything. The stalker is after *me*,

and I don't need or want your advice or your brand of help. The fact is you've done way more than enough for me already.'' She stood up, her slim body hardened into fighter stance.

''You're taking this all wrong, Jodie.''

''Forget it, Ray. Let yourself out. I'll explain to Grams why you couldn't stay.'' The words sliced the air as she turned on her heel and strode away without a backward glance.

JODIE PUSHED THE screen door open and slid through it, thankful the agonizing dinner for two was finally over and the kitchen was back in ship shape. Grams hadn't bought for a second her feeble story about Ray's suddenly remembering a previous engagement. She'd grilled Jodie like a piece of red meat.

Who did he have to run off and meet so suddenly? Why didn't he just telephone if he couldn't make it to dinner instead of coming all the way over? Why didn't he at least step into the kitchen and make his apologies to her? After all, she was the one who'd invited him for dinner.

Jodie had stammered and hemhawed with answers. Lying was not her forte, although she was getting better at it since necessity had made it a way of life. And the first set of lies all traced back to a rainy night twenty-two months ago. Her heart constricted at the memories, poignant and bittersweet.

She took a deep breath, consuming the scents of a southern fall. Damp leaves harboring fallen pecans, perfume from the clusters of blooming chrysanthemums that bordered the fence line. The wind picked up, shuffling the carpet of leaves and sending a cascade of new ones swirling to the ground.

She stood still, suddenly cold and shaking. It was as if she could feel someone's gaze crawling her body.

"I thought you might be out here."

The scratchy male voice came from nowhere. In a split second, her hands wrapped about the only weapon in sight. Twirling, she raised the flowerpot over her head.

"Sorry, Miss Jodie. I didn't mean to frighten you."

A giant stepped from behind the hedge that bordered the house and sheltered the backyard from traffic on the street. Breath escaped her body in a surge, leaving her so light-headed she leaned against the porch railing for support.

"Gentle Ben," she said, her voice quaking with relief.

"It sure is me. And I'd hate to know who you were expectin' to greet with that flowerpot."

"No one," she lied. "Just my big-city reflexes in top form." She sat the flowerpot back in its appointed spot and gave Ben a quick hug. Fifteen years of tending the yard and garden and keeping the fishing boat in good condition had elevated him to family status.

He stood back and gave her an appraising look. "Well, if living in the big city makes you that jumpy, you need to move right on back down here with your grandmother." He slid his hands into the pockets of a pair of new-looking overalls. "She pines away for you all the time. Worries about you, too. New York ain't the place for a pretty southern girl like you."

"Thank you. For the pretty part," she added, "but not the advice. Most of the time New York is the perfect spot for me." Jodie attempted a reassuring smile. "Besides, you know you're exaggerating, Ben. Grams is not the type to pine away."

"Maybe not, but she misses you just the same. We both do."

"From what I hear, you haven't been around enough to miss me. When did you get back in town?"

"Tonight. I called Miss Emily to tell her I'd be at work

in the morning. That's when she said you were here. She said it would be all right if I dropped over to say howdy.''

"Of course it's all right. Is your son better?''

"As good as he's ever been. He wasn't near as sick as he let on. He just had me up there waiting on him.''

"He's lucky to have a father who cares enough to come running when he needs you.''

"Yeah. 'Cept he don't know that.'' A dog's barking interrupted him, a growl that dissolved into a mournful howl. Ben got up and walked to the edge of the porch, staring into the darkness. "Full moon tonight. It riles the animals. People, too. Makes 'em restless and uneasy. Makes 'em do things they oughtn't.''

Like send flowers, Jodie thought, wrapping her hands and arms about her body to ward off a sudden chill. Only some people didn't need a full moon to cause their darker side to surface. "Does the moon affect your moods, Ben?'' she asked, more to make conversation than anything else, to shift her thoughts from her own troubles.

"Yeah.'' He nodded his head, still staring into space. "I guess maybe it does, seeing as how I feel right now. A little crazy, a little wild with fighting feelings I shouldn't have.'' He turned and gave Jodie a nervous smile. "I reckon it's a good thing full moons don't last too long.''

Heavy footsteps interrupted Ben's words. Jodie's gaze flew to the corner of the house, but this time she didn't go for the flowerpot. She should have. It would have fit nicely on the top of Ray's head, and the dirt could have spilled deliciously over his shirt, streaking the snowy white with muddy gunks of earth.

She stared icily but didn't say a word while Ray and Ben exchanged greetings, offering a smile only when Ben excused himself and made his exit. And then the smile was only for Ben. The ice in her stare remained for her newest caller.

"What are you doing here, Ray?"

"Is that the way you greet guests in New York? It seems awfully unfriendly."

"Good. Then you got the message."

He dropped to the swing beside her. "I vote we cut the games, Jodie. We've been friends too long."

Friends. There it was again. All she had to do was forget they'd ever made love, that she had lain awake for nights afterward, reliving every touch of his hands, his lips, his body merged with hers. Forget that he hadn't returned her phone calls. Forget that he had fathered sons he wanted no part of.

"If you're here to renew an old friendship, you're wasting your time. Our definitions of friendship don't correlate."

"No, I came back because I'm worried about you." His hand closed over hers. "This terrorizing routine has got to stop."

"What a novel idea."

"Sarcasm doesn't become you, but I can understand it. Nothing is more frightening or frustrating than an enemy who won't come out in the open. It's a coward's way, but it works. I have a few ideas for stopping it."

"Your memory is short," she said, scooting to the far edge of the wooden swing. "It hasn't been two hours since I told you to stay out of my life."

"And when this madman is caught, I'll heed your wishes, if that's still what you want. But I'm not turning my back on you now, so you might as well accept my help." He leaned forward and planted his feet on the porch, stopping the motion of the swing. "How much do you know about stalkers, Jodie?"

"The typical profile information." Jodie got up from the swing and paced the porch, quickly realizing there would be no getting rid of Ray before he was ready to go. No wonder he had the reputation for being a barracuda attorney. Telephone solicitors were less persistent.

"And what do you consider typical?" He stood up and walked to the railing of the porch, leaning against it easily as if they were talking about the weather or the brightness of the moon.

"They usually follow a path of increasingly obsessive behavior. They're usually former lovers or spouses, but not always." She was quoting the literature now, the way the cops always did. "Occasionally they're total strangers who pick you out for some unknown reason. Apparently my stalker falls into that category."

The howling started again. This time she felt dark shadows of the madness Ben had talked about. It built and shivered inside her, pushing her closer to the edge of hopelessness.

"But my stalker always leaves a calling card."

"But not his name?"

"No. A red heart. Sometimes it's a cutout, sometimes a sticker or a printed pattern like the one that came with the flowers. More often, it's drawn with a red crayon." Her voice caught. Natchitoches had seemed so safe. Until tonight. "Sometimes he adds a message."

"What kind of message?"

"A warning. He tells me things that let me know he's watching me. He says I need to be a good girl, that he wants me to save myself for him. If I do, he'll continue to love me and make sure I'm safe. If I don't, I'll have to pay the ultimate price, like the others did."

Ray reached out and grabbed her arm, pulling her to him. His eyes bore into hers, penetrating her resolve. "What others?"

"He never says."

His hand tightened on her arm possessively. "You need

to be more careful, Jodie. Stop jogging alone in isolated areas.''

''You said yourself, just because he sent flowers doesn't mean he'll actually travel from New York to Natchitoches. Besides, I left easy-to-follow clues that I would be in San Francisco. If he goes anywhere, he should go there.''

''If you believed that you wouldn't have turned into a shivering mass of nerves when the flowers were delivered. Just do what I say, Jodie. Don't go out alone, unless you're going to very public places, at least not until we know if this guy's in town.''

''So you think I should let this lunatic keep me prisoner and hope for the best. I certainly can't afford a bodyguard.''

''I can.'' The words were a hoarse whisper. ''And if it comes to that, I'll hire one. But right now, I'm in town and you can work your schedule of solitary errands around times when Ben or I can go out with you.''

''You're not my keeper, Ray. I'm not ready to trade one stalker for another.''

''Maybe not. But at least you know I'm not dangerous.''

Jodie met his gaze, and her heart settled like lead in her chest. Danger had many faces. So did pain. ''I can handle this. It's not your concern.''

He ran his fingers the length of her arms and back up again, sliding his arm across her shoulders, riding the strained lines of her neck with his thumb. Her pulse quickened, and she willed it to slow. But still she couldn't make herself pull away.

He leaned closer, his lips inches from hers. And then they met, soft and tickling, like the brush of a feather. So quick she had no time to stop him or the impulses that churned inside her. A touch and then he pulled away.

''Now go in and tell Miss Emily you'll be back in a few minutes,'' he said, his voice suddenly hoarse. ''Gloria Bigger is expecting us at the flower shop.''

"Does she remember something about the man who ordered the flowers?" Her voice rose optimistically.

"Only that he called in the order, which means my theory about his still being in New York is probably right."

"Lots of people order flowers for local delivery."

"Not stalkers. When you order by phone, you have to give a credit card number. Mrs. Bigger said she's sure she checked the number out with Visa. That's the only way she accepts orders from strangers. If we have his name and the number of his account, we can identify him."

Jodie shook her head, doubts hammering away at the sliver of hope Ray offered. "He's smarter than that." But a surge of adrenaline rippled through her veins. The cops always said he'd make a mistake sooner or later. Maybe this would be the time. "I'll tell Grams," she said, "and meet you at Gloria's."

"We'll go together."

She didn't argue the point. Maybe it was the effect of the full moon addling her senses, or maybe she just didn't want to be alone. Whatever the cause, she was suddenly glad they were facing this thing together.

RAY SPUN THE steering wheel of his red Porsche, rounding the corner onto Front Street. It was eight-fifteen on a Monday night and the main street of town was all but deserted. The only visible sign of life was a couple of hand-clasped young lovers peering into the window of a store already filled with bright colored Christmas ornaments and a waving Santa.

The window display was a reminder of just how much Natchitoches would change in the next few weeks. When the light extravaganza was turned on along the river, visitors would flood the small town. The number of lights had grown steadily over the years. So had the crowds, especially for the first weekend of the popular Festival of Lights.

"How much did you tell Gloria?" Jodie asked, finally breaking the silence she'd imposed since climbing into his car.

He turned to face her. She was chewing on her bottom lip, the way she always did when she was worried. He would love to get his hands on the trash who was causing her this kind of grief. The last time he'd been with her she'd been—

He shook his head, pushing the memories from his mind once more, the way he had been trying to do ever since his trip to New York. "I told her the truth," he finally answered. "At least a partial truth. I said you were being harassed by someone and you wanted to verify the name of the person who sent the flowers. We'll get the credit card information and turn it over to the police."

"And I can hear them now. It is not against the law to send flowers, Miss Gahagen. Then they'll hand me hundreds of yards of bureaucratic tape and no action."

"That was New York. This is Natchitoches. There's not a hundred yards of tape in the whole town." Ray leaned closer, and the soft scent of gardenias washed over him, weakening his resistance and playing havoc with the promise he'd made himself earlier this evening. He was a friend helping out in an emergency.

He wouldn't make the same mistake he'd made in New York again, wouldn't give Jodie any reason to think of him as a man to hook her dreams of permanence on. They rode in silence until he pulled to the curb in front of the flower shop.

"Gloria must not be here yet." Jodie scooted closer to the passenger door but didn't open it. "The shop is pitch dark."

"Yeah, but that looks like her green sedan in front of

us, and it looks empty. Wait in the car. I want to look around a minute.''

''No.'' Her fingers dug into his arm, holding him back. ''Something's wrong. I can't explain how I know. It's just something I feel, a dread that crawls across my skin when *he's* been around.'' Fear stole her voice, reducing her words to a whisper.

Ray wrapped an arm about her trembling body, pulling her close. Too close. His heart constricted and other body parts, ones far more traitorous, came to life. He struggled for control.

''Okay, Jodie, we'll go in together. Gloria's probably in the back of the shop going over the order slips as we speak. There's no possible reason for your stalker to show up at the flower shop. He couldn't suspect you were going to rush down here after closing to go over the records.''

He eased open the driver's side door, one arm still about her shoulders. ''Besides, like I told you before, the chances are slim to none the crackpot's traveled all the way to Natchitoches to make trouble.''

Jodie pulled from his arms and swung open her own door. ''I hope you're right,'' she said, rounding the corner of the front fender and heading straight for Gloria's car. ''But I wouldn't make bets on it.''

Chapter Three

Ray joined Jodie, peering through the windshield of Gloria's parked car. "See. The car's empty, except for a stack of papers and a McDonald's bag." He slid his hand over the hood. "And the motor's still warm. She must have beat us here by no more than a few minutes."

A sigh of what he hoped was relief escaped Jodie's lips in a whoosh. He followed her to the door, his gaze tracing the line of shrubs that bordered the side of the shop. For the first time since he'd arrived in Natchitoches, he felt the pangs of apprehension, the wariness of deserted places he'd learned to accept as commonplace in New Orleans.

But the shrubs were still and the only noises were Jodie's footsteps and the eerie rasping of the metal sign above the door as it caught the wind. He was letting Jodie's faceless fears set him on edge, and he couldn't allow that to happen.

He needed a clear head. If the suspicions rolling through his mind were true, Jodie was in real danger. The stalker she described had the earmarks of a serial killer, a man who chose his victims and then tormented them before leading them to their death. He'd have to walk a thin line, make Jodie ever cautious without scaring her to death.

Ray stepped in front of Jodie and banged his fist against the weathered wood. The door creaked open a few inches, then stopped. He pushed against it, but it didn't budge.

"What is it?"

"I can't tell exactly." Slowly, his eyes adjusted to the blackness of the room. He stepped inside, poking at the mass that blocked the door with the toe of his leather moccasin. A soft moan gurgled from the mass.

He dropped to his knees. Jodie draped over him and reached past him to grab the limp arm that lay across the cold tiles of the entrance way.

"Is that you, Ray Kostner?"

Jodie gave him no time to answer. She'd already squeezed her slender body through the partially opened door.

"Mrs. Bigger, what happened? Are you all right?" Jodie's voice rose to an uneven pitch.

"No, honey. Call an...ambulance and...tell them to hurry." Gloria Bigger's breath came in quick gasps, and her body jerked convulsively.

Ray managed to shove the door open a few more inches and squeeze through. His fingers searched the wall and found the light switch. Jodie dived for the phone, and Ray kneeled beside the suffering woman.

Illumination did not make the situation better. Gloria was white as a sheet, and her left hand clutched the material of her blouse at a spot over her heart.

He checked her pulse only to find that it was as weak as he expected. But at least she still had one. "We're getting help, Mrs. Bigger."

She coughed and tried to raise her head. "The flower order."

"Don't worry about that," he assured her, massaging her cold hands. "Don't worry about anything. We'll have you to the hospital in no time."

"The man..." She stopped in midsentence, whimpering in pain.

"Don't try to talk now. Just relax. Everything's under

control." He gave her hand a gentle squeeze. After what seemed hours to him, Jodie hung up the phone and dropped to the floor beside them, brushing a tissue she'd found somewhere across Mrs. Bigger's sweating brow.

"I'm sorry," Jodie whispered, her voice shaking. "I didn't mean to drag you into this."

"Not…your fault."

Half of Mrs. Bigger's words were swallowed in a moan. But the expression on Jodie's face was proof to Ray that Jodie believed all of this was her fault. Hers and the stalker's.

Ray relinquished Gloria's hand to Jodie's as the cry of approaching sirens attacked the night.

"You'll be just fine after Dr. Creighton works his magic," Jodie whispered, her face close to the florist's ear.

Ray hoped the good doc had a double dose of the magic. The woman on the floor would need it.

JODIE GROUND HER TEETH and stared at Butch Deaton while he scribbled down notes on a pad of paper. It was about time he did something besides walk around the flower shop scratching his head.

She had known Butch ever since she'd moved to Natchitoches, even dated him a few times during her senior year in high school. Watching him tonight, she couldn't imagine what she'd seen in him. He was far more arrogant than sympathetic, and his competence, seriously in question.

"It looks like a routine emergency to me," he said, tapping his stub of a pencil on the pad. "The woman had a heart attack from natural causes."

"Papers and folders are scattered all over her desk," Jodie protested. "And the top drawer of the file cabinet has obviously been rifled through."

He leaned against the counter, one hand propped on the

handle of the revolver that peeked from his holster. "I know the place is a mess, Jodie."

"Exactly. Because the man who sent me the flowers must have realized too late that he could be traced through his credit card information. He broke in here tonight to get the same records we were looking for. Only he beat us to them. That's why they're not here."

"Then Mrs. Bigger arrived unexpectedly and caught him in the act. He frightened her into a coronary." Butch finished her scenario for her, a patronizing smile splitting his lips. "I'm sure your theory sounds reasonable to you, but you don't understand police work."

"The theory sounds plausible to me, too, Butch, and I do understand criminal activity."

Butch stared at Ray as if he were a bug he'd like to stamp. "If the man was worried about being tracked down, he would have never called in an order and given a credit card number in the first place. Even a defense attorney should be able to figure that out."

"Maybe he didn't think about the card being used to trace him until after the fact."

"Sounds like a pretty stupid stalker to me."

"Or one who made a mistake. It happens. Surely even cops make mistakes occasionally." Ray stared him down.

"Occasionally." This time he directed his remarks to Jodie, stepping closer, putting a hand on her arm, invading her space. "We can't go jumping to any criminal conclusions, Jodie. I know you mean well, but you have to leave the professional decisions to the police department."

She backed away from him. "Then you really believe Mrs. Bigger trashed her own office?" Jodie's patience could stretch no further.

"It's not unusual. Fact is, it happens all the time. The family calls us in, sure someone's heart attack was provoked by a break-in. Later we find out that when the pain hit, the person kind of went wild for a minute or two, all panicky, slinging things everywhere.''

"But Gloria Bigger wasn't even in the office when we found her. She was at the front door, as if she'd just arrived.''

"Or trying to get help.''

Jodie blew a blast of steam from between pursed lips. Arguing with Butch was useless. She should have known that from the moment she'd told him that she thought Gloria Bigger had been attacked by an unknown stalker who had followed her to Natchitoches from New York City. The way he had rolled his eyes at his partner had told her more than his feeble attempts to humor her. He thought she was a fruitcake.

"You don't need to worry, Jodie. I'll follow up on this. If Mrs. Bigger pulls through, she'll be able to tell us herself if she encountered somebody in the shop.''

"If she pulls through.''

"She has a good chance. In the meantime, you call me direct if you get any more flowers or see anyone suspicious looking hanging around the house.'' He pressed his business card into her hand. "You can always reach me if you call the beeper number.''

"But you will get a team down here to check for fingerprints?'' Ray asked, reminding him of his earlier promise.

"Yeah, Kostner. I always do what I say I will.'' His gaze left Ray and sought out Jodie's. "I can give you a lift to your grandmother's if you'd like. I'm going that way.''

"That won't be necessary,'' Ray answered for her. "I'll see that Jodie gets home safely.''

He took her arm and urged her to the door. Reluctantly, she let herself be escorted out. The only real clue she'd located had been a stack of acknowledgment cards stamped with a border of red hearts, just like the one that had come with her flowers. Valentine leftovers, Jodie suspected.

But the heart cards had been in the back corner of the supply desk, and a larger stack of cards had been in the front, all decorated with fall leaves and pumpkins. Mrs. Bigger would have surely chosen one of those unless the caller had specifically requested something with a red heart.

The only thing that didn't add up in her mind was that the stalker had left red roses on her doorstep before, but never yellow ones. The shift in color probably had some symbolic meaning, but it was lost on her.

She was sure the stalker had sent the flowers. She had no admirers in Natchitoches. But did tormenting her give him such pleasure he would follow her all the way across the country? Had he been here, in this very office, frightening Gloria Bigger into a heart attack? Or was Jodie just the running-scared neurotic everyone took her to be?

By the time she reached the curb, her head was pounding. Ray opened the door for her and then climbed in on his side, settling under the steering wheel and firing the ignition. Seconds later, he pulled out of the parking spot, taking the curve at a speed that sent her flying in his direction.

"You told me earlier that this maniac you're so afraid of has never touched you. Were you telling me the whole truth?" Ray held a death grip on the wheel.

"I'm asking again, Jodie. Has this man ever laid a hand on you?"

"I'm not on the witness stand, counselor. And I don't have to tell you anything. This isn't your problem." Besides, she'd told him more truth than he'd wanted to believe already. And the rest of the truth...

Fear surged again, moving through her veins like ice water. The rest of the truth might be so gory even she couldn't bear to think of it. Only she could think of nothing else. Not since the night she'd been called to identify the body. And still the police hadn't believed her. So why would anyone else?

"Hey, wait a minute," she protested, realizing that Ray was heading in the opposite direction from her house. "I need to check on Grams and the boys, and I want to go home *now*."

"You can call them. Besides, you'll be home soon enough. I just need to make one quick stop."

"I should have ridden home with Officer Unfriendly."

"You had your chance."

"So, where is this stop you have to make?"

"My house. I need to pick up a few things."

"Like what?"

"Like underwear. A pair of pajamas, if I can find them. A shaving kit."

An unexpected lump gathered in her throat. She spoke past it, determined not to let anything Ray did bother her ever again. "Sounds like a slumber party," she quipped. "How fun. Too bad you had to keep the party hostess waiting."

Her attempt at uncaring sarcasm came out like the farce it was. She sat in silence, curses rolling through her mind like the blackest of Louisiana storm clouds.

But he was doing her a favor. Knowing he was heartless enough to throw his plans for being with another woman into her face was just the kind of reminder she needed to put him out of her mind for good.

"Actually the hostess doesn't know I'm coming." He picked up his cellular phone and punched in a series of numbers before sticking it in her hands. "Why don't you tell her she'll have a houseguest for a few days?"

Before Jodie could slam the phone into the side of his head, she heard Grams's voice at the other end of the connection.

JODIE PUSHED OPEN the screen door and Ray followed her inside, swinging a quickly packed duffel at his side. The house was dark except for the welcoming light in the hall. That could only mean Grams was asleep.

Of course Grams would have been up and ready to receive her guest with open arms if Jodie had given her the message he'd told her to deliver. But Jodie had no intention of frightening her grandmother or of putting her in danger. That left her only one choice and it did not encompass having a past lover move back into her life as a temporary bodyguard.

"Where do you want me to put this?" Ray asked, lifting his duffel a little higher.

She choked back her first choice of an answer. "Shhh." She placed a finger over her lips. "Don't wake up Grams. I told you I don't want her to know you're here."

"Don't you think she'll figure it out when I come down the stairs for morning coffee in my bathrobe?"

The image flashed through Jodie's head. Ray, clean-shaven with the hint of aftershave lingering in the air. Ray, his hair damp from the shower, his mouth minty fresh. Memories filled her mind, making her body weak but strengthening her resolve.

"Wait in the kitchen," she whispered. "I'm going upstairs to check on the boys. When I get back, we'll talk."

"It's pushing midnight, a little late for chatting."

"This conversation won't take long." She turned her back on him and hurried to the boys' room. She needed to see them sleeping safely in their beds. Needed to hear the soft sounds of their breathing and see their tiny chests rise and fall beneath their cuddly sleepers. Needed to feel that something was all right with the world.

The night-light glowed softly, illuminating her steps enough that she avoided colliding with the wooden rocking horse and a stuffed tiger one of the twins had obviously tossed from his bed. Neither of the boys stirred from slumber as she tiptoed across the thick carpet.

Grams had chosen the perfect room for a nursery and then raided not only her attic but her neighbor's to find two cribs, the rocking horse and bright-colored paintings of Louisiana pelicans and sailboats. Only the mattresses had to be purchased.

The hasty exit from New York had forced Jodie to bring only necessary items. Clothing, photographs and a few of the boys' favorite toys had topped her list.

This time she'd have to travel with a whole lot less. Her heart constricted in pain at the thought of leaving her sons, but pain and heartbreak couldn't change what she had to do.

She tiptoed to the side of Blake's bed. Shadows from the teddy bear mobile danced along the pale yellow walls, and she shivered. The boys had been sleeping this soundly the night she had found the note tucked inside Blake's empty bed. The night the killer had been as close to her babies as she was right now. The night she'd vowed he would never touch her sons again.

Her fingers tightened around the crib railing, as she stared down at her firstborn son, her eyes adjusting to the faint light. Blake had kicked off the covers, and, thumb in mouth, was sucking away. She touched her fingers to her lips and then to his cheek before tucking the light blanket over him, knowing he would kick it off again before she made it back down the stairs.

The second crib was across the room, next to the window seat. Blair wriggled as she approached, his lips breaking into a smile as he slept. "Pleasant dreams," she whispered. "May you always have them, pumpkin."

The room was warm, but a sudden chill shook Jodie's body. They were not alone. A human-shaped shadow moved along the wall, and she jerked around in time to see Ray's back as he disappeared through the nursery door.

He'd intruded and then walked away. So like him. But the loss was all his. At least she was no longer tormented with whether or not she should tell a man who wanted no part of responsibility, of commitment, that he had two wonderful sons. Now it was he who had made the choice of denial.

A tear slid down her cheek as she turned from the cribs. It was time to let the past die. Today was more than enough to deal with. And dealing with it meant keeping her boys safe at all costs.

RAY STOOD at the kitchen door and stared into the blackness of a night that had started with bright moonlight and a heaven full of stars. Now dark clouds punctuated by ragged streaks of lightning pummeled the serenity.

And here he was back in Natchitoches, being sucked into a life he wanted no part of. Dealing with his disapproving dad by day, and now Jodie by night.

Jodie by night. The words had the ring of a song title, maybe even a romantic sonnet. Jodie, hot with passion, sex siren in a cotton gown, warming up a New York night with a blaze all her own.

Suddenly, heat suffused his body. He pulled at the collar of his shirt and went to the refrigerator. Retrieving a pitcher of cold lemonade, he searched the cabinets above the sink for a glass. Before he'd finished pouring, Jodie made her entrance, and the cold challenge in her eyes made a cool drink unnecessary.

He set the pitcher on the table. "Were the boys all right?"

"Sound asleep," she answered, playing along with him, pretending she hadn't seem him watching the tucking-in procedures from the shadows. "And so is Grams."

"As are most people in Natchitoches this close to the bewitching hour. I suggest we turn in, too. You've had a rough evening."

"Not nearly as rough as Gloria Bigger's."

"And none of that was your fault. The woman had a heart attack, her second according to the report we got when we called the hospital. And the last report said she was holding her own."

He took her hand. She pulled it away, as if his touch might defile her.

"It's possible you and Butch are right about the stalker not frightening her into a heart attack. It's also possible you are wrong. At any rate the flowers this afternoon were from the stalker."

"That's circumstantial evidence."

"Okay, I *believe* they were from the stalker. I also believe there's a good chance he is either in town or on his way. Call me crazy. I don't care. But this man is obsessed with me in some sick fashion. Obsessed enough to travel across the country to find me. I don't understand it. I just know it's true."

"I'm sure there have been many men obsessed with you, Jodie. I remember a few."

"Don't make light of this. You don't know the whole story."

Her eyes watered, dark depths of fear, and Ray fought the urge to take her in his arms. But comfort would not release the devils that were tormenting her. Talk might at least help him to understand them. "Go on, Jodie. You've been skirting the truth all night." He pulled out a straight-backed kitchen chair and led her to it. "Tell me the rest of the story."

She perched on the front edge of the seat, her eyes staring at a spot somewhere over the kitchen range, her hands

on the table, clasped tightly. "It would be a waste of time.
You wouldn't believe me any more than anyone else did."

"Try me."

"Okay." She took a deep breath. "I worked late at the
office one night."

Her voice was hollow, as if she were delivering a mem-
orized speech that had nothing to do with her. Ray listened
carefully, his attorney's mind honing in on every detail.

"I had to finish up a presentation for a client. Max Roling, one of the college interns stayed to help. I told him I'd
treat for dinner."

"And did you go to dinner?" he asked, when she appeared stuck in the mire.

"Yes, at a restaurant close to the office. It was late, past
ten when we finally stopped to eat. We had a glass of wine.
I guess the combination of zinfandel and fatigue got to me.
I opened up for the first time to him about the stalker who
was wreaking havoc on my ability to sleep or concentrate."

"What was his reaction?"

"No signs of guilt, if that's what you're thinking. He
was surprised, and understanding. We finished the meal,
and he hailed me a cab. I offered to have the taxi drop him
off at his place, but he refused. He was supposed to meet
a friend later, a waitress at a restaurant in the theater district."

Pain hammered at Ray's left temple. He had a good idea
where the story was going. "I know this is tough on you,
but tell me everything, Jodie. And be as accurate as you
can."

"I'll try. The facts are entangled with emotions." A frustrated sigh escaped her lips. "Max hugged me tightly before I got into the cab. But instead of his arms, it was
someone's gaze that I felt."

She shook her head, rearranging the unruly curls that
hugged her cheeks. "I know. It sounds crazy. Several of-

ficers of the NYPD already assured me of that, in kinder words, of course. But *he* was watching us. I felt him, the same way I felt him tonight.''

''It's not crazy, Jodie. Survival is a sixth sense sometimes. You can't take it to court, but that doesn't mean it's not real.''

''I got a call in the middle of the night from the police department,'' she continued, a finger tracing the outline of a vine in the tablecloth. ''Max had my business card on him, and they needed someone to identify the body.''

''Oh, jeez! And you had to be the one they called.'' This time Ray's body refused to heed his own survival warnings. He rounded the table in quick steps and all but lifted Jodie from her chair, steadying her on her feet and cradling her in his arms.

''One week later, I woke in the middle of the night, shaking and afraid. That's the night I found the note tucked inside Blake's crib.''

Her voice dissolved into a shaky whisper. ''And that's when I ran. Until today, I'd thought I'd made the right decision.''

''You did. You definitely did.'' Ray tightened his arms about her, and she swayed closer. She felt so good in his arms, so right. His brain went numb. His body grew warm.

When he'd left New York two years ago, Jodie Gahagen had been so embedded in his senses, it had taken months for him to even begin to get over her. Months before he could fall into bed at night without aching to hold her. Months before he had woken up in the morning without reaching for her.

Now it was all coming back, and he was powerless to stop the feelings that raged inside him. Her head was on his shoulders, her hair painting the front of his shirt with a tangle of bright red curls, her fragrance filling him like some exotic aphrodisiac.

It was all wrong. His brain whispered the warning. But his body shouted his need. He pulled away only enough to slip a thumb under her chin, to tilt her face upward. Her lips trembled, and he touched them with his own, softly at first, then harder, hungrily.

The world swam around them, and he was powerless to control the desire that choked away his will. Jodie finally did, pulling away, her eyes fiery, and her soft lips still swollen from his kiss.

"Why did you do that?" she asked, meeting his gaze head-on. "Why did you kiss me?"

"I don't know. An impulse."

"A be-nice-to-the-scared-lady kiss?" She walked to the other side of the table, putting a tangible barrier between them. "I don't need that kind of comfort. The truth is I don't need anything from you. I want you to leave here, tonight."

"I can't do that."

"Of course you can. You just pick up your bag and walk out the door. No phone calls. No cards and letters. You just leave and then nothing. You're good at it. I've seen you in action."

"If you're talking about New York, I had my reasons, Jodie."

"They don't matter, not now."

"Maybe not, but I'm not leaving until we know for sure if this lunatic of yours is in town."

"You have work to do. You can't be my bodyguard twenty-four hours a day."

"I won't have to. Ben will be here during the day. I'll be here at night. You and the boys will be safe, and if the man shows up, we'll nab him."

"He'll show up, but you'll never see him. No one will, until he wants to be seen."

"I'll stop him," he said, knowing that he had to protect

Jodie, no matter what being around her every night did to him.

"You can stay here tonight, Ray. I'll make up some excuse to Grams as to why you're here. I'll have to tell her so many lies to make my plan of action work that one more won't matter."

"And what happens after tonight?"

"I'll be out of here," she said, her voice trembling.

"No way. You are not running away again. The chase has to stop somewhere, and it should be here where you have friends and family."

"And a policeman who gives credence to my story?"

"Butch said he'd check everything out. Besides, you can't keep uprooting the twins' lives trying to outrun a madman."

"The twins are not your concern. But you're right. I won't be taking the twins with me. This time I'll run alone and hope the stalker catches up with me. If I can see him, I can go to the cops with a description. I want this over, once and for all, one way or another."

"Now you're talking crazy, Jodie. I will not let you do this."

"Then you better come up with a hell of a way to stop me."

She spun toward the door, her hair flying. Ray thought hard for a comeback, but his mind drew only blanks while he watched her march her shapely little body out the door.

Chapter Four

The grandfather clock in the downstairs hall struck three. Jodie counted the chimes as she stared at the ceiling. Alone in the dark, memories played havoc with her determination and trounced on her will. Memories and proximity. Ray Kostner was in the next room, separated from her by a few feet and a wall. And an impenetrable barrier of regrets and denial.

She tossed again, mauling the sheets and wallowing in images that would be best forgotten. With all the complications in her life, all the hopelessness of running from a madman who wouldn't give up, Ray had still managed to slip back into her heart. She had learned nothing from years of mistakes.

As a teenager, it had been the relentless infatuation with the town bad boy. He'd always been a little bigger than life, more daring than the other boys in town, and far more exciting. He'd been the teenager who collected speeding tickets like baseball cards, ran away to New Orleans for a wild weekend when most of his classmates dared go no farther than Shreveport. He'd been the one kicked off the football team for ignoring the coach's orders and having his head shaved in Mohawk fashion, just to be cool.

He would have probably never made it through high school if his dad hadn't been the pillar of the community.

Still, half the adolescent female population in Natchitoches had drooled over him since grade school.

Actually, Jodie had been a late bloomer. She'd been all of fourteen before she'd fallen under his spell. Ray had been a senior in high school then, and he had stopped by her house with her older cousin for a slice of her birthday cake. Too bad he'd liked Grams's coconut cake so much— he'd thanked the birthday girl with a kiss on the cheek.

The kiss.

Her first kiss. And it had to be from Ray Kostner. Not that it was much of a kiss. But she hadn't washed her face for days. She'd have waited longer if she hadn't gone up to Shreveport to the state fair and eaten that wad of sticky cotton candy. She'd waited for years for him to kiss her again.

God, she'd been stupid. Then she'd had youth for an excuse. Tonight she had only her own weakness to blame. She'd ignored every warning her brain had issued and asked for his help. Once again he'd torn her heart from her chest and stamped on it.

He'd denied his own sons.

She could live with his rejection, but as long as she had breath in her body, her sons wouldn't have to.

Jodie kicked her feet, entangling them even worse in a sheet that seemed to be fighting back. She gave up and attacked the pillow instead, pounding it into submission, and wishing for daylight.

She closed her eyes, for seconds, mere seconds. That's when she heard the noise. A cry of pure pain, and it was coming from the nursery. She jumped from the bed and raced down the hall. Before she was out her door, the second twin had joined in the wailing chorus.

Ray beat her to the nursery. "What's wrong with them?" he asked, from his position between the two cribs.

"I don't know. Maybe they don't like having strangers in the house."

"I'll introduce myself. The name's Ray Kostner. I'm here to help your mom."

Blake quit crying and stood, sinking his teeth into the top railing of the crib. He was all smiles now that company had arrived. Jodie nudged Ray out of the way and reached over the railing to check on Blair. He'd stopped wailing the second he'd caught sight of her too, but he looked none too happy. His lips were trembling, his eyes red from tears.

She let her fingers linger on his brow. "He has a fever," she said, picking him up and holding him close.

"I can drive you to the hospital."

"You don't rush babies to the hospital every time they have a fever. But I do want to check it. Could you get the thermometer for me? It's on the table over there."

Ray fumbled through the assortment of baby implements while Jodie changed Blair's diaper. "I don't see a thermometer."

"You have your hands on it."

"Really? Odd-looking contraption."

"Just hand it over." She took it and inserted it in Blair's ear.

"I thought you put those things in their mouth."

"Go back to bed, Ray. I'm not doing a class in Baby 101 tonight."

"If you're sure you don't need any help."

"I'm positive."

Relief eased the lines in his face. "I'll wait and see how high his fever is, though. High fever's not good for a kid. I do know that much."

"A hundred and one. You can go to bed."

"Does that mean you don't have to worry?"

"No, it means I don't have to panic. I'll give him something to bring the fever down and take him to the doctor in the morning. It's probably an ear infection. He's prone to those.''

Ray backed to the door. Jodie settled in the rocker and cuddled Blair in her arms. Blake assessed the situation and figured he was the loser. He released a mournful wail.

"Do you think he has a fever, too?" Ray asked, slinking back inside the room.

"No. Probably just brotherly sympathy pains. Of course, he might need his diaper changed."

The look on Ray's face was one of pure panic.

"You could change him and see if that calms him," Jodie said sweetly, knowing she was scaring the wits out of the usually confident attorney and enjoying every second of it. "Staying here was your idea, you know. You might as well be useful."

Blake increased his volume level considerably when no one moved in his direction. "Okay, boy, quiet down now. You'll wake your great-grandmother." Ray stepped closer, his hands still at his side. "I...ah...I don't know how to change a diaper," he finally admitted.

"It's easy. I'll give you step-by-step instructions."

He looked doubtful. "What if I stick him with a pin? That would be a lot worse than a wet diaper."

"Diapers don't have pins anymore. Get one out of the package on the dressing table. You can change him in the bed. All you have to do is unsnap his jammies and take off the wet diaper. Slip the new one under and over his bottom and attach the tabs. Surely a high-powered lawyer can handle a simple task like that."

"We didn't cover changing diapers in law school."

No, she was sure they didn't. If they had, he would be an expert, like he was at everything else he did. She was the one who was a slow learner.

She watched his awkward movements as he changed the diaper of a son he'd never wanted and didn't claim, the amusement she'd felt initially dissolving into a lump that settled in her chest, choking her breath away.

In the morning she'd insist he leave the house. Gentle Ben would stay over at night if she asked him. He'd done it before.

"All done." Ray's voice interrupted her thoughts. "What do I do with this thing?" He held the wet diaper with two fingers, at arm's length, as if it contained radio-active material.

"Dump it in the plastic container in the corner."

"Disposable. I like it." The smile on his face forecast his pride in his dubious achievements. And either the dry diaper or the attention had worked. Blake was lying on his back, sucking his right thumb and kicking his legs con-tentedly.

"Do you need me to do anything else?" Ray asked.

"No."

"You still look upset, Jodie. I'll call the doctor for you if you want."

"No." She placed her lips on her son's head. "He's cooler now that he's stopped crying. I'll rock him until he falls asleep."

Ray leaned on the door, watching her. She rocked faster, suddenly aware of the thinness of her nightshirt, the warmth in the room. "Go to bed," she whispered.

"Well, if you're sure you don't need me..."

"No, I don't need you." She almost choked on the words. She needed him. She couldn't lie to herself. But it was a need she would bury deep inside her, so deep she would forget it existed.

She closed her eyes, holding Blair so close she could feel the beating of his tiny heart as Ray turned and walked from the room.

THE SOUND OF a lullaby filled Ray's ears as he made his way back down the narrow hallway to the guest bedroom.

What in the hell was he doing here? Two years ago he'd walked away from Jodie Gahagen, knowing he could never let her back in his life.

Tonight he was more convinced than ever he had made the right decision. She was the marrying kind, the type of woman who made love to you like there was no tomorrow and then had you planning a future of…of changing diapers and going to Little League games. The type of life he didn't want and couldn't handle.

So why was he here?

Jodie was in danger, that's why. *Pay the ultimate price, like the others did.* Even now the words settled like cold lead in his gut. If the man who wrote that note wasn't stopped, Jodie could wind up dead.

He couldn't let that happen.

Doubts rose inside him bitter as bile. He was nobody's savior. Ask his mom, his dad, his high school coach. Make demands, and Ray Kostner buckled under like an empty cardboard box.

Only in his professional life was he a man of might. And that's how he had to keep this. Impersonal. It was the only way.

He dropped to the side of his bed and flicked on the lamp, grabbing a pen and paper. He was wide awake now; he might as well work on the problems at hand. Number one: how to trace the identity of the man who was terrorizing Jodie. Number two: how to keep his hands and lips to himself when Jodie was around.

He closed his eyes as he heard the clock, praying he would get some sleep and not dream of anything that had happened nearly two years ago in New York City. Even he had his limits of endurance.

TENSION THICK AS a bowl of Grams's grits hovered over the kitchen table. The last thing Jodie had wanted was to pull her grandmother into this. But with the local police already calling the house, it was only a matter of time before she figured it out on her own.

"Why didn't you tell me this before, Jodie?" Grams fingered her coffee cup, running a bony digit around the edge of the delicate china handle.

Jodie reached a hand across the table and wrapped it around one of Grams's. "I didn't want you to worry."

"Well, of course, you didn't want to worry me, child. But I'm family. It's my duty to worry." She got up, refilled everyone's coffee cup and then sat back down at the head of the table. "Now, Mr. Attorney, what are you going to do about this?"

"I'm—"

Jodie cut him off. "It's not Ray's problem, Grams. It's mine, and *I* can handle it."

"Pooh. If you could handle it, you would have done it already. Besides, you've got mothering to do, and Ray here doesn't do anything but run around town all day in one of those fancy starched shirts and neck-choking ties bleeding people dry with those confounded lawsuits. A little worthwhile work would do him good."

Ray's laughter filled the air. "You do know how to cut to the chase, Miss Emily." He stirred cream into his coffee and took a slow sip before continuing. "Jodie came to Natchitoches for help and we're going to be sure that she gets it. In fact, I'm going to get started on it right after you cook that bacon and eggs you've been threatening me with."

"Good." She pushed her glasses farther back on her nose. "What can I do to help?"

"Just keep everything under your flowered sunbonnet. The fewer people who know about all of this, the easier the hunt will be. I'll tell Ben, though. I want him to keep an eye on all of you during the day.''

"And Selda. I have to tell Selda. The woman's been my next-door neighbor for thirty years. And you can't keep a secret from that nosy woman anyway." Grams was already up and busy, peeling off thick slices of honey-cured bacon.

"Okay, Grams. You can tell Selda, but no one else. In fact, I'll go over with you after I've fed the boys their breakfast," Jodie offered.

"No need for that. She's already called. Said she had something she wanted to bring over for the twins, but I bet she already heard about what happened last night at Gloria's shop. She'll be over before the dishes are wiped to get an earful."

The baby monitor on the counter buzzed with the sounds of wriggling movement and toddler babbling. "The boys are waking up," Jodie said, grateful for an excuse to leave Grams and Ray at each other's mercy.

"And I've got to eat and get back to those disgusting lawsuits," Ray said with a conspiratorial wink. "If I don't see you before I leave, I'll pick you up at twelve-thirty for lunch, Jodie."

"I have plans."

"Change them. I worked up a list of priorities last night, and I want to go over them with you. Also, I'll need information about everyone you came in contact with in New York on any regular basis. I'll need descriptions, when you've seen them last, anything unusual about the way they act around you. That type of thing."

"You're not my attorney."

"I'll take care of that," Grams said, cracking eggs into a pottery bowl. "I'll hire him."

"I accept the assignment."

Jodie shook her head in exasperation. She'd save her strength for a battle she could win. She'd handle Ray her own way, outside Grams's earshot. "I'll see you at lunch, counselor," she said defiantly before marching out of the kitchen.

LASYONE'S WAS BUSTLING at 12:30, tourists and locals alike crowded at the small wooden tables. Ray pushed through the door and then held it open for Jodie, ushering her into the spot he frequently referred to as aroma heaven.

The potent odors of hot spices drifted in from the kitchen where the miniature meat pies browned in huge pots of hot grease and oysters and shrimp danced on sizzling grills.

A waitress, blond and willowy and no more than twenty, flashed him a smile and wiped her hands on her apron. "Smoking or nonsmoking?" she said, sidling up next to him.

"Nonsmoking, unless there's a long wait."

She flashed her eyes flirtatiously. "I got a table just opening up in the back. It won't take but a minute to get it cleaned and set up."

"Sounds perfect."

They followed the sashaying waitress through ill-formed rows of tables, all covered in plastic cloths and most filled with huge helpings of red beans and rice, potato salad and the famous meat pies. A group of young men in jeans and work shirts looked up from their food as they passed. The waitress was prancing, but it was Jodie their eyes were on.

Ray didn't blame them a bit. Even in loose slacks and a cotton blouse, the figure beneath the mane of bright red hair was enough to make a man turn primal. He should know.

But the figure wasn't the only thing that drew men's attention. She wore the look of a challenge, forbidden, too self-satisfied. But Ray knew better than to buy the look. He'd kissed it from her face before, knew that beneath the cool exterior, there was enough heat to seriously threaten the polar ice caps.

Keep it cool. Impersonal. All business. The warnings flooded his brain.

He held a chair for Jodie and then took the one to her right, making sure his hand didn't brush her shoulder or tangle in her hair.

"Do you have a recommendation?" she asked, burying her head behind the well-worn menu the waitress had left.

"I've never had a bad dish here. Of course, I like my food spicy. Save room for dessert, though. The Cane River Cream Pie is the best in town, next to Miss Emily's, of course. I've been known to go for seconds."

"Everything looks good. Unfortunately, I don't have much of an appetite these days."

Ray studied the lines in her face. In most people, the kind of fear and worry she'd been living with would have drawn and drained their features, making them look tired and years older. It obviously didn't work that way with Jodie.

Her beauty wasn't at all diminished. If anything, the new seriousness made her more woman, more desirable even than the whirlwind of vivacious energy he remembered.

He smiled thankfully as the waitress returned with two tall glasses of iced tea. He was falling into the trap again. He wasn't sure who set the trap, Jodie or his own memories, his own needs and fantasies. All he was certain of was that he felt the clamps tightening every time he was around her.

But the traps would never hold. That's why he had to remember that Jodie was off-limits. Friend in need, and nothing more. He owed that to both of them.

Bending over, he reached into the briefcase at his feet and pulled out a yellow legal pad. No use to put off the inevitable.

"I spent the morning on the phone to the NYPD," he said, looking over his notes. "It took some persistence, but I finally managed to talk to the detective who's investigating your complaints."

"Detective Cappan?

"One and the same. Seems like a sharp guy."

"Not as sharp as the stalker."

"Maybe not. But he's out there trying. He thinks you did the right thing by getting out of New York. For the record, so do I."

"Right. We may as well make the stalker work a little harder at his tormenting business. Now, he, too, can give up his job and apartment, if he had one, and travel to beautiful downtown Natchitoches. Maybe we should put up a banner welcoming him."

"I wouldn't. We have no evidence Deaton wasn't correct in his initial assessment. Panic and pain caused Gloria to knock the files to the floor. The man isn't likely to travel this far from his home haunting grounds, not when New York City is overrun with replacement victims."

"No, and Cappan didn't think he would move beyond leaving notes. He almost had me convinced until Max Roling turned up dead. And all the poor man did to deserve losing his life was give me a comforting hug. Come to think of it, Ray, you may be treading dangerous ground yourself. I should probably come with a warning label."

The frustration in her voice tore at his resolve. He battled the urge to take her hands in his, relying on words instead. "According to Cappan, Roling was murdered in a robbery attempt. The murder rate in Manhattan is down, but not extinct."

"I've heard Cappan's theory. It's old news. And wrong."

"You can't be sure of that." Ray ran his fingers up and down his glass, tracing a drop of condensation. "Stalking's a cowardly thing. In almost every case, the perpetrator waits until the victim is alone to act, just like yours has done. If there's no history of violence, the stalker usually doesn't escalate to that state.''

"Thank you, counselor. I couldn't have quoted the police procedural manual better myself. It doesn't do a damn thing for bringing Max back to life though.'' She unclasped the napkin she'd been twisting and picked up her knife, spreading a layer of butter on a wedge of French bread and then wagging the utensil at him. ''Besides, I doubt the murderer has a copy of the manual. Perhaps you and Cappan could send him one. It would make his life and mine a lot easier.''

"We could have just left one for him in your apartment.''

"What's that supposed to mean?''

"He came back, evidently the night after you moved out.''

Jodie winced at his words and sucked in her breath, letting it out in a heavy sigh. ''How do they know that?''

"Evidently the neighbor who purchased your furniture didn't get it all the first afternoon. When she came back the next day to pick up the bed and chifforobe, she found the door cracked open and the sheets on the bed wadded into knots, as if someone had slept there, or something. She was sure she'd left the door locked.''

"So it took less than twenty-four hours for the man to realize I'd run out. Fortunately, it took a month for him to track me to Natchitoches. Better than having him do it overnight. This way we know he's not psychic as well as crazy.''

"All we know is that he made a lucky guess about your destination. He could have talked to almost anyone who knows you and found out you were from here. At any rate, we have to put a stop to the harassment.''

"Not we, Ray. You have a short memory. *I* will put a stop to it."

The determination in her voice caught him off guard. He met her gaze, and what he saw worried him even more than the fear he'd seen the night she received the flowers. The fight that burned in the deep recesses of her pupils now was the kind he'd seen in desperate clients, right before they'd ignored his counsel and taken matters into their own hands.

"You're no match for the likes of this man. Especially if it turns out he really is a killer."

His words of caution were lost in the clatter of dishes being set in front of them. A huge plate of catfish for him, a shrimp salad for Jodie, and a bowl of fried okra for nibbling. He waited while the waitress gave her "Anything else for you?" spiel before continuing his lecture.

"When we get back to my office, I want descriptions of every man who's made a pass at you in the last year, even if you think it was totally innocent. I know a man in New Orleans who does unbelievably accurate drawings from verbal descriptions. I want to send them to Cappan and have him look through his mug books. Chances are this man has a record. Breaking and entering can get you time even in New York."

"I've been through the suspect list with Cappan already." Jodie nibbled on a shrimp, taking her time chewing and swallowing, her eyes everywhere but focused in his direction. "And I don't have time to go through it again today," she said finally, nudging a piece of lettuce with her fork. "I have an appointment at three o'clock in Shreveport. I'm hiring a nanny."

"That makes sense. Tending to those two would be too much for anyone."

"No, they're not too much for me." She took a deep breath and straightened her shoulders, as if gearing up for a battle she hated to fight. "But they'll be too much for Grams when I go back to New York."

The bite of catfish stopped midway down Ray's throat. He coughed it loose, his body suddenly tighter than a spring. "You are not going back to New York. Not until this thing is settled. For God's sake, Jodie, I just told you, the man was in your apartment the night after you left. If you'd been there…"

"Next time I will be there. It's the only way to stop him. If he followed me here, and I believe he did, he'll follow me back to New York. I'll let him know I want to see him, talk to him, find out who he is and what he wants from me. Then I can go to the police and have at least a chance of stopping him. But I have to do it alone. I have to protect Blake and Blair."

"So you'll get their mother killed, or…"

"Or I could bring the nightmare to an end. You and Cappan both said the man is likely harmless. Besides, something has to be done. I can't just keep running. As it is now, I've put the boys and Grams in danger. And even you."

"I can take care of all of you."

"We're not your responsibility."

Ray put down his fork and wiped his mouth. Civilized dining was obviously over. He couldn't believe he was having this conversation, not with Jodie Gahagen. She'd always been headstrong, but in the past she'd at least been sensible. Now she was spouting pure lunacy.

What he wanted to do was just put his foot down and order her to do what he said. In the same breath he might order the Mississippi River to change its course or the sun to rise at midnight.

He'd have to think of something more democratic, and persuasive. After all, he was the top defense lawyer at Fowler, Glenn, Kostner and Grange. The top one in the south since the Greer murder trial if he gave credence to the press. He could damn sure argue a point. If he could find one.

The beeper at his waist vibrated. He pushed his plate back, leaving half a catfish. His appetite was suddenly shot to hell, but Jodie's had blossomed. While he stewed, she was cleaning her plate, evidently feeling much better now that her ridiculous plan was out in the open.

"I have to make a call. Will you excuse me?" he said, punching in the beeper and making a mental note of the number.

"Of course. I think I might try a piece of that pie you were talking about. Can I order one for you?"

"No, thanks. Just coffee for me. And if she has some left in the bottom of a pot, tell her to warm that up for me. I need it strong."

He opted to make the call from his car phone. It would be much quieter there, and if the beep was the one he was expecting he wanted to hear the caller clearly. He exited the restaurant and slid into the front seat of his unlocked car. Grabbing the phone, he punched in the number. The credit card administrator answered on the third ring.

"I have the information you requested about Mrs. Gloria Bigger's reported credits, Mr. Kostner. I hope this is helpful to her."

"I'm sure it will be. And thanks for getting on this so fast."

"No problem. Since you faxed us documentation that the Kostner firm has the legal authority to handle all business decisions for the flower shop, we are glad to be of assistance."

Ray took out his pen and waited for the name and address of the person who had charged an order for a dozen roses yesterday afternoon. He scribbled it down and thanked the woman before slamming the cover shut on the phone. Everything he needed to know in two little words. Nasty words that blew his and Cappan's theories into shrapnel.

Now all he had to do was tell Jodie she'd been right all along. Statistics lied. Her survivor instincts had not. The card used to order the flowers had belonged to Max Roling. Ray shoved his knotted fists deep into the pockets of his trousers.

Jodie going to New York to face a killer. Like hell she was. He'd stay with her twenty-four hours a day if that's what it took to keep her in Natchitoches until the man was caught. Eat with her, work with her at his side, even sleep with her if he had to.

Sleep with Jodie Gahagen, and then walk away. He'd done it once. He'd sooner go hand-to-hand with a grizzly than try that again.

Chapter Five

Jodie stared at the walls of Ray's temporary Natchitoches office, the blood draining from her head, her mouth so dry she couldn't swallow. In her heart she'd always known the person who was stalking her had been the same man who'd plunged a knife deep into Max Roling's heart, twisting the blade until his life had spilled out on the street like used crankcase oil.

But somewhere inside her, she must have hoped otherwise. Why else would Ray's words be turning her stomach inside out?

"He's dead because of me." Strain tore at her voice, breaking the silence that hung in the air between them.

"He's dead because a lunatic took his life. This isn't your doing, Jodie." Ray paced the room, then stopped in front of her, rolling a chair closer and propping on the edge. He took her hands in his, holding them firmly, easing their cold shaking. "It's the work of a madman who has to be stopped."

"Right. Only no one stops him. I couldn't even get the police to seriously consider he was Max's murderer. They were so sure it was some punk kid, coming off a high and looking for a few bucks to start a new climb."

"They'll listen now. You just sit tight. The fact that Max's credit card is tied in with the flowers will force them to listen. With this new bit of evidence, they'll have a lot more motivation for finding and stopping the man who's ruining your life. And when they try him for murder one, he can be locked behind bars for the rest of his natural life.''

Ray made it sound so easy. Sit tight and the police would handle everything. Trust justice. And put more people in danger, people she cared about more than life itself. ''I can't do that,'' she told him, pulling away. ''Especially not now.''

She stood and walked to the window. Clouds were forming in the west, a new frontal system on the way, painting the old courthouse that stood across the street in shades of shadowy gray. The present building had been there since 1896, sturdy, unchanging, like the town. Perhaps its walls had seen murderers before. Perhaps the town had seen men as evil as the one who was either here now or on his way.

Perhaps not. All she knew was that she couldn't be the one that brought him to these streets. She couldn't be the cause of another death. Burning moisture gathered at the back of her eyelids. She tried to blink it away, but a tear escaped, sliding down her cheek. She whisked it away with the back of her hand, silently cursing it for exposing her weakness.

Ray eased behind her, so close she could hear his breathing, feel the warmth of it on the back of her neck. She kept her gaze riveted to a distant point outside the window. ''I have to leave. It's the only way I can make sure the boys are safe. And Grams. And even you, Ray, and anyone else who befriends me.''

''No.''

There was no pleading in his voice. The word was a command, direct, final.

''I'm not doing this out of some death wish. I'm not

looking forward to it, but I have no other choice. You're an intelligent man. Surely you can see that."

His hands pressed into her shoulders, tugging and forcing her to turn and face him. She met his gaze, and the intensity in his dark eyes sent a new wave of chills skidding along her nerves.

"I'm not letting you leave, Jodie. Not as long as this killer's on the loose." His grip loosened, but his hands didn't leave her body. His thumbs moved along the veins in her neck, sweeping up to her earlobes and back down again, a slow hypnotizing rhythm.

"Why, Ray, why now? Why are you all of a sudden so concerned about my well-being? Nearly two years ago, you spent a week in my apartment. You danced with me on Broadway at two in the morning, shared hot pastrami sandwiches with me at daybreak, rode the carousel with me in Central Park. And then just walked away with a simple goodbye."

"That was different."

"Obviously." Different in a million ways. Then he had slept beside her in bed, made love to her until every muscle in her body had ached with delicious pain. And when the week was over, he had said his goodbyes hurriedly, as if their time together had been a careless holiday he was ready to put behind him.

"You never even returned my calls. So what in the world makes you think you can just stroll back into my life now and give orders?"

She was shaking inside, but somehow she forced the outside to play the game, to hang tough when she was dragging her heartbreak out for public display. "Why now?" she insisted again.

"Because..." He backed her to the wall, his hands on her shoulders. His body was so close the front of his white dress shirt brushed against the smooth cotton of her blouse.

"Because, I…I can't stop myself."

She didn't get the chance to argue. Before she could open her mouth, his lips were pressed against hers. She pushed her hands into his chest, hard, afraid of the feelings that wrestled with her feeble hold on control. Control lost. The world spun around her, and instead of pushing, her hands and arms wrapped around him, pulling him closer.

His kiss deepened, his body pressing into hers, rocking her against the wall. Passion dipped inside her, exciting parts of her body she'd never known existed until the week she'd spent with him in New York. Now it was as if he'd never left. As if the nightmare of the stalker didn't exist.

She parted her kiss-swollen lips, and the play of his tongue tangling with hers left her weak and struggling for air. But still she couldn't pull her mouth away, couldn't bear to have his arms not around her, his fingers not digging into the flesh of her back. Tiny moans gurgled inside her, and she arched her body, pressing her hips against his, reveling in the hardness that she had brought to life.

The intercom on the desk buzzed. She barely heard it. It buzzed again, persistently, and Ray managed to pull away, grabbing the receiver. His "What's up?" was hoarse, strained with the passion that had to be tearing at him the way it was her. The receiver bobbled between his cheek and shoulder while he straightened his tie and rubbed at the wrinkles in his shirt.

"Put him through."

Jodie's pulse slowly returned to somewhere near normal. Ray was obviously talking to someone with the NYPD, giving them the facts about the credit card. The rest of the conversation made no sense at all.

"What was that all about?" she asked when he'd hung up the phone.

He tossed the legal pad he'd been scribbling on across the desk. "The kiss or the phone call?"

"Both. You can start with the phone call. The kiss we'll discuss later."

His gaze raked across her. "The investigation into the stalker has officially escalated to a homicide case. And, they believe your stalker is still in New York City."

"Why would they believe that? They have no idea who he is."

"A watch engraved with Max Roling's initials turned up in a pawnshop this morning. His sister identified it. She'd given it to him last Christmas."

"Oh, poor Janie. They were so close. Neither of them had married yet, and they spent lots of weekends together. They both loved the city. They were from a little town in Illinois." She was rambling. She couldn't help it.

"Concentrate on the positive, Jodie. If the man is in New York, then he's not here."

"*Ifs* are not reliable."

"They're as reliable as anything else we have to go on. And that means, you, the boys, your grandmother, all of you are perfectly safe. In fact, until this thing is wrapped up, this is the best place for you."

"And if the police are wrong? If the man is here in Natchitoches? If he frightened Gloria Bigger into her heart attack?"

"Then we'll know soon enough. Gloria's condition is listed as stable. If someone was in her shop last night, she'll be able to describe him. But the evidence points to the fact that your stalker's in New York. If he is, he can't hurt you or the boys."

"I can't take that chance."

"You have to, for all the reasons you mentioned before. You have two babies who depend on you for everything. They need you alive."

Two babies who needed her. Ray was right. No matter how badly she wanted the lunacy to end, she couldn't willingly put her life in danger. Not if there was any other way to stop the madness.

"What if you and the police are wrong, if the man is already here, watching and waiting?"

"Then you'll still be safe. Ben will be with you and Grams and the boys during the day. I'll be there at night."

"It sounds too simple, too easy."

"Not simple, just safe. So forget this nonsense about leaving town."

Jodie closed her eyes, determined to think with reason. Everyone had advice, but they didn't know this man, not the way she did. He was the terror she woke with in the morning and climbed into bed with at night.

Still, if she could stay here with the boys and know they were safe, know Grams was safe... "I can't promise you anything, Ray, except that I'll think about it and that I won't act foolishly."

"That's a start." He slipped a finger under her chin and tilted it upward. "Just hang in there, Jodie, and give the wheels of justice a little time."

"You never answered my question, Ray. Why are you so concerned about what happens to me?"

He slid a finger down her nose and across her mouth, then slowly traced the lines of her bottom lip. "I think I did answer the question a minute ago, for both of us. It's just that the answer has flaws."

"Flaws or limitations?"

"Both."

Flaws and limitations, the story of her life. She didn't even want to imagine what kind of limitations could go with a kiss so powerful, they had both been left as weak and disoriented as midday drunks.

"We'll talk about it tonight," he said, moving back to his desk. "Right now I have an appointment with a fee-paying client. One of Dad's regulars. He keeps the firm on retainer just so he can have instant attention.''

''I can take a cab back to Gram's.''

''No cabs. No strangers. I've already arranged for Dale to drive you home. He's the student worker from the university. Six-four and built like a wrestler. You'll be in good hands.'' Stretching across the desk, he punched the intercom button and asked his dad's secretary to find Dale.

Jodie slung her handbag over her shoulder. ''I'll see you tonight,'' she said. He only nodded, his head already bent over a manila folder of typed forms.

She opened the door and went to wait for Dale. The outer office was chilly, a forecast of the cold front that was dropping the outside temperature by the minute. Still, a flicker of heat ran through Jodie's blood. Flaws and limitations or not, the kiss had proved one thing.

She had not imagined the passion she and Ray had shared in New York. And it was still alive, not just inside her but burning in him as well, easily raised to four-alarm status.

When all of this was over, if it ever was, she wanted one more chance with Ray Kostner, not as her bodyguard, but as her lover. One chance to see if what she felt was love or just a young girl's fantasy that didn't know when to die.

And one more chance to see if he had what it took to be a husband and father. Either the flaws would win or she would.

THE EARLY AFTERNOON showers ended, leaving cooler temperatures and earth that squished instead of crunched beneath Jodie's rubber boots. She trudged along, tugging the wagon carrying Blake, Blair and a conglomeration of stuffed animals and plastic toys behind her. Fortunately, Grams's lot was large, nearly an acre, a yard size unheard of in New York. It gave Jodie and the boys room to roam without leaving the protection of home.

Especially with this, she thought, patting the walkie-talkie attached to a belt loop at her waist. One for her, one for Grams and one for Ben. Instant communication. Another of Ray's ideas. Another ploy to convince her to stay in Natchitoches.

Ray was determined that she was not going to leave. His reasoning was still a mystery to her. It would have made sense if he'd believed her when she'd told him the boys were his. Surely any decent man would feel obliged to protect the mother of his sons.

But he believed what he chose to believe. Mr. No Commitment turned macho protector from a stalker he kept insisting was thousands of miles away. His actions did not match his claims. If he'd really believed there was no danger, he'd be sleeping in his own bed at night, not camped out in Grams's guest room.

She stopped and pointed out a scurrying squirrel to the boys. Blake clapped his hands, and Blair tried to crawl out of the wagon. If he could see it, he wanted it. The simple logic of childhood. She could use a little simple logic herself these days.

"Jodie, is everything all right?"

She jumped, startled by the voice.

"I'm fine, Ben. Where are you?"

"Down by the boathouse, cleaning up some gardening tools. I just thought I'd check on you."

"We're fine."

"Then over and out."

Checking and playing with his new toy. He and Grams both were acting like troopers. Actually, more like children playing espionage. And, if Ray's scenario held true, it would stay that way. No one would get hurt.

She shuddered and looked around, a sense of uneasiness

shrouding the peace of the garden. It wasn't fair. A man too cowardly to identify himself had drawn her and her family into his circle of fear, robbed her of her right to live without terror.

And she was not the first woman to face this kind of nightmare. It happened far too often, according to Cappan and the literature she'd read on the subject. But usually the woman knew who was watching and following her, threatening her privacy and often her life. Somehow, Jodie was sure knowing would be easier. It was impossible to fight an identity without form.

She'd spent all of the boys' afternoon nap time sitting on the back porch, following Ray's orders. Searching hidden crevices of memory, she'd conjured up everyone she'd come in contact with in New York in the past year. If there was even the most remote chance they might be the stalker, she'd listed their name, as detailed a description as she could come up with and anything else she knew about them.

Tomorrow Ray would fax the names to Detective Cappan. He could check the ones she'd added since she'd given him the original suspect list and see if any one of them had a record. Ray would also fax the descriptions to his friend André in New Orleans. Ray wanted the drawings of possible suspects shown to everyone in the apartment building where she had lived. If someone had seen one of the men hanging around, either coming or going, they would have something to go on.

Anything would be miles ahead of where they were now.

Her list of possible suspects had grown. A few of her past clients, a couple of neighbors, an intern she'd fired for making unwanted advances to her secretary, a guy who worked at the deli by the office. Once she'd started, the list had grown, broadened to people she hadn't considered before.

The basic similarities were that they were all male. They all flirted, a little. They all looked at her in that way men do when they want you to know they like what they see. And none of them seemed nearly as sick as the man who had sent the bizarre notes.

Bits and pieces from the notes he'd left stabbed their way into her mind, impervious to the miles that hopefully separated her from the man who knew more about her than any lover she'd ever known. Descriptions of the way she looked after her shower, her wet hair dripping onto the tattered blue robe. Sensual details about the fragrance she wore, the way she shook her hair under the dryer, the way she applied creams to her face and body.

She stopped beneath a tree, her chest closing tight, stealing her breath. If she ever saw this man, surely she would recognize him. Evil that strong had to leave its mark, must surely haunt the eyes.

The police disagreed with her, telling her it could be anyone. More than likely, he would blend into a crowd, one of the masses. But she couldn't buy it. She'd felt him, not his touch, but his aura. It had been cold, dark, frightening.

The way it had been last night at the flower shop. She shivered and tugged her sweater tighter. Maybe the feeling wasn't reliable after all. It was almost as if *he* were here now, behind a bush, on the other side of the fence, maybe in the boathouse. But he wasn't. The watch he'd stolen from Roling had hit the pawnshop today.

Which meant *he* had to be in New York and she was freaking out again. She started walking, slowly, still deep in thought. Blake put up a howl. She stopped and bent to kiss his pudgy little cheek. "So, you like speed, do you?"

He waved his hands at her and managed to throw his bear over the high sides of the wagon. She picked him up and brushed a giant magnolia leaf from his tummy. The bear hairs were a little damp from his overboard experience, but fortunately he'd missed the mud.

"So, you want to play rough." She tickled Blake's stomach with the head of the soft bear, and he erupted in giggles. "And I guess you want action, too," she said, pulling Blair in on the fun. After a minute of play, she renewed the walk, heading down to the river, this time at a pace that kept the boys happy.

"Two babies and a pretty lady surrounded by the glories of nature. A Kodak moment."

Jodie's heart slammed into her chest like a runaway train. She spun around and stared in the direction the voice had come from, her fingers tightening around the walkie-talkie. "What do you want?" she asked, staring into a smiling face that peeked over the wooden fence.

"I'm sorry. I didn't mean to startle you. I just heard laughter and had to check it out. I'm glad I did. A pretty woman is always a refreshing sight." He stuck a hand over the fence, extended for her to shake. "My name's Greg Johnson."

She studied his eyes. They were brown, deep-set and huddled under thin blond brows, but no more evil than any other eyes she'd ever seen. Still, she ignored his outstretched hand and kept her distance. "What are you doing in the Mayans's backyard?"

"Getting a little fresh air. Admiring the view. I'm Miss Selda's new tenant. She gives me the run of the place, yard included, so I'm not trespassing, if that's why you're looking at me like I might be a gypsy out to kidnap you."

"I wasn't aware Miss Selda had a new tenant," she said, still watching his eyes.

"She does now. I moved in two days ago. She had a note posted on the bulletin board at the drugstore. I saw it, called her, and, as they say, the rest is history."

Jodie let her gaze move past the eyes. The man was

slightly older than her, thirty-five or so. His ears were too big, his nose a little pointed, but the grin that spread over his face more than made up for the minor flaws. In her prestalker life, she would have instantly warmed up to him. Today, it was only frigid caution that ran through her blood. She searched her brain for a snatch of memory, something to let her know if she'd seen this man before.

"What are you doing in Natchitoches?" she asked, bending to pull Blair's cap down over his ears.

"Taking pictures. I was just thinking, you and the boys, down by the river, maybe in the motorboat. That would make a great shot for your Christmas cards."

"No." The word flew from her mouth.

"Okay, just a thought. I wasn't going to charge you."

"It's not that." She started to explain, but thought better of it. She studied his face again, memorizing the shape of his nose, the cut of his sun-bleached hair, the way his brows hung low. If nothing else, doing the descriptions for Ray had taught her that she was not nearly observant enough. This time she would be.

"Are they the kind of pictures you usually take, family photographs?" She fished for more facts.

"No. I'm a freelancer, which means I shoot anything someone will buy. I'm on my own for this assignment, though. A friend of mine and I are doing a book on Cane River plantations. Hopefully we can get an editor to bite on it."

"Where are you from?" She tried to sound casual.

"Everywhere. Nowhere. I was homeless before it got all the press. This town a while, and then I move on. That way my photos don't have time to get stale."

The wind picked up, whistling through the trees, like a woman moaning, or crying for help. Blair tried to stand up, impatient to be moving again. She resettled him in the wagon, handing him a stuffed raccoon Grams had sent him for his first birthday.

"Where was your last assignment?"

"Up north. They've already had their first snowstorm. I was glad to relocate. What about you?" he asked, his gaze raking across her.

Blair started to cry as if on cue. "I have to be going," she said. "My sons are getting hungry." She turned the wagon and started back toward the house.

"I hope to see you again, soon. After all, we're neighbors now."

"I don't have time to visit much."

"Yeah. I'll bet. Babies are a lot of work even when they don't come in pairs." He walked his side of the fence, keeping up with her. "Anyway, I'm glad we met. I was watching you this afternoon."

"Why were you watching me?" Suspicion gnawed at her control.

"I can see your back porch from my room. The first time I'd looked out it was still raining. When I looked again, all I could see was your red hair, shining in the sun. I said to myself then, you should have been a hair model."

"Thank you."

"It's not from a bottle, is it?"

"What?"

"The red. Your hair."

"No. Why do you ask?" She was walking faster now, but he was matching her stride, her on one side of the fence, him on the other. A wall of wood between them, instant communication on her hip, Ben somewhere nearby, so why was her heart beating like the drums in a hard rock recording?

"I like natural stuff," he answered. "You know, women who don't try to gussy up too much, fool men into thinking they're something they're not. Funny, but fake comes through in a photograph easier than it does in real life. Maybe because everything stops in a picture, suspended in time, forever. The image is still there even when the people are gone.''

A door slammed, and Jodie looked to the house. Ray was there on the porch, watching her. She looked back to Greg Johnson, but the fence line was deserted. Her visitor had disappeared as quickly as he'd materialized.

Ray walked toward her, his unbuttoned suit jacket swinging with the rhythm of his gait, his tie already loosened and pulled away from his neck. Tall, familiar and confident. She took a deep and thankful breath. He had never looked better in his life.

HE YANKED THE TAB on the can of cola and took a long swig, letting the liquid roll down his throat. The last taste of powdery pills washed down with the cola. The medicine controlled the impulses that drove him, buried them beneath a thin layer of sanity. At least it was supposed to. But sometimes the feelings hit too hard, like a boxer delivering the killer blow. When that happened, the pills were useless.

He'd been on the verge of that yesterday, and it had made him make a costly mistake. He shouldn't have used Max Roling's credit card. Cops didn't worry about one woman with an admirer who didn't quite play by the rules. Murder was different.

But the impulses had taken over, and he had picked up the phone and ordered the flowers. The mistake had left him no alternative but to go to the florist shop last night. Destroy the order form with the card number and name so no one would be the wiser. And he'd done just that, though the fool woman had complicated matters, walking in seconds before he'd have been out the door.

He would have killed her to keep her quiet, if he hadn't been sure she was going to die anyway. A nice, natural heart attack, just like the others. Only this time, he wouldn't have had to waste his precious resources.

But the old broad was tough. Still, he was sure she couldn't have gotten a good look at him in the dark. At least, he was almost sure.

He took another long drag on the soda. Whiskey would have been better, but the pills didn't mix well with alcohol, and he had to stay focused, especially now.

Lay low. Just a man doing his job. He'd fooled everybody for years, and he would do it again. It was easy when he stayed focused, when he was the one in control. Amazingly easy.

He finished the drink and crushed the can between his fingers.

Jodie was a good girl, not like the others. Only a man was sleeping in her house. *If he ever found out the two of them had been together…*

Then it would be all over. For both of them. Even if the man wasn't defiling Jodie, it would be over soon, one way or another. It was time for him to make his move.

Chapter Six

Three days had passed since the arrival of the yellow roses. The cops had no news, police checks into the background of Selda's tenant had turned up zero and Gloria Bigger remembered nothing. Everything was back to the way it had been a few weeks ago except now Jodie was in Natchitoches instead of New York, waiting for the next horror to drop into her life.

"You're playing instead of eating," she said, picking up the spoon herself and coaxing Blair to open his mouth. Instead, his hand flew into the offering, sending the tiny green peas scattering across his tray.

Ray picked that opportune time to stroll into the kitchen. "Say, aren't you supposed to put the food in their mouths?"

"Very funny."

Not to be outdone, Blake put his lips together and blew, demonstrating a new noise he'd perfected in the last couple of days. Drool bubbled from his mouth and rolled down his chin as he banged his hands on the tray of his high chair.

"That's telling him, Blake," she said, pushing a slice of cooked carrot in front of him. "Now, open up and try this." He closed his lips tight.

"Can't say I blame you, Blake. I'd hold out for pizza."

Ray walked to the kitchen counter and poured himself a cup of coffee. "Do you want a cup?" he asked, lifting his in Jodie's direction.

"No, I have my hands full right now. And after this it's bath time."

"It's a good thing. Either that or you'll need to hose them down." He dropped into the chair closest to hers. "How did you learn to do this mothering stuff? Do babies come with some secret set of instructions for parents only?"

"Trial and error." She gave up on the carrots and went back to the peas and baby food chicken. "Mostly error. Although, fortunately, there are lots of good books on raising children."

"You must have read them all when you found out you were getting double trouble."

She kept working, suddenly aware that Ray was watching her every movement. He was asking questions, but she was sure he didn't want truthful answers. "I panicked at first, but the idea grew on me."

"You do a good job. I've known women who couldn't handle one, and you take care of two like it was fun and games."

"It is fun. It's also lots of work."

"And no pay."

"Wrong." Blair stuck his finger out, reaching for her face, his own brand of intimacy. He touched her lips and she kissed his sticky fingertips. "I've never had this kind of reward from anything else I've ever done."

"Then, I'd say those are two very lucky kids."

"I'm the fortunate one, Ray. I can't imagine life without them." And he was the unlucky one. Except he had everything he'd ever said he wanted. He'd left Natchitoches behind and made it big in a city where the lights never dimmed and the party never stopped.

He talked a good story, but here he was back in town, helping his father out in an emergency and risking his life to protect hers. That reeked of responsibility. Maybe she'd misjudged him. Maybe he'd misjudged himself.

"You look worried. You're not thinking about Selda's new tenant again, are you?" he asked, scooting his chair out of the line of fire of a pea that shot from Blair's spoon.

"No. I was thinking that I could use some help bathing the boys. What are you doing for the next half hour?"

His face screwed into perplexed wrinkles, and his fingers circled the near empty mug nervously. He tilted his mug high, drinking the last drops of the coffee as if it had some power to save him from her impossible request. When he set it back on the table, the clacking of pottery on wood filled the room.

"Okay," he said, his eyes narrowed. "I'm game. But remember, I'm a novice at this."

Jodie felt tight fingers of anxiety circling her heart. What had she been thinking? Surely not that exposure to parenting would change Ray Kostner.

"Everyone's a novice the first time." She wiped a layer of sticky dinner remains from Blair's face. "And only the tough survive."

"You make this sound like some kind of test."

"Do I?" she asked.

"Yeah." Ray got up from his chair and walked over to stand beside her, the cocky half smile he'd perfected to irresistible levels, splitting his lips. He took Blair from her arms, his hands brushing her breasts in the process, an innocent touch that took her breath away.

"Why would I give you a test?" she asked, her voice catching on the question.

"I don't know. Maybe because you know I can't resist a challenge. Maybe you just want to see if I'm the coward around babies I told you I am.'' He turned his back before she had a chance to think of a worthy response.

She followed him up the stairs to the bathroom, a wriggling Blake tucked under her arms. Bath time with Ray Kostner. She had to be losing her mind. To him this was a new game, one you could leave behind when something more exciting came along. And she'd be left to deal with more painful memories.

Minutes later, the boys were naked and fastened into bath safety seats that kept them from climbing and falling in the slippery water. One child she might have handled without the seats. Two left her seriously shorthanded.

''Hey, this isn't so bad.'' Ray scooted a toy boat across the water, making putt-putt noises as the boys laughed and splashed.

Jodie soaped a soft baby cloth and handed it to him. ''Then you're ready to advance to the actual cleaning stage.''

Ray took the soapy cloth. ''What do I do with this?''

''You scrub. Just pretend Blair's your Porsche and you're taking off a little road dust.''

''You mean I have to treat this splash machine like he's gold?''

This time *she* splashed *him*. ''He's a lot more valuable than that mass of metal and chrome you drive.''

Ray flicked a stream of water in her direction. ''Your mother's vicious,'' he teased, dabbing Blair's stomach with the soapy cloth. ''But I'll pay her back later.''

''I'm really worried. A man who can't handle bathing a small boy is no match for me.''

''What do you mean, can't handle the job? We're doing just fine. Tell her, big boy.''

''I don't know about the Porsche, but dabbing gently at a few exposed parts doesn't get it with little boys.'' She demonstrated the correct process, wiping Blake's face, getting the ears and under both chins while he tugged at the cloth and tried to wriggle out of her grasp. "You have to leave no spot untouched."

"No spot untouched, uh?" Ray's voice fell to a husky drawl.

His gaze raked across her, from the tip of her disheveled hair, down her water-splattered blouse to settle on her jeaned bottom that stuck out behind her as she knelt on the bath rug. Awareness sizzled inside her, and she wrung the cloth in her hands into a tight wad.

"Maybe we should try the bath routine again later, when the boys are in bed. I'll soap, you rinse."

Desire rose up inside her, sweet and choking. She pulled away. It was crazy to think like this. She had too much at stake here to let Ray take control of her feelings, building fires when he had no intention of staying around long enough to keep them burning.

If she let him, this would be New York all over again. Fun and games, only then it had been *sans* babies. They had laughed and played and made love in every corner of her tiny apartment. When the week was over, he had walked away without a backward glance. And she had been left with new life inside her, growing just beneath her breaking heart.

Blair splashed his hands across the surface of the water, and a spray of soap bubbles flew up and landed on the front of Jodie's blouse. Ray ran his fingers across the bubbles, scraping off a fluffy pile and flipping them back into the tub. The circle of dampness left by the dissolving bubbles gave her away. Her right nipple was hard and erect pushing at the lacy fabric of her bra and blouse.

He dabbed at the pinkish outline, massaging with the corner of a hand towel he'd dipped into the tub. The bath-water was only comfortably warm, but invisible steam rose between. Ray leaned closer, his eyes smoky with desire, his lips inches from hers.

When they touched, her breath rushed from her body, leaving her too weak, too dizzy to think. A shower of splashing water from Blake's hands hit her just in time. She lunged past Ray and grabbed a towel.

"They're clean enough," she said, her voice low and shaky.

"Too bad. I was just beginning to enjoy this."

"Good." Bending low to extract Blake from his seat, she lifted his dripping body and handed him to Ray. "If you like bath time, you'll love slipping these wriggling arms and legs into pajamas."

"*Undressing* was always my speciality."

Heat climbed her body and flushed her face as new images tangoed through her mind. A trail of clothes, hastily shed, leading to any surface big enough for two naked bodies. The sofa, the floor, the shower. Her mind reeled as she rescued Blair from the tub and started down the hall, Ray and Blake a step behind.

"Humpty Dumpty sat on a wall." Ray's boisterous rhyming echoed down the hall.

"Why, Ray, I didn't know they taught nursery rhymes in law school," she quipped, doing a poor imitation of a mother without worries.

"Oh, yeah. It's basic first-year trial procedure. Did Humpty really topple on his own, or was the wall's poor construction the reason for the fall?"

"And what was the verdict?"

"The jury's still out."

"I can identify with that."

Ray caught up with her as she reached the door. One arm around a wriggling Blair, he used the other to grab her elbow and pull her to a stop. "The jury is in on your case.

The man is as good as caught, and he will be tried and convicted.''

''You sound so sure.'' He was, of course, but he didn't know the way this man could move in and out of a building, an apartment, a bedroom without being seen. He didn't know the cold aura of terror this man carried as a shield.

''I am sure.'' His fingers trailed down her arm. ''I've made mistakes before. This time I won't.''

Mistakes, flaws, limitations. Easy excuses that got him off the hook, let him walk away from responsibility, let him pick and choose when and how much to risk.

She watched Blake climb Ray's chest, his red head bobbing up and over his father's shoulder, a father he and his brother might never get the chance to love.

And that might be Ray's biggest mistake of all.

Her heart constricted. The last thing she wanted for her boys was a father who'd turn his back on them, taint their lives with rejection, poison their self-confidence with denial.

She hugged Blair to her, her lips burying in the whisper soft baby hair. She loved her boys so much she had to protect them at all costs from any source of danger or heartbreak. That was the only fact she was sure of.

That and the knowledge that she couldn't let Ray tear the heart from her again.

JODIE PULLED A light yellow sweater over her head and smoothed it over the top of her brown flannel skirt. The temperature was hovering in the high fifties, and in Natchitoches that constituted sweater weather. Cotton, of course. Wool was about as useful to Louisianians as steak to a vegetarian.

Bending at the waist, Jodie let her hair fall free, fluffing it with her hands and then straightened to standing position. Loose curls bounced around her shoulders, falling into casual disarray, wild, the way Ray liked it. A quick stroke of blush and a swipe of bronze lipstick finished her grooming routine.

Turning sideways, she checked her profile in the full-length oval mirror that swung from a frame of cherry. Not bad for the mother of twins, she acknowledged, running her fingers along the smooth lines of her stomach. She was five pounds less than her prepregnancy size.

Too bad her petite figure had only worked against her. Another trait the stalker found appealing. It was spelled out in one of his notes, in red, and in words that still sent icy shivers through her.

She hugged her arms about her. A week ago, she'd just begun to relax, to believe that moving to Natchitoches had been the solution she searched for.

But now she was walking the tightrope again. The only difference was that this time she was never alone. Ben was nearby during the day and well into the night, under orders from Ray not to leave until he arrived.

Which was getting later and later. She might have enlisted his aid in bathing the boys once, but, as always, Ray had his own priorities, and they obviously didn't include baby-sitting.

The last two nights he'd arrived at Grams's house after the boys were asleep, and he'd dressed and disappeared in the mornings without stopping in the kitchen for more than a fast cup of coffee.

Jodie suspected he'd have preferred to have had that in his dad's law offices if he'd been sure Grams wouldn't have followed him down there to make sure he drank one of hers. She was upset enough he wouldn't binge on bacon and eggs and other artery-choking breakfasts.

Ray Kostner, man of the hour, ready to play. Ready to boss and protect. Her guess was his hour was up and he was sorry he'd ever jumped into the macho male protector role. Maybe he'd tell her that this afternoon after they visited the hospital.

Finally, Gloria's doctors had agreed to let their recovering patient have visitors outside the immediate family and the police. Detective Butch Deaton had spoken with Gloria once. He'd left her bed convinced Gloria had been alone in the shop when her heart had dived into a state of massive shutdown.

He'd delivered the message to Jodie in person, staying for dinner at Grams's invitation, assuring them both that he was watching the house even though the evidence pointed to the stalker's being in New York.

Jodie wished she shared his certainty. But if he was wrong, if the stalker had been at the florist shop that night, then his face might be embedded somewhere in Gloria Bigger's subconscious. All they had to do was pull the description out of her, and she could put a face to the formless monster.

A last glance in the mirror, and Jodie decided to tie her hair back from her face. Ray liked it flying loose, and she had no desire to ignite desire. She'd make sure he knew she was with him only because he had insisted on bullying his way back into her life, not to set a husband trap.

She slid open the top drawer of the dresser. The usually neat stack of scarves were fluffed instead of folded, as if someone had tossed them and let them parachute into place. Ice water coursed her veins.

Trembling, she clutched the top edge of the dresser for support. She was overreacting. The stalker couldn't have been here in her bedroom. They had been home every day. But even as she whispered the denial, she knew her words were a lie.

She ran her fingers beneath the scarves, searching until they encountered the prickly edge of the scrap of paper she knew she'd find. She pulled it out, her heart racing, blood rushing to her head in dizzying spurts.

This time the note was a Valentine, homemade from red construction paper and a thin parchment doily. The words were written in red ink. She forced her gaze to fasten on them, shimmying as they were between her shaking fingers.

> Roses are red
> My heart is blue
> Don't run away again
> Or you'll pay the price, too

Pay the price, too. Like Roling. Her insides churned sickeningly. A man who killed for no reason except some sickness that festered in his mind, and he had been here, in this room. Steps away from her sons. Steps away from Grams.

But the killer wanted her.

The hinges on the door creaked behind Jodie, and she spun around. Ben stood in the shadow of the door, watching her. He stepped inside and closed the door behind him.

Jodie stuffed the note in the front pocket of her slacks. "You frightened me, Ben." She struggled to steady her voice. "Is something the matter?"

"Yea, ma'am. I need to talk to you."

His gaze darted about the room, and he fingered a baseball cap, bending the soiled bill, the muscles in his arms strained as if it were a task worthy of his strength. Her heart beat erratically.

"Has something happened? Did you see someone?"

"Oh, no ma'am. It's nothing like that. It's just, well, it's my son, Grady."

"Grady?" She tried to focus on Ben's words instead of the fear that twisted inside her. "Is he sick again?"

"No. It's not that. But he's here."

"In the house?" Her mind skittered crazily over every frightening possibility.

"No, of course not. In Natchitoches."

"You mean he's back for a visit?"

"No. He's packed up and left New York. Moved back in my place. Says he got fired and couldn't afford to pay his half of the rent up in Brooklyn. I think his roommate kicked him out, though he wouldn't admit it. He always defends those so-called friends of his."

She shook her head. "But he didn't live in Brooklyn. He lived in Pittsburgh."

"Not for six months or more. Didn't Miss Emily tell you?"

"No, she must have forgotten. Are you saying that you were in New York all the time you were out of town?"

"Yes ma'am. I thought you knew."

"Why didn't you call me, Ben? Why didn't you visit me?"

"I don't cotton to those subways much." He stared at the carpet. "Besides, you didn't ask me to."

"I didn't know you were in town. When did Grady arrive in Natchitoches?" she asked, her mind whirling with frightening suspicions.

"A few days ago. He needs a job."

She knew what Ben was after, but the last thing she wanted was his son hanging around the house. There was little chance he was the stalker, but she couldn't take even little chances. "Maybe he can find employment in town," she suggested, trying to sound positive.

"Yes ma'am. Maybe so."

"With the Festival of Lights preparations in full swing and the Christmas tourists about to invade, I'm sure there are several local businesses that can use some extra personnel."

He looked at her doubtfully, and shrugged his shoulders.

"Any other time, Ben. But things are not going well." She reached in her pocket and wrapped her fingers around the note. Her flesh crawled and her hands grew clammy. The madman had held this same note in his hands. Maybe minutes ago.

"What is it, Miss Jodie? You look like a ghost's walking over your grave."

"The stalker. He was here, Ben, in this room."

"He couldn't have been. I was here all the time, Miss Jodie. I had the walkie-talkie on every second."

"I'm not blaming you, Ben," she said quickly. "It's no one's fault. It's always like this. He moves silently, invisibly, like a phantom."

"What do you want me to do, Miss Jodie?"

"I need you to stay here in the house with Grams and the boys while I go to the hospital to see Gloria Bigger. I wouldn't go now, but it's necessary."

"I won't leave them for a second."

"I don't know what we'd do without you, Ben."

"With all Miss Emily's done for me over the years, I'm just glad to be on the doing end for a change. Besides, I like you a whole bunch, Miss Jodie. You know that."

He studied his shoes. "I was wondering, Miss Jodie, do you think I could bunk in the boathouse for a while? That way I'd be here on the premises all the time, and Mr. Kostner could just come and go like he wanted. He wouldn't have to come around at all when he was working late."

Unexpected disappointment settled in her stomach, cold and hard. It was so like Ray to weasel out of a responsibility she'd never asked him to take on. "Is this Ray's idea?" Her words came out rougher than she intended, more like an accusation.

"No, ma'am. I haven't even talked to him about this. I know he's helping out around here now, but I don't see as where I live is any of his business."

A little resentment leaked from his tone. It took Jodie by surprise. It was out of character for Ben, at least out of the character he showed around her. Maybe Ben ran a lot deeper than the easygoing surface he displayed when she was around.

"I haven't talked to Miss Emily, either." He shuffled his feet and twisted the cap in his hand. "Not yet, anyway. I thought I'd ask you first. Truth is I was thinking about moving in the boathouse anyway, before I knew you were moving back home. That was if Miss Emily didn't object. She needs someone to keep an eye on her, what with her memory coming and going like fireflies on a starry night."

"And she's very lucky to have you looking out for her. It's fine with me if you move in. I'm sure it would be fine with Grams, too. But what about your son? He might not be too happy about your running off and leaving him."

"Not that boy. He don't care a good two cents about my company. It's the freebies he's here for. I don't fool myself. Not anymore. He don't have no more use for me than his momma did."

"In that case, we'd love having you. If you need anything, we can raid the attic. There's enough furniture up there to fill a couple of plantation homes."

"I don't need a thing. Those old bunk beds that used to be in your room are out there. A TV, too. And Miss Emily put a microwave out there last winter so's I could warm my lunch and make me some of that instant hot chocolate when my old bones got chilled. And if I get a notion to do more than open a can or two, why that old range your grandpa used to fry fish on still works. They don't make 'em like that any more."

"Then it sounds like you're all set."

The purr of Ray's engine drifted through the open window. "I have to go now, Ben. Just watch the boys and Grams until I get back. And if anything happens, anything at all, call Butch Deaton at once.'' She scribbled down a couple of phone numbers. ''The top one's his office, the bottom one's his beeper.''

''Did you tell him the stalker's been here?''

''No, but I will. I'll call from Ray's car phone.''

''Take care, Miss Jodie. A woman like you, so pretty and sweet. You can't trust a man. Not any man.''

''I'll take care, Ben. But I do trust some men. I trust you.''

She gave him a quick hug and walked to the boys' room. Before she left the house, she needed a second alone with them. She was the one the stalker wanted, and there was no reason to believe he'd hurt her children. Still, even the thought of his evil invading their lives filled her heart with overwhelming dread.

She couldn't sit back and wait any longer. The note beneath the scarves had robbed her of that choice.

Chapter Seven

Jodie climbed into the passenger seat of Ray's car without waiting for him to play gentleman. He slid under the wheel and started the motor.

"You look upset," he said, backing out of the driveway and into the street.

"I had a visitor today."

"Who was that?"

"The stalker."

He turned to face her, deep grooves forming in his forehead. "What happened?"

She told him the story of finding the note. He let her talk uninterrupted, the muscles in his arms straining the fabric of his shirt, the veins in his neck and face popping out like the lines on a road map. A car pulled in front of him, and he slammed on the brakes, a string of curses flying from his lips. She was sure the car had not provoked his fury.

"How did he get inside the house without being seen or heard?"

"If I knew that I could stop him." She reached for the cellular phone. "I have to call Butch Deaton. I'm supposed to tell him at the first sign of the stalker."

Ray listened while she shared the story again, but this time he reached over and wrapped his hand around hers.

"Tell him to get someone out there on the double. Check

every door and window for forced entry. And comb every inch of your bedroom for fingerprints.''

She repeated his directions into the phone.

"Who's coaching you, Jodie? It wouldn't be Ray Kostner, would it?''

"Ray and I are on the way to the hospital to talk to Gloria Bigger.''

"I've already talked to her. She doesn't remember anything about that night.''

"I know, Butch. But I'll feel better if I talk to her myself.''

"I understand. I know how tough this is on you. We'll find the man, Jodie. I'll have a crime scene team at your house in minutes.''

"I appreciate that.''

"I'll get back with you later today. And don't worry about a thing. The NYPD might not have caught him, but we will.''

She finished the conversation and hung up the phone as Ray swerved into the hospital parking lot.

The harsh odors of disinfectants blended with the sweet smells of gladioli and daisies as Jodie and Ray stepped into the hospital room. Sunlight peeked through half-open blinds, creating lined patterns of shadows on the bleached white bedsheets and the chrome of the side railings.

"Company. It's about time.'' Gloria greeted them from an almost upright position, propped as she was on three pillows. Her face was a pasty hue, her eyes encircled by gray layers of puckered skin.

Jodie stopped, knowing she shouldn't stare, but unable to look away. She'd run into Gloria at the checkout counter of Wal-Mart a couple of weeks ago. That image haunted her now. Then Gloria had been the picture of health, a chubby middle-aged matron full of gossip and glowing comments about the twins.

"How are you?" Jodie asked, stepping closer and taking Gloria's hand.

"Too puny to be half as ornery as I like, but I'm getting there."

A smile wrapped around Jodie's heart. The woman might be weak, but the zest for living was still there.

"You were never ornery," Ray said, flashing a smile and his charm. "Belligerent at times, but never ornery. You managed to control me in Sunday School for a couple of years if I remember correctly."

Gloria scooted up higher in the bed, her thin lips breaking into a smile. "That's an attorney for you. Always changing your words to say the same thing in a different way, just so no one knows what they're talking about. His dad's the same way."

The three of them chatted for a few minutes, the way people do who've known each other's families for all their lives but have never been close, touching the surface of safe topics. Today, the talk was mostly about doctors and their fading bedside manners and about the growing size of injection needles.

It was ten minutes into the visit before Ray managed to steer the conversation into focus. "Did anything unusual happen at the shop the night you had your coronary?"

"You mean besides nearly dying?"

"That was bad enough, I know, but did something happen to frighten you before the attack?"

"To tell you the truth, I don't remember much of anything that happened that night. I know I was going there to meet the two of you, something about a ticket you wanted me to check. Did you find it?"

"No, but that's okay." Jodie scooted to the front edge of the uncomfortable chair. "We think someone might have been in the shop that night when you got there. Do you remember seeing anyone?"

A dark shadow robbed the light from Gloria's eyes. Shivering she hugged her arms across her chest.

Jodie felt the same chill that inundated Gloria, but this time the cold was heated with hope. "Don't be afraid, Gloria. Just tell us if someone was there."

"I'm not afraid. Never have been. But this medicine. It makes you dream, you know, strange things. A man stealing your breath away, an ambulance that never reaches the hospital. The weirdest images pop into my head, but I can't give them credence."

"What kind of images?" Jodie's pulse was racing now, and she had to keep Gloria talking.

"Last night I could have sworn someone slipped into my room, and told me he had to kill me. I woke up screaming."

"You mean someone tried to kill you here, in your hospital room?"

"No, honey. It's the medicine. Dr. Creighton says it makes people imagine all kinds of things."

"But what about at the flower shop? You weren't taking medicine or having nightmares then. Was someone there?" Desperation clawed at Jodie's insides. "Did you see someone in your shop?"

"No. I don't even remember seeing you and Ray, but I'm sure glad you showed up when you did."

Ray walked over to stand behind Jodie. He massaged her shoulders, but the tight coils of pressure didn't loosen. She couldn't walk away again empty-handed.

"I'm trying to find someone Gloria." She struggled to keep her voice calm. "I think he's the one who ordered the bouquet of flowers from you, the yellow roses you delivered to me at Grams's house. I think he might have even broken into your shop."

"Why would he do a thing like that? I sent the flowers just like he said. Well, now that's not exactly true. He wanted red roses, but I was fresh out. But the yellow ones were nice, and I even found a card with a heart on it. He was bound and determined the card have a heart on it some-where.''

"Did he say why?''

"No. He had a nice voice, though, real friendly like. I think he likes you.''

Jodie rubbed a stabbing pain in her right temple. It was time to try a new tack. "What did the man in your dream look like, the one who tried to strangle your breath away?'' She was clutching for any shred of hope now, but she couldn't leave without trying everything. It was possible the fear she wasn't ready to face consciously was mani-festing itself in her dream.

"I don't know. Nightmares, they're more a feeling than a movie, at least mine are. A bunch of shadowy images that make you wake up shaking.''

"But was he tall? What color was his hair?''

Gloria shook her head, and squinted her eyes half shut. "I don't know. Officer Deaton asked me the same thing. I told him I don't remember a thing, but I promised to call him immediately if I do.''

"Then we have the bases covered.'' Ray tightened his grip on Jodie's shoulders. "We'll go now, Miss Gloria, and let you get some rest, hopefully the nonnightmare kind.''

"I've had enough rest. That's all they let you do in this place.''

"For good reason, so you'll get well fast. Your doctor already warned us not to wear you out.'' Ray took Jodie's hand and led her to the door. She managed a proper good-bye and kept a semblance of calm until the door shut be-hind them.

"He was there,'' she said, when they were out of Glo-ria's earshot. "I could see it in Gloria's eyes when we first asked if she'd seen someone in her shop that night.''

"All I saw was confusion.''

"No. He was there. For some reason, she's blocked it from her mind. Or maybe the medicine has."

"We'll find him, Jodie. I faxed the names of your possible suspects to Cappan and your descriptions to the artist in New Orleans. He wants to talk to you about a couple of them. We can call him from my office."

She rubbed a spot between her temples, fighting the beginning of a headache that threatened to be a zinger.

Ray dropped an arm around her shoulders. "Are you okay?"

"I'm disappointed." She leaned for a second, needing the support of his strength.

"A description from Gloria would have been nice. But, don't worry, baby, it'll be over soon."

Baby. An arm around her shoulder. All the right actions, from the wrong kind of man. "You don't have to do any of this Ray. I've told you before. It's not your battle."

"You're wrong. I do have to do it."

"Why?"

"You need me."

She pulled away. "I never told you that."

"I know. You're too stubborn." He took her hand and tugged her along at a snail's pace. "Right now you're even doing a good *imitation* of a mule."

"Just take me home, Ray. You can pick up your things and move back into your own home. You can go on with your life."

"My life right now is protecting you. And I'm taking you back to my office. We have a killer to catch."

"WHAT ABOUT THIS MAN?"

Kostner was grilling, falling into his lawyer routine, and he could tell Jodie was rebelling. Her responses were growing so sharp, he could feel the prick. But he had to get to the bottom of this for both their sakes. She was in danger of losing her life.

He was in danger of ruining his, of making a colossal mistake, by falling for Jodie Gahagen so hard he'd never be able to walk away. He'd escaped by the skin of his teeth before. Yet the second he was near her, his well-rehearsed inhibitions flew out the window.

He tapped the eraser end of his pencil on the description she'd labeled number five. Dark hair cut short, medium build, in his early twenties. Nice-looking. He asked his question again, rephrasing it slightly. ''What's your contact been with this man?''

''We've been over his description before. We've been over all the descriptions before, several times.'' She uncrossed her right leg and crossed her left, this time swinging her foot toward him.

''We talked about him, but you didn't say much. All I have in my notes about this guy is a two-sentence description and the fact that he works at a deli by your office.''

''It *was* my office. Past tense. And you don't have any more about him because that's all there is. He flirts with me when I buy fresh fruit. Innocent flirting. He does the same with every female. You told me to list every possible suspect. I did.''

''You overlooked one.''

''The mayor of New York City? We don't run in the same circles.''

''So how about your sons' father? You must have run in the same circles with him, a least for a while.''

She stopped swinging her leg. Her brows drew together, and her eyes shot daggers. Just like earlier, the mere mention of the boys' father put her on edge. There was a story there, but Ray wasn't sure he wanted to hear it.

Either the man was a complete jerk, and Jodie had found out in time not to marry him or he was the biggest fool in the world. He'd walked away from one of the best catches of all time. Gorgeous, smart, good sense of humor, at least most of the time. And so sexy she could heat a room to boiling point in thirty seconds flat.

Ray let out a heated breath. Maybe the boys' father was only runner-up to the biggest fool in the world. Still, it wasn't as if Ray had walked away without reason. He was just smart enough to know he didn't fill the bill as husband or father material. He couldn't be counted on when the going got rough. He'd proved it one time too many.

His dad's secretary buzzed in from the outer office. He switched the speaker on.

"You told me I could have the afternoon off for my grandson's birthday party. I'll be leaving in about five minutes. Do you need anything before I go?"

"Not that I can think of, Barbara." At least not anything she knew how to do. A one-man law office with no paralegals. One secretary, one part-time student research assistant. Life in the dark ages. "Enjoy yourself."

"I will."

The interruption over, he zeroed in again. "Back to the subject of the boys' father. Ex-lovers are at the head of the suspect heap when you're trying to identify a mystery stalker, Jodie. You know that."

"The boys' father is not a suspect."

"Were you in love with him?" God, where did that question come from? Not only was it irrelevant, it was none of his business. And Jodie would mince no words in telling him so. She'd probably march out the door as well.

"Yes."

The answer caught him off guard, pounding him squarely in the gut with the force of a boxer's punch. Her gaze was fixed on him, her eyes smoky, but not with anger. He wished it had been. Anger, hate, anything but the dark, hazy passion he saw swimming in their depths.

The same look she'd given him time and again during his week in New York City, always after they were quiet and spent, his love still inside her, his arms still wrapped around the curves of her seductive body.

Today the look was for someone else. Someone who had come into her life within weeks after he'd left. While he was in New Orleans trying to get her out of his mind, some other guy was...

Tension crawled Ray's spine, tightening every nerve and muscle into painful knots. And he had asked for this kind of misery.

"I think we've covered enough for one day." He yanked open the top drawer of his desk and slammed the legal pad he'd been making notes on inside. "I'll drive you home and then come back here and try to finish up before midnight." He stood up and grabbed his suit coat from the back of his chair. "Trying to keep my career afloat while taking care of Dad's is a major effort."

"Sit back down, Ray. Now it's my turn to talk."

He didn't sit. It wasn't his style to be equal with a sparring partner, and from the tone of Jodie's voice, a big-time confrontation was brewing. Instead he leaned against the front edge of his desk, his suit jacket hooked on a thumb swung over his shoulder, his gaze locked with hers.

"There's absolutely no reason for you to continue to stay at Grams's house," she continued, her shoulders straight as a lamppost, and just as unyielding. "Not only are the police going to watch the house now that they know the stalker is a murderer, but Ben is moving into the boathouse."

"When did this develop?"

"This afternoon, right before you picked me up."

"Does my being there bother you that much, Jodie?"

"How could it? I never see you. Since I asked you to help with the boys the other night, you've managed to stay away until we're all fast asleep. I don't blame you. You never know about these single mothers and the traps they lay to get a husband.''

''Is that what you think?'' His hands gripped the edge of the desk. ''That I've been staying away because I didn't want to be with you?''

''What else was there for me to think?''

What else? The truth. That the more he saw her, the more he wanted her. That every nerve in his body, and a few parts that didn't classify as nerves grew hard just thinking about her in the next room, dressed in some clingy little nightie, her body stretched across a crisp white sheet, her hair falling like fire over shoulders as soft as fresh cream.

He left his desk and walked over to the office door, turning the lock.

''What are you doing?''

''Come here, and I'll show you. I don't want there to be any more confusion about why I don't come back to Miss Emily's at night until I'm so tired I can't think.''

She stood up, but she didn't come closer. She didn't get the chance. Ray crossed the room in a split second, dropping his jacket on a chair as he went. His arms wrapped around her, pulling her close while his mouth sought her lips. The taste of her rocketed through him, bringing him alive deep in his soul.

Her lips parted beneath his, warm, loving, the Jodie he remembered from a hundred sleepless nights. Nights when hours of New Orleans revelry had dimmed his wit but not his memories. Nights when every sound, every smell, every female voice reminded him of Jodie Gahagen and one week in New York City.

The memories merged with the present. His hands skimmed her back, his fingers digging into the threads of the soft sweater. Her body was supple, soft and yielding, but her mouth was hot and demanding. Her tongue pushed its way between his lips, seeking out his own and the dark recesses of his mouth.

Breathless, he pulled his mouth away, but not his body. "This is why I stayed away, Jodie. Why I can't see you except in public places." He buried his face in her hair. "Because I can't be around you without wanting you like this."

She swallowed his words with her mouth. "Want me, Ray. Want me like this. I'm tired of fear and running. Tired of men who sneak through closed doors and hide behind notes and gifts." She trembled against him. "I need to be held, to be loved, like this."

He drowned in her kiss, and all he could think about was wanting more. His hands slipped under her sweater. The first touch of his fingers to her heated skin sent shock waves coursing through him. He worked at the clasp of her bra until it let her breasts fall loose, soft mounds of flesh resting against him. His thumbs circled the nipples, pink and perfect and berry hard.

It was the wrong place, the wrong time, but he was powerless to stop himself. He worked his lips down her neck, and then touched them to her breasts. She moaned, soft gurgling cries that tore at him, releasing new waves of desire so primal he had to take his hands off of her or take her right there. He backed her against the wall, his body against hers, his hands pushing into the painted wood above her shoulders.

Jodie came up for air only to tear at the buttons on his shirt, pulling them loose and pushing the fabric aside until she could rake his bare chest with her fingertips. Each touch was like flames licking at his self control. If they'd been anywhere else but his office...

"I want you, Ray. Now. This minute." Her words were more demand than pleadings.

"In a law office?" Doubts shook from his lips.

''The door's locked.''

True. And the way he felt right now he could take her on Front Street with the whole town looking on. He lifted her in his arms and carried her to the desk, setting her down on the edge. With one free arm, he swept his hand across the polished surface, raking papers and folders into a pile at one end, more than a few falling to the carpet.

His fingers fumbled with the buttons of her blouse, hers with his zipper. Somewhere deep in his mind, he knew he was breaking the rules he'd set, forgetting the boundaries. But somewhere else, somewhere much closer to his heart, he was following dictates that couldn't be ignored.

Moments later, Jodie's cries filled the room, and he exploded inside her.

His strength returned slowly. Finally, he moved, stretching to an upright position and yanking his trousers into place. It was then he heard the sound, slight, like muffled movement in the outer office. Tilting his head, he listened, but there was nothing more.

Overactive nerves, he guessed, as Jodie stirred beside him, the smoky look he remembered so well dancing in her eyes. And this time it was all for him.

Chapter Eight

"You should have seen the man. He was a sight. Out in my backyard on his all fours shooting a picture of a regular old armadillo like he was on some African safari."

"That's some tenant you got yourself this time, Selda. Next thing you know he's liable to stick that camera in the wrong animal's face. He'll be coming in smelling like a polecat and you'll have to fumigate the whole upstairs."

Jodie only half listened to the two women's conversation and laughter. Selda and Grams had been neighbors ever since Selda had married, over thirty years ago. They'd hugged and cried through the deaths of both husbands, bonding the way only women who've celebrated and suffered together can.

Selda was twenty years younger than Grams, spry as a fox before the hunt, and she kept a keen eye out for her neighbor. There wasn't much they didn't know about each other, but every time they got together, they still gossiped and giggled like a couple of teenage girls.

Jodie smiled in spite of herself. In a world of constant change, it was nice to know some things never varied. Emily and Selda definitely fit into the latter category.

"Did you meet him yet, Jodie? Jodie?"

"I'm sorry, Selda, did you say something to me?"

"My word, child, your mind must be a thousand miles

away. I was just asking if you'd met my new tenant yet. He's a nice-looking guy. A Yankee, but you're used to those northern men, you might like him.''

"I met him a few days ago." Jodie looked up from her position on the sitting room floor. One twin was climbing over her, the other was pulling apart a string of colored plastic links. "But don't get any matchmaking ideas," she added.

"Well, of course not. I wouldn't think of it. Would you, Emily?"

"I don't know. He'd have to be a sight better than having a lawyer in the family. I keep telling her don't get mixed up with the likes of Ray Kostner. Too handsome for his own good.''

Reverse psychology. Jodie wasn't fooled for a minute. Grams smiled like a Cheshire cat the minute Ray appeared, and she'd like nothing better than seeing her granddaughter married to the man. If she knew what Jodie had done a couple of afternoons ago in the Kostner law office…

No, she'd never believe it.

Jodie stretched her legs, and the gentle ache in her thighs reminded her of something else that never changed. The way she felt about Ray Kostner.

Not that she needed a reminder. The man who'd eaten, drunk, slept, laughed and loved in her apartment for a week two years ago was alive and well, and had crept back into her life. And either he was as crazy about her as she was about him or he did the best imitation she'd ever witnessed.

But no matter how he felt about her, it didn't alter facts. When he finished helping her and his dad out of their respective jams, he'd walk away again just like he had before.

Marriage, commitment, family life, they simply weren't part of his future. Neither were two of life's most wonderful blessings. She reached down and picked up Blake, hugging his lively body to her before letting him wriggle out of her clutches.

Her babies needed a father, a willing father, one who loved them unconditionally. The way love had surrounded her growing up, constant and reinforcing, a buffer for all of life's blows. And when the small plane had gone down robbing her of her parents, her grandmother had stepped in, opening her arms so wide, Jodie had become lost in their comfort. So lost, she was able to find herself again, secure in knowing that was what her parents would have wanted.

She leaned back on her elbows and watched the boys, one of them half crawling, half scooting across the carpet, the other tasting a plastic link to see if it could measure up to ice cream. Both totally adorable.

Her stomach churned, the familiar tension-induced indigestion that didn't respond to antacids. She'd tried to tell Ray about his sons when she'd learned she was pregnant. He'd refused to return her phone calls, breaking her heart in the process. She'd tried again when they were born, and again the night the stalker had laid his murderous hands on Blake.

When she'd finally found the courage to tell him outright that he was the father of her sons, he'd refused to believe her, preferring to think she'd lie than to believe he had fathered two magnificent boys.

The pain stabbed at her again, a dull knife pricking at an old wound. When Ray was with her, holding her in his arms, she saw only what she wanted to see, only what her heart would let her see. And that was the greatest tragedy of all, that she could love so completely a man who could only play at love.

But life wasn't a steak you could order prepared to your taste. She didn't want a stalker either, but nonetheless a madman was wrecking her life. Grams didn't want to lose her memory and her vitality, but the years were still taking their toll.

She and Grams were measuring up when they had to. Maybe, underneath the facade of money and glory, Ray had enough strength to do what was right, too.

"Jodie, honey, would you mind giving that pot of vegetable soup on the burner a stir? And add a little salt and pepper to it. I haven't put the seasonings in yet. Selda and I'll keep an eye on the boys."

This time Jodie heard the request. "I'll be happy to," she said, standing up and starting for the door. She padded down the carpeted hall in her stockinged feet.

The aroma hit her as she lifted the lid of the big stew pot, mouthwatering odors that took her back to being ten and ravenous, visiting Grams's house for summer vacation, running in from playing ball or jumping rope. Corn, okra, green beans, carrots, all picked in the summer from the vegetable patch Ben tended behind the house and frozen or canned by Selda and Grams.

She took a soupspoon and ran it across the top, scooping up a sampling of the bubbling liquid and blowing across it to keep it from burning her mouth. It was always better to taste Grams's concoctions before adding seasonings. Sometimes she forgot salt and pepper altogether, sometimes she gave it a double dose.

The hot juices washed over her tongue, a medley of flavors. And seasoned just right.

The doorbell jangled loudly, and Jodie jumped nearly from her skin, dropping the lid back onto the pot with an unmelodic clang. Grams hadn't mentioned expecting company. Her fingers stroked the walkie-talkie at her waist, caution running along every nerve. Better to be safe than sorry."

"Ben, are you there?" The seconds of silence seemed like minutes.

"I'm here, Miss Jodie. Do you need me?"

"No. Someone's at the door, but I'm sure it's nothing to worry about. I just wanted to make sure this thing works."

"It's working just fine. I'm out at the boathouse washing up, but if you need me, just give a holler."

"I will. Thanks, Ben."

"No trouble, Miss Jodie. Nothing I do for you is a mite of trouble."

Jodie headed for the door, but Grams beat her to it. She was already ushering in Butch Deaton, making a fuss over him the way she did anyone who stopped by, her southern hospitality in top form.

"Well, of course you're not inconveniencing us. You just come right on in. Selda and I were just having a cup of tea. Could I get you one?"

"No, ma'am. I just stopped in to talk to Jodie for a few..."

He'd spotted her coming down the hall before he finished his sentence.

"Anything new?" she asked, not daring to hope for much.

"A few developments. Can we talk in private?"

"I'll stay here and help Emily with the boys. You talk as long as you need to," Selda offered without waiting to be asked.

Jodie thanked her and led Butch out to the back porch, although she wasn't sure how private it was. Selda's tenant might be perched at his upstairs window doing his voyeurism routine. But unless Butch planned on yelling, he wouldn't be able to hear their conversation.

"We don't have a match back on the prints taken from the dresser," Butch said as the screen door closed behind them. "But they were all small, probably yours or Grams's."

"So we're nowhere."

"Pretty much. I talked to Cappan this afternoon. It seems like he's been doing a lot of conversing with Ray Kostner." A frown pulled at his lips, and his eyebrows bunched.

"Ray said they've talked. I'm sure Cappan will tell you the same things he tells him."

"I don't know why he's telling Kostner anything. He's a lawyer, not an officer of the law. He doesn't have a damn bit of authority. Pardon my French, Jodie, but it makes me madder than hell. The man's not even a local lawyer. He's just here on a little vacation, helping his dad out in an emergency."

She put her hand up to silence his tirade. "Look, Butch, if you have a fight with Cappan or Kostner, take it up with them. I have enough problems."

"I'm sorry, Jodie. You're right. But you know how Kostner is. Ever since he substituted for me and took you to your senior prom, he acts like he owns you. I'm tired of his trying to hog the ball."

"Well, I guess you'll just have to take it away from him and run with it yourself," she said, her patience so thin she considered breaking all of Grams's hospitality rules and throwing him out. "To tell you the truth, Butch, I don't care who runs with it. I just don't want it dropped. I have too much at stake. Do you understand?"

"Of course, I understand. I'm the detective in charge here. But I don't want Kostner messing things up."

"They're already *messed* up." She bit her tongue. Jumping down Butch's throat wouldn't help matters. Still, at times like this, she longed for the anonymity she'd had in New York. A world where she hadn't dated the cop in charge of the investigation. A town where she'd never slept with the lawyer who'd decided to name himself as her public defender and bodyguard.

"Let's start over, Butch. Hello, it's good to see you. Now, is there anything else I need to know?"

"I'm afraid so. I hate to be the one to have to tell you."

Right. That's why he'd rushed right over. "Just tell me, Butch. I can take it."

"They picked up the man who hocked the watch. A young good-looking actor wanna-be who lives in the area around the pawnshop. Problem is, he's not our guy."

"But he had Max's watch."

"He told them he was walking home near daybreak and just happened on the body. According to him, your friend Max was already dead. He couldn't do anything to help him, so he gave in to temptation. Grabbed a plastic bag from the corner trash bin and helped himself to the watch and a ring. He still had the ring when the police apprehended him."

"What makes them think he's telling the truth?"

"He passed the lie detector test."

"That can't be one hundred percent reliable." Frustration drained her spirits until she felt as if she'd been washed and wrung into twisted knots. "How can they be sure he's not the man who's been stalking me, that he's not the one who killed Max?"

"You're not his type."

"I'm a woman."

"Bingo."

She dropped into a chair, too limp to stand. Her best hope had just collapsed at her feet. Butch hooked a chair with one foot and dragged it next to hers. He sat down, too close, invading her space.

"He's not off the hook yet, but chances are slim he's the man. Cappan's not giving up, though. They're still watching the area around the apartment you moved out of. I don't know how they'd notice anybody new there, though.

The place is crawling with strangers, some a lot stranger than others.''

She nudged the toe of her shoe against a splinter that had split away from the porch floorboards. ''How do you know about the area around my apartment?''

''You really know how to deflate a guy. I was there, last summer. I'd hoped you'd remember.''

She blew a rush of hot air out of her mouth. Goofed again. ''Sorry, Butch. I do remember. We went to dinner at Sardi's.''

''Yeah. All my life I'd heard of that place. You wore a black dress, with little cutouts at the waist, and a neckline that cut clear down to here.'' He reached over and ran a finger from her neck to the swell of her breasts.

The movement came from nowhere, and she jumped up tipping her chair over backward. It clattered across the porch, bouncing off a small table.

''I'm sorry. I just got carried away, talking with my hands, you know. I didn't mean to frighten you.''

''You didn't frighten me. You touched me. Inappropriately. Don't let it happen again. Not if you want to continue to be friends.''

''At one time we were a lot more than friends.''

''We *dated*. In high school. And even then everything below the neck was off-limits. Just so we both know the rules. Touch now is relegated to handshakes. That's the way I conduct business.''

''I'd like to do more than work together, Jodie. I've always liked you. You know that. If I hadn't upset you by getting in that fight and breaking my nose the day before your prom, we might have kept dating after you graduated from high school. You might have been the one I married instead of that two-timing hussy I got hung up with.''

This absolutely could not be happening. She had known Butch ever since she moved to Natchitoches. They had dated a few times during high school. If they'd even kissed, she didn't remember it. Now he was acting as if they'd been partners in some torrid fling. They obviously shared a different set of memories.

"Look, Butch, let's just forget today happened."

"I'm sorry. I was out of line. How about letting me take you to dinner, to make up for it. Hands to myself. I promise." His lips split in an easy smile.

"Not now, Butch. I'm terrible company. I will be until the stalker is stopped."

He picked up the chair she'd sent careening across the porch and set it upright. "I understand. You just be careful. And it's none of my business, but I'd watch out for Ray Kostner if I were you."

The screech of the side gate sliding on its hinges caught them by surprise. Jodie swung around in time to see Ray rounding the side of the house. She wondered if he ever used front doors.

He walked up and put a possessive arm around her waist. "Why should she watch out for me, Butch?"

Jodie stepped back, watching the interplay of fiery emotion that crackled between the two men. For a minute she thought they might come to blows. The idea of grown men fighting over her would have been hilarious if the situation weren't so serious.

Butch backed down first, the muscles in his face and arms relaxing, the fake smile finding his lips again. "She should watch out for you because you're a big-city boy now. We hometown folks always keep our women home and our money in our pockets when you guys come around."

"Good idea. Only Jodie's not your woman. The truth is, you don't have anything I want, Butch, so you can quit worrying."

"I'm not worried, Kostner. Count on it. And I can handle

my own business. So, unless you're planning on running for chief of police, I expect you to leave the criminal investigating up to me. After I catch the criminals, you can go to court and try to get them off. That is what you do, isn't it, put the killers back on the street so they can harass innocent people like Jodie?''

"I like to think of my clients as innocent until proven guilty. And if I take their case, I believe they're innocent."

"Good. You don't interfere with my investigation, and I won't try your case."

"Fair enough."

This time, Ray gave a few inches. Jodie excused herself while the two men shook hands and hopefully agreed to disagree more amiably. She had babies to feed and bathe, bedtime stories to read, and lullabies to sing.

BEN PACED the narrow boathouse, glaring at his son, not trying to hide the anger that was twisting his gut into ragged steel. "I told you not to come out to Miss Emily's house."

"Why not? I'm family, and this is where you're shacking up now."

"I'm staying here to keep an eye on things."

"To keep an eye on Miss Jodie. I could handle that job for you. But then that was always a task you enjoyed taking care of yourself."

"Don't smart mouth me, Grady. I don't know why you came back home in the first place. You never liked it here. You only make trouble. Butch Deaton told you last time he wasn't cutting you any more slack."

"I missed you, Dad. Besides, I don't need any of Butch's slack. My nose is clean. I just came back to Natchitoches to escape the New York winter. They're brutal, not like the mint julep season down here. The only ice you get is in your drink glass."

Grady pushed back the shabby curtains and stared out

the window. Ben watched him, knowing he hadn't stopped by just to visit, but not sure what he wanted. He never knew with Grady. He'd thought the time he'd spent with him in Brooklyn might have drawn them closer. Instead it had only pushed them further apart.

Grady had asked him to come, to stay with him while he recovered from stomach surgery. Medical complications had drawn the intended week into eight. Way too long to suit Ben. Grady took pain pills by the handful and drank way too much. Still, he was his son, and all the family he had left.

"Look, son, I'll give you a few dollars if you need it. But I want you to get out of here. I can't afford any trouble with Miss Emily or with Jodie. They've taken care of me, and I'm going to take care of them."

"I don't need your money. Not tonight. I've got a friend waiting for me in the car out front, and he's got plenty of money. Zackery Lambkin, you remember him. You met him in New York, another one of my friends you didn't like. Creepy, I think that's how you described him."

"He's trouble, that's what he is. And he's a long way from home."

"Nah. He's originally from Shreveport. Disney has it right. It's a small, small world. He wanted to know where my dad worked, so I thought I'd show him. He's impressed."

"Where are you going when you leave here?"

"Out."

"No trouble, Grady. You know what happened last time you got mixed up with those buddies of yours."

"I spent a night in jail. No big deal. Not when my dad's got friends like Miss Emily and Parker Kostner." He sauntered to the mini fridge and yanked open the door. "Do you have any beer around here?"

"No, just a couple of soft drinks."

"Soft drinks. You're a good man, Dad. Too bad Mom didn't see it that way."

Grady grabbed a cola and left, slamming the door behind him and not bothering to say goodbye. Ben didn't take offense, not at his son's lack of manners. He was used to that. Everything he'd tried to teach his son had backfired, and Grady had picked up the exact opposite traits. Evidently his mother had been the better teacher.

Ben walked out of the boathouse. The night was still, but his joints ached. That meant either rain or trouble, and there wasn't a cloud in the sky.

JODIE FLICKED the switch on the tape recorder by the bed, filling the darkness with a recorded lullaby. Bending over, she tucked Blair in for the night, smoothing the light blanket over his backside. "Sweet dreams, darling," she whispered, kissing his cheek lightly.

Moving to Blake's bed, she repeated the routine. So precious, in his blue jammies, his thumb stuck between his lips, a thin red curl flipping about his ear. Two years ago, she'd been a career woman, thoughts of babies and diapers floating in the back of her subconscious only as a distant dream.

Now they were the only things in her life that really mattered.

She padded down the narrow hallway. The house was whisper quiet, and dark shadows climbed the walls of the narrow hall. From nowhere, the taste of fear pooled on her taste buds, and the smell of it choked her lungs. She stopped walking and leaned against the wall, her heart racing as an unexpected shot of adrenaline fueled her body.

The fear was unfounded. She was safe. Grams was safe. Her boys were safe. Butch had a patrol car passing the house at regular intervals, ready to answer a 911 call in seconds. She sucked in a ragged breath and listened.

An old English shepherd's song seeped from under the crack of the boys' door and wafted down the hallway. The sound of light snoring came from Grams's room. And any minute Ray would be returning from his visit with his parents.

Hands steady, she turned the knob on her bedroom door and slipped inside. A wisp of wind caught the gingham curtain, unfurling it like a sheet hanging out to dry. Funny, she didn't remember leaving the window open. Perhaps the cleaning girl had.

Her finger fondled the walkie-talkie. One call and Ben would rush to her side. He'd walk every inch of the house with her, put her fears to rest. But there was no reason to call him. It was just her nerves playing tricks on her.

The room was neat as a pin, nothing bothered, nothing out of place. But the stalker had never left a mess. He'd only rearranged things, moved her intimate belongings around, touched them, stretched them into bizarre shapes.

Her fingers trembled as she cracked open the dresser drawer. Her hand brushed the silky softness of her scarves. They were folded exactly as she had left them. One more drawer. The stalker's favorite. Her breath caught and held as she eased it open, but the panties and bras were in their places. No one had been here.

Shivering, she hugged her arms across her chest and walked over to close the windows. They were French, the kind that swung out and let in plenty of fresh air. Once in high school, she'd climbed through in the middle of the night, stretching onto an overhanging branch of the pecan tree.

The tree was still there, but trimmed so that the nearest branch was much farther from the house. She got on her knees in the window seat and leaned out. If someone really wanted to, he might be able to climb the tree and swing in through an open window.

She shook her head. No one had, and from now on she'd make sure the window stayed locked tight. She closed the shutters and stepped out of her shoes, unzipping her skirt and letting it slide to the floor. She needed a shower, hot, sudsy. Enough to warm her inside and wash away the stench of fear.

Wriggling out of the rest of her clothes, she pulled back the shower curtain.

And the horror hit home again.

Chapter Nine

Ray pulled into the driveway in front of the Gahagen house and skidded his car to a stop. It had been a long night, most of it spent haggling with his dad over minute details of a case he could have handled in his sleep. In New Orleans, he might be a legend, but at the office of Parker Kostner, he was still the son who never quite made the grade. Bygones were never bygones.

If Jodie hadn't needed him, Ray would have packed his bags and headed back to New Orleans in a New York second. New York. Just the words piled on another layer of fatigue.

Two years ago New York had been just another city in North America, one he could well do without. But a week in the city, in a tiny apartment that could have fit into the bedroom of his own spacious living quarters in New Orleans, and his satisfying life-style had been turned into so much muck.

All of a sudden the man who had everything he thought he wanted or needed had realized how much he was missing. Now fate had hurled him and Jodie back together in a game of wits with a madman. He banged one fist on the steering wheel. Life just wasn't fair.

This afternoon's escapade in his temporary office might be his biggest mistake yet. Making love to Jodie was like an addict's fix. It satisfied for a short time, only to whet the desire for more and more and more. Even now... He pushed the thought aside. What he needed was sleep.

Grabbing his briefcase, he stepped into the cool night air. He sucked in a huge gulp, hoping it would clear his mind. It didn't. Once thoughts of Jodie invaded his brain, neither mind nor body was easily put to rest.

He glanced at her window and then at his watch. Half past midnight, and her light was still on. His pace quickened, the fatigue that had been weighing him down growing lighter with the seductive prospect of seeing her again.

Fumbling for the newest key on his chain, he fitted it in the hole and turned it, opening the door and stepping into the foyer. The house was quiet. He tiptoed up the stairs, trying unsuccessfully to avoid the creaks of a house that should have finished settling half a century ago.

He stopped at the guest room first, depositing his briefcase and suit jacket and pouring two fingers of whiskey from the crystal decanter Miss Emily had set out for him as soon as she realized he was a semipermanent guest.

She'd made a production of the amenity, placing the decanter and shot glasses on a silver tray atop the mahogany secretary that she'd proudly pointed out dated to Civil War days. She saw him as a prospective grandson-in-law. Ray could all but see the designing wheels turning through her nearly translucent skin.

Of course, that was only because she didn't know the real Ray Kostner. Perhaps she should talk to the judge, ask him why he gave up the career he loved when it was in full swing.

Ray downed the drink in a single swig and poured another. He should just drop into bed like he'd planned before he'd noticed the light in Jodie's window. Jodie, forbidden fruit, delectable and luscious, so damned tempting his mouth watered at the thought of her. He slipped out of his

Play the
"LAS VEGAS"
GAME
GET 3 FREE GIFTS!
FREE GIFTS!
FREE GIFTS!
FREE GIFTS!
TURN THE PAGE TO PLAY!
Details inside!

Play the
"LAS VEGAS" Game
and get
3 FREE GIFTS!

1. Pull back all 3 tabs on the card at right. Then check the claim chart to see what we have for you — 2 FREE BOOKS and a gift — ALL YOURS! ALL FREE!

2. Send back this card and you'll receive brand-new Harlequin Intrigue® novels. These books have a cover price of $3.99 each, but they are yours to keep absolutely free.

3. There's no catch. You're under no obligation to buy anything. We charge nothing — ZERO — for your first shipment. And you don't have to make any minimum number of purchases — not even one!

4. The fact is thousands of readers enjoy receiving books by mail from the Harlequin Reader Service™. They like the convenience of home delivery... they like getting the best new novels BEFORE they're available in stores... and they love our discount prices!

5. We hope that after receiving your free books you'll want to remain a subscriber. But the choice is yours — to continue or cancel, any time at all! So why not take us up on our invitation, with no risk of any kind. You'll be glad you did!

Yours Free!

FREE!
No Obligation to Buy!
No Purchase Necessary!

BUSINESS REPLY MAIL
FIRST-CLASS MAIL   PERMIT NO. 717   BUFFALO NY

POSTAGE WILL BE PAID BY ADDRESSEE

HARLEQUIN READER SERVICE
3010 WALDEN AVE
PO BOX 1867
BUFFALO NY 14240-9952

NO POSTAGE
NECESSARY
IF MAILED
IN THE
UNITED STATES

shoes and loosened his tie before dropping all pretense of giving up the chance to see her tonight.

A minute later, he tapped lightly on her door.

"Come in, Ray."

"How did you know it was me?" he said pushing the door open and stepping inside.

"I heard you drive up."

Jodie's voice was low, strained, and her skin had turned shades of ghostly white. "What's wrong?" he asked the question, but he knew the answer. It was written in the fear that glazed her eyes and pulled her lips into thin, trembling lines, the same way it had the night the bouquet of roses had been delivered.

"You heard from him again, didn't you?"

"A present." She motioned toward an opened package that sat beside her on the bed. "I found it in the bathroom, behind the shower curtain."

"That worthless piece of trash." He walked over to the bed and picked up the box. It rested in a nest of red, shimmery paper, a shiny red bow as topping. Cradling it in his hand, he lifted the lid.

The soft tinkling sounds of music escaped, the serenade to accompany a pair of lovers who twirled round and round inside a glass gazebo.

"A music box?"

"Right, one that plays 'New York, New York.' A perfectly harmless reminder that no matter how many police are watching, he can walk into my house at will."

"Where did you find it?"

"It was in my bathtub. So thoughtful of him to go to the trouble to hide a present in the spot where he knows I strip to nothing, where he knows I won't even be able to shower now without fearing he's just a step away."

She stood, her hands knotted into fists, her eyes the deep

emerald of a tossing sea. "And if that wasn't enough, he left his calling card."

"A red heart."

"Yes, with another message."

She walked to the dresser and opened the top drawer, taking out a folded construction paper heart. He took it from her and unfolded it.

The message was printed in black crayon.

"Save yourself." He read it again, this time to himself.

"I don't know what this lunatic wants from me. I don't have a clue who he is. Which means I'm exactly where I was when this whole thing started. Except now I've given up my job and traveled from one end of the country to the other to escape him."

"You're not where you were." He took her hand in his. She was rigid, torn with frustration. "Butch has turned this into a full-scale investigation."

"And in spite of that, the man walked into my house and deposited a wrapped package in my bathtub."

Ray felt the tightening in his jaw, the urge to bury a fist into something, anything. But he had to fake a calm he didn't feel.

He could all but see Jodie on the next plane to New York, walking the streets like a vigilante patrol. Setting herself up to be the next victim. He wasn't about to let that happen. So he had better start talking.

"My guess is the man will be identified and arrested within the week."

"And my guess is Mars will collide with Venus, and the New Orleans Saints will win the Super Bowl."

Ray switched tactics. "I know you're upset, Jodie, anyone would be under the circumstances. That's why this is not the time to make rash decisions."

"It's past time. I will not play games with a madman under Grams's roof. I have to protect her. I have to protect

Blake and Blair. If anything happened to them..." Her voice dissolved into a shaky whisper.

"Nothing will happen to them. Ben's here. I'm here. Cops are watching the house."

"That's not good enough. Not anymore. I have a plan, Ray, but I'll need your help. Don't panic, it doesn't involve baby-sitting, and I won't be going to New York, at least not yet."

"So, why am I not relieved?"

"I want the stalker to contact me."

"He just did."

"No, I mean I want a face-to-face confrontation. No strike and disappear. I can't deal with a phantom."

"How do you propose to arrange this meeting?"

"Don't laugh. I've given this a lot of thought. I'm going to take out an ad in the personal column. A note to my stalker that I'd like to meet him, thank him in person for all the gifts. I'll have it framed inside a heart."

"What makes you think he reads the personals?"

"He writes. Maybe he reads. Do you have any better ideas?"

"The police..."

"The police have taken weeks to find out the man killed Max. Even if I fail miserably, I can't do much worse." She walked over to the dresser and picked up a notepad. "This is what I have in mind," she said, pointing at a lengthy list scribbled in longhand.

Ray read silently, detail by detail, the knots in his stomach pulling tighter with every word. Her plan was dangerous at best, deadly at worst. She wouldn't listen to reason, not in the mind-set she was in now. Which meant he had to make a few plans of his own.

"You can't talk me out of this, Ray, so don't even try," she announced, when he'd finished reading her bizarre scheme to use herself as bait to trap a murderer.

"Okay."

Surprise drew her brows into auburn arches.

"You are a very brave woman." He kissed the tip of her nose. "And I'm sure you will not put the mother of your sons into unnecessary danger." A new tactic, probably also useless.

"I'm not trying to be a hero. I just need my life back. I have to know my babies are safe."

This time the pain inside her broke through her determination, shattering her voice into shaky cries. He held her in his arms rocking her to him, absorbing the sobs that shook her body. He eased her down, placing her head on the pillow, his arms still locked around her.

He held her like that, her hair across his shoulder, the warmth of her breath against his skin until she was fast asleep.

JODIE TWISTED beneath the sheet, curling her knees up to her waist. Slowly, she opened her eyes, rubbing until the moonlit bedroom took form. The last thing she remembered was Ray holding her while torrents of tears finally broke loose.

The room was empty now. Flexing her feet, she pulled them over the side of the bed. Her mouth was so dry she could barely swallow. Sliding into her slippers, she went to the bathroom and filled a paper cup with water from the tap, drinking it down in thirst-quenching gulps.

The baby monitor was quiet. She checked it, overly cautious, just to make sure it was turned on. It was. The boys were obviously sleeping soundly. Still, she felt the need to see them. As she'd done so many nights lately, she grabbed a quilt from the top of the bed and threw it over her shoulders, padding down the hallway to sit in the rocker and watch them sleep. It was far more effective than tranquilizers or aspirin to calm her ragged nerves.

She pushed into their room. The rocking chair swayed, and her heart plunged to her toes before the shadowy form took shape. She leaned against the door frame, her heart still racing. "What are you doing in here?"

"Watching my sons sleep." Ray's words sank in slowly, like feet in quicksand.

"What did you say?"

"I'm watching my sons sleep."

Alarms went off in her head, shaking her from the dregs of sleep into full wakefulness. Ray stood, his frame catching the moonlight that peeked through the window and casting a shadow that engulfed her. Slowly, almost silently, he walked to Blair's crib and towered over the sleeping child.

"He's perfect. They both are. Innocent and trusting. They deserve so much. Instead they got a father who denied them." Ray reached into the crib and touched the back of his fingers to Blair's cheek.

Jodie's heart constricted. Father and son. Picture-perfect. Except for the tension that filled the air, suffocating, burning, a stifling blanket of fear and confusion.

Blair squirmed in his bed, waking to the noise of voices invading his dreams.

"This isn't the place to talk, Ray." She turned and walked out, his footsteps following behind her. She considered the kitchen and coffee, buying time to think, but Ray caught up with her and took her arm, leading her into her bedroom.

The moment of truth had come, but there were no feelings of exhilaration, just a dull throbbing in her temples and a duller ache in her heart.

Ray closed the door and leaned against it, his dark eyes glazed and unreadable.

Jodie struggled for calm. "What makes you suddenly think the boys are yours?"

"Not think, Jodie. I know they're mine. What I don't know is why you didn't tell me when you first found out you were pregnant."

"I called you. You didn't return my calls."

"You never indicated there was a problem. You merely said you missed me and wanted to hear my voice."

She met his accusing stare. "Believe me, one part of me longed to tell you the truth from the very beginning. But the other part of me, the sensible part, knew you meant what you said. You wanted no part of commitment. So I did what I thought was best for my sons. I want Blake and Blair to know unconditional love, not rejection."

He stepped closer, his breath hot on her flesh. "Jodie Gahagen, the perfect mother. It was too bad you were seduced by a man who was never worthy of you."

"Not seduced, Ray. I made love to a man I loved. Together we created two individuals, so precious I can't bear to think of life without them."

"So you went through the pregnancy and the birth all alone. You were always a fighter." He turned his back on her and paced the room before finally stopping to stare out the window.

Jodie stepped behind him. "You didn't answer my question, Ray. Why are you suddenly so sure Blair and Blake are your sons?"

He turned, wrapping his fingers about the flesh of her upper arms, his gaze meeting hers. "Because you're too strong to be reduced to lies even in the face of death."

"It took you a long time to figure that out."

"Too damned long." His voice grew hoarse. "Or maybe I knew it all along. Maybe I'm just not as strong as you are, Jodie. Maybe I ran from the truth the way I've run from a lot of things in my life."

"But now you have it all figured out?"

"No. Not at all. I'm still not sure how it happened. We were careful. We used protection."

"Nothing is one hundred percent except abstinence. We pushed the odds that week."

"You know I never meant for this to happen." Ray walked to the dressing table and picked up a silver-framed picture of Jodie and the boys outside her New York apartment. The images couldn't have been clear in the muted glow of moonlight, but he studied the snapshot as if he were memorizing every line.

Finally he returned it to its spot of honor. "I should have been there." The self-accusation in his voice surprised her.

"Why? You told me all along you didn't want any commitments. You were honest."

"I told you I wasn't husband material. I'm still not."

"Then I guess you don't have any problems. You're not a husband."

His eyes raked over her and he crossed the room, stopping inches away, looking for all the world like a man who had no desire to run away. One hand under her chin, he tilted it upward until their gaze locked. "You're a remarkable woman. Knowing all you did about me, you still chose to have my babies."

"I didn't choose anything. I missed my period and went to the doctor. He confirmed what the drugstore test indicated. I was pregnant." She backed away.

"You had a choice. A choice that might have been better for you, for your career, for your life-style. People make it every day. But you chose to give our sons life. And I didn't even have the courage to return your phone calls."

"You didn't know."

"I'm not sure I could have handled things differently if I had. That's the scary part." He walked away from her. Dropping to the window seat, he patted the spot beside him. "Sit by me," he whispered.

She hesitated, then gave in to her own need to be close to him. She could convince herself of anything in the bright light of day, almost believe she didn't care at all if he chose to have to nothing to do with her or their sons. But this was the middle of the night, and her needs lay naked and exposed.

"It's so hard to accept that I'm a father," he whispered, reaching for her hand.

"Is that why you chose not to believe me when I told you they were yours?"

"No. That was pure fear. I've let down everyone who ever needed me, everyone who ever mattered to me. I couldn't handle knowing I was doing it again." He knotted his hands into fists and then stretched them out again in repetitive motions.

"But I think I always knew they were my sons, at least at some level. When I first found out you had given birth to twins, I tried to picture you with another man, making love the way we made love."

She swallowed a surge of pain. "And did you get comfort from those thoughts?"

"The same kind of comfort I'd get from a rattlesnake bite." His hands knotted into fists again.

"I'm a simple woman, Ray, not nearly so complicated as you. If you want me to understand you, you'll have to spell things out for me, make your feelings crystal clear."

"My feelings? They change by the minute. Elated? Confused? Nervous? Petrified?"

"That runs the gamut. Throw in morning sickness and the awkwardness of carrying around a twenty-pound stomach and you pretty much have the same symptoms I had during the pregnancy." She wasn't being vindictive, just honest.

His muscles were taut, a man geared for a fight, but it was his own demons he was battling. The skirmish was far from over, and she had no idea who'd come out the winner. Still, she needed a few questions answered, now while Ray was dealing with the truth and with his own feelings of inadequacy.

"Why didn't you return my calls, Ray? We'd been acquaintances forever and good friends since the night of my senior prom. Earlier, if you count the kiss on the cheek at my fourteenth birthday party as a sign of friendship."

"Do you still remember that?" he asked, his eyebrows raised in surprise.

"Of course, I didn't wash my face for days. You were my first case of serious puppy love."

"Before you found out I was really a dog."

"I've never thought that. I just thought you had a twisted sense of values. Money and fame at any cost, and get as far away from family as you could. That's why I avoided contact in Baton Rouge when I was in college and you were in law school at LSU. No matter how I felt about you, I knew it wouldn't work."

"You were wise for your years."

"I thought so at the time. But you seemed so different that week in New York. You were fun, romantic, thoughtful. The new Ray Kostner. I had high hopes for you."

"And *you* were a sex-crazed goddess." He trailed a finger down her arm.

"I was not sex-crazed. Intimately uninhibited, maybe. And I don't remember your complaining."

"You *were* sex-crazed, and I loved it. But you made me *feel* and that scared the wits out of me."

"You find me so tempting, you avoid me. I'm missing something here."

He leaned against the side of the window, watching her. "It's pretty simple. When I'm with you, I forget who and what I am, start thinking that we're right together, start thinking I could be the husband and father you'd expect me to be. The truth is, it's not going to happen.''

"Men have careers and families all the time, and do both well. Look at your dad.''

His mood changed instantly. Tension stormed between them, so heavy she could feel the weight of it crushing against her chest.

"Sure,'' he said. "Parker Kostner. The Judge. Everything to everybody. Well, to almost everybody.''

She shuddered, chilled by the bitterness that dripped from every word. "Is there trouble between you and your father?''

"Trouble? How could there be? The Judge is the perfect father. Too bad he got royally shortchanged on sons.''

A shiver skidded her spine. This was a scene from a bad movie, the story of someone else's life. Not Ray Kostner's. He had it all. "You're obviously upset about something, but you're not making sense. Your dad is proud of you. He's always been.''

"Is that what the world sees? Good. He'd like that.'' Ray gestured a sign of surrender. "Can we just drop this, Jodie? I'm not here to blackball my father. He is what he is. I am what I am.''

"And what is it that you think you are?''

"A tough lawyer who's damn good at what I do, because I do what I'm good at. I don't cut the mustard as a son, and I don't have a chance of making it as a husband or a father. So, it looks like you and the boys drew a bad deal, the same as my dad. The truth is I can't be counted on.'' He stood up and paced the room.

This was incredulous. Ray was calling on the most feeble excuses she'd ever heard. If he tried this in court, the prosecuting attorney would bury him. "Let me see if I have this straight. Just because you don't think your dad appreciates you, you're willing to give up the chance to have a family of your own."

"Drop it, Jodie. This isn't about an argument. It's about me and what I am and am not capable of."

"Don't talk in riddles, not to me. I've been through too much these past few months. If you prefer a life void of commitments, I can buy that. I have no intention of trapping you. But if you think you can walk out of my life with some cock-and-bull story about caring about me too much to hurt me, about not having what it takes to be a father when you've never even tried, you have another thing coming."

"Don't read anything into a few nice deeds, Jodie. It's the week in New York that's the lie, a pretense that I was someone else. I'll do right by you and the boys. You'll never want for anything, but I can't become someone I'm not."

"So why are you here, Ray, pushing your way back into my life, making demands, risking your life to protect mine?"

"To trap a stalker. I'm not the man to hang your hopes on, but that doesn't mean I'll let some murderous lunatic threaten you and walk the streets to do it again. I told you I won't stop until this man is behind bars."

"But just don't depend on you to be there when I need you, right?"

"Right."

He started to walk away. She grabbed both of his arms and stopped him. Rising to the tips of her toes, she placed her lips on his. The kiss was wet and sweet, and so exciting she felt it tumble along every nerve ending.

"And don't expect me to be here all warm and eager waiting for you when you decide you need me too much to walk away," she said, pushing him toward the door.

He looked at her for long painful seconds before he disappeared down the hallway.

Jodie watched him go. The man might be a brilliant attorney, but he didn't have a clue when it came to his own virtues. When this was over, she'd gladly hang her hopes and her dreams on him. That is, if she was still alive to do so.

JODIE SPENT the next morning perfecting the ad. It would start its run on the Saturday before Thanksgiving, three days away. The details were fine-tuned, ready to run like a well-geared car.

The ad was simple: "To my secret admirer, The flowers were beautiful, the music box was delightful. I'm saving myself, for you."

The rest was in small print. If he wanted to meet her in private, he was to call her. The telephone company was connecting the line today. Grams had bought the explanation that the line was for business purposes, although Jodie had no idea what she thought her business was.

The only activity she'd involved herself with that remotely resembled employment was the journal she was keeping on the life of the stalked. Hopefully, she'd live to see her experiences published in an article that would help other women in the same predicament.

Even if the stalker saw the ad, he might not call. The man was smart, and this smelled of a trap. But the man was also mentally off balance, and she saw his attempts as a sick way of reaching out to her. This might be the type of opening he was looking for to reveal himself.

The danger would be minimal. All the calls would be taped. In essence, she was bugging herself. If he called, she would meet him. It was up to the police to figure out how they would keep her safe and make the arrest. That was the one weakness of her plan, the one element she couldn't control.

Ray was furious. Butch claimed she was crazy. But it was not their lives that were being split into a thousand splintered parts.

She was meeting with Butch this afternoon to set up the finer points of their strategy.

JODIE SAT IN Butch Deaton's cramped office, listening to one side of a long-winded phone conversation. The woman on the other end of the line was obviously complaining about her neighbor's barking dog.

Bored and restless, Jodie's gaze took in the room. A spiderweb in the far corner of the ceiling, a shamrock-shaped stain on the carpet, a silver-framed photograph of a young blond woman with smiling eyes and heavy makeup on the top of a chipped file cabinet.

Finally, Butch dropped the receiver into the cradle and looked her way. "Sorry to keep you waiting," he said, rummaging through the clutter on his desk to recover a manila file folder.

"You said something important had come up and for me to rush right over. What is it?"

"The nurse at the hospital called. Apparently Gloria Bigger's memory is returning. She asked to speak to you."

"Then why did the nurse call you?"

"Because this is police business, Jodie. No one wants to see you hurt, least of all me."

"When did the nurse call?"

"This morning, about ten."

"And we're waiting until two in the afternoon to talk to her?"

"I had things to take care of. Besides, we've waited days for this description. A few hours won't change anything."

"Can we go now?"

"Absolutely. You can ride with me if you don't mind a squad car."

"As long as we leave the flashing blues turned off."

"I thought you were in a hurry."

"The hospital is only five minutes away. The barking dog has already taken twenty."

"It's a small town. We keep our taxpayers happy when we can. Besides, Gloria's not going anywhere."

Ten minutes later they pushed through the door of Gloria's hospital room. The sheets were pulled up over an empty bed. The nurse stopped in the door, sympathy written all over her face as she told them the patient had died a little over an hour ago.

Chapter Ten

The drive back to the police station was cloaked in silence. The nurse had said Gloria Bigger died from a heart attack. It had come on suddenly, and it had been massive. The only good thing was she hadn't lived long enough to suffer much.

This time even Jodie couldn't blame the stalker.

Butch led her back into his office. "We can talk about your plans later, Jodie. I know Gloria's death has you upset. I'm a little shaky myself."

"I'd rather get this over with, Butch." She tapped the cover of a spiral-bound notebook. "My plans are outlined in here. They're pretty much the same as when we talked on the phone."

"Mind if I have a look before we talk?"

She stood and walked over, opening the notebook and placing it in front of him. "Like I told you, the ad starts Saturday. I plan to meet the stalker if he calls. I'd like for you or one of your officers to tail me."

"If the man's got any brain cells at all, he won't fall for this. He's wanted for murder."

"He doesn't know that. He broke into the florist shop and stole the incriminating record."

"In a state of panic. I'm sure after he calmed down he

realized how easy it would be to trace the credit card information from the company.''

"So we know he makes mistakes." She took her seat again. "I think he'll come, Butch. I can't explain it, but I feel this man is desperate and he's calling out to me. What's the point of following me, of leaving me notes and gifts, of letting me know he's obsessed with me if he thinks it's going nowhere?"

"Oh, he'll come to you, Jodie. But it will be when you least expect it, when he can't stand keeping his identity a secret another second."

"Maybe he's to that point now."

"I hope not. I plan to stop him before he reaches that stage. I could do it more effectively if you'd let me handle the investigation without interference."

"I appreciate your concern, Butch, but I have to do this."

"Then it's my job to protect you. You're a citizen, misguided, but still a citizen. Besides, you and I go back a long way."

"This is not about friendship, Butch. I need your help as a police officer."

"And you'll have it. One hundred percent, but that doesn't mean I like it."

"But you do think you can protect me?"

"In theory it should be easy. In reality, anything can happen."

"What do you think of my choice of meeting places?"

"The old Coxlin place. Great choice. For the stalker. It's isolated, large and rambling and in ruins, surrounded by acres of woods."

"Which means there's also hiding places for you or one of your officers. I could wear a wired microphone, maybe even get a taped confession that he murdered Max."

"You read too many detective books. Even if the man

reads the ad and falls for the trap, this type of setup doesn't come with guarantees.''

''I trust you.''

''You could be making a fatal mistake.''

''Let's hope it's the stalker who makes the mistake.''

''And I definitely wouldn't count on that.'' He closed her notebook and scooted it to the back of his desk. ''I'll take a ride out to the Coxlin place later and see what I think. Do you want to go with me?'' Pushing his chair back, he stood up, raking his hair back with his hands.

''Yes. What about tomorrow? That way we can decide exactly how to handle the situation, where your man will be hiding and how I can signal him.''

''I'd like to talk you out of this, Jodie.''

''I wish it wasn't necessary. But the man has to be stopped before he loses all control and someone else ends up dead, the way Max did.''

He walked her to the door. ''I just don't want that someone to be you.''

''Neither do I, Butch. Neither do I.''

JODIE LEFT the police station at half past three. Gloria Bigger was on her mind as she pulled to a stop at the traffic light on Front Street. Tears moistened her eyes. Another death. There was no way of knowing if her stalker was behind it. But somehow, she was sure he was.

On impulse, Jodie pulled into the semicircle of parking that followed the paths and grassy areas along the river— the peaceful oasis in the middle of the oldest part of town.

The sun peeked over the tops of oak and cottonwood trees, shaking a tail of glimmery gold over the river. A fishing boat motored past, the man at the bow tipping his hat to a tall, slender woman who was being walked by a prancing Pomeranian on a jeweled leash. Two preschoolers played chase around the circular pavilion that was already strung with bright colored lights for the upcoming festival.

Life as usual. For everyone but her. Opening the car door, she slid from beneath the wheel, and stepped out. She grabbed her handbag in lieu of locking the door. The fall nip in the air made a cup of coffee at The Bakery seem too good to pass up.

She was sorry for the decision the minute she walked through the door. Sara Kostner was at the counter, paying for a bag of pastries. Not that she had anything against Sara, but today was not the time she wanted to make small talk with Ray's mother. Not the time to pile on guilt either, but seeing Sara did just that.

In the end, Ray might be willing to walk away from his sons, but Jodie doubted Sara would be as easily deterred from knowing her grandsons. Another complication, another knot in the spidery web that had entangled Jodie's life with Ray's. Sara turned, and a smile curved her lips and lit up her face.

"Jodie Gahagen, what a nice surprise." She picked up her bag of pastries and hurried in Jodie's direction.

"Hello, Sara." She extended her hand. Sara ignored it and went for a hug.

"We've been so worried about you. Ray said you had some lunatic bothering you in New York and that's why you came down here to stay for a while. Have they caught the man yet?"

"Not that I know of." Funny, she hadn't even considered that Ray had told his parents about her situation, but then he had to come up with some explanation for sleeping over every night. Left to her own conclusions, Sara would have been hard-pressed not to expect the worst. And a loose woman would not meet with Sara Kostner's approval.

"Then it's a good thing you came back home. I know your grandmother would love it if you decided to stay permanently. We feel the same about Ray, but he won't even talk about moving back.''

"His work is in New Orleans."

"It could be here. Parker would love for him to take over the firm.'' The smile vanished from her face. "Not that he'd ever ask him. And not that Ray would consider it if he did."

"No, your son seems to like his life as it is."

"But I don't have a clue why. Working day and night. Living alone. It's time he settled down and had a family."

Jodie remained silent. The responses that flitted through her head were much better left unsaid.

"I'd love to stay and chat a bit," Sara said, glancing at her watch. "But I don't like to leave Parker long. He's mending nicely, but I worry about him. He complains when I fuss over him, but I can't help it."

"Perhaps I can stop by one day for a visit."

"Parker would be delighted. And bring the boys. We'd love to see them. I live for the day Ray decides on one woman and gives me some grandchildren."

Jodie nodded past the lump that had settled in her throat without warning. Denial cast a long shadow. She said a quick goodbye and watched Sara walk out the door. A minute later Jodie followed behind her. Her taste for coffee was lost. Now the only craving she had was to go home and hug her boys.

The parking area was nearly empty by the time she returned to her car. A pickup truck parked near the water, a blue Ford parked under the biggest oak.

She fished the car keys from her pocket and slid into the driver's seat, turning the key in the ignition. The silence was ominous, an instant dread that ground in her stomach. She turned the key again. No reassuring hum. Not even an angry growl or sputter.

This had happened once before, right before she left New

York. The car had been working fine when she'd parked it. When she'd returned, the engine hadn't started. A chill stole her breath. She lowered the window and sucked in a gulp of air.

This was Natchitoches, not New York City. She was surrounded by family friends, business owners who knew her grandmother, who had gone to school with her dad, who knew her name and where she lived. Today she'd go home to Grams and the boys.

That day she'd gone home to a gift, a pair of gloves to warm her hands after being stranded in the dark, in a cold car whose engine wouldn't respond.

The message had been clear. The stalker had been watching and then had beaten her to her apartment to put the gift in place.

She fit her trembling hands around the key again and gave it one last try. The engine didn't respond. She stepped out of the car. She'd find a phone booth and call Selda.

"Hello neighbor. Having car trouble?"

The voice startled her, triggering a rush of adrenaline. She spun around and stared at the man who'd come up behind her. Recognition was instant. Selda's new tenant was staring at her, a smile splitting his face, his eyes laughing.

"The engine won't start."

"I'll take a look at it if you like. If we can't start it, I can give you a ride."

"Is that your blue car?"

"That's it. I was taking some pictures of the old courthouse but the workers on the other side of the river caught my eye. This Festival of Lights must be some display."

"I thought you were in town to photograph plantation homes."

"I am. But lucky for you I stopped off in town before

heading home. Why don't you pop the hood and let me take a look?''

"It was running fine earlier," she said, opening the door and releasing the hood catch.

"Does this happen often?"

"No. Only once before."

"What was the matter with it then?"

"I don't remember," she lied, not sure why she felt the need.

He rolled up his sleeves and propped the hood on the safety rod before his head disappeared inside. "Here's your problem."

She walked around the car and peeped under the hood. Wires, valves, belts and thingamabobs. A greasy puzzle with no cheat sheet. If the whole thing had been installed backward, she wouldn't have known. "I don't see a problem."

"This little wire's your culprit. It's supposed to be connected right here."

He demonstrated, fitting the wire into place and tightening the connector on the battery. That was the one part she could identify. She'd had to have it replaced once. New York winters ate batteries like monkeys ate bananas. That's what her mechanic had said when explaining why she should purchase the most expensive one he had.

"Now try it," Greg said, pulling a white handkerchief from his pocket and adding a little more grease to the black stain that was already there.

She did. This time it hummed beautifully. "You saved the day, Mr. Johnson, isn't it?"

"My pleasure. And the name's Greg, especially when a beautiful redhead is asking."

"Then, thank you, Greg. But I'm curious," she said, "what would have made the wire disconnect?"

"A bad bounce in the road. Maybe nothing. Sometimes

they just work loose. Or maybe fate just wanted us to meet again.''

''I doubt that. Fate hasn't been on my side lately.''

''Then maybe it's my fate, and you just got caught up in the undertow.''

''Well, for whatever reason, I appreciate the assistance. If I can ever return the favor—''

''You can,'' he answered, too quickly.

She eyed him warily.

''You could have dinner with me tonight. Tell me if I'm jumping to conclusions or out of line in inviting you, but I don't see a ring on your finger.''

''Well, it's a long story,'' she joked, realizing she was beginning to feel at ease with the lanky photographer with the easy smile. She wasn't entirely sure that was good, but he did seem harmless.

''Then will you have dinner with me?''

''Why? All you know about me is that I have two sons and a car that dies at inopportune times.''

''I know a lot about you.''

''How would you?'' The wariness intensified as quickly as it had faded.

''My landlady loves to talk. Besides, like I told you, I have a good view of your back porch from my window. That seems to be one of your favorite resting spots.''

''When do you work if you're always watching me?''

''When the light is right. So, are we on for dinner? I promise not to bore you with stories of the big shots that got away.''

''I'm afraid not. My life is in a state of flux right now. And, to be perfectly honest, there is someone else.''

Jodie sensed a change in her rescuer. Not in the smile. It never left his face. It was the eyes that changed, grew darker, more intense.

''I'm disappointed.''

"Don't be," she said. "In my present situation, I would be lousy company. And if the situation changes, you never know, I just may take you up on your offer."

"Then you better hurry, or you might miss your chance."

"It won't be the first time."

"Or hopefully the last." He tipped his hat and walked away.

A strange man, she decided, friendly, but a little quirky. *Everyone you know is a suspect.* Ray's words echoed in her brain. She tried to picture Greg Johnson sneaking into her house or plunging a knife in Max Roling. The thoughts made her blood run cold, but they didn't ring true.

Shifting into reverse, she backed out of her parking place and headed home. Hopefully not to another gift.

RAY KOSTNER STRETCHED, his mouth opening into a killer yawn. Keeping up with his own business long distance and running his dad's office had turned into a lot more work than he'd anticipated. But that was not what was dragging him down.

It was the past, attacking him without mercy, digging into dark crevices of his brain and pulling out memories he'd thought were buried too deep to be unearthed. Another reason Natchitoches was no good for him.

"You're a disappointment, son. You've gone too far this time. I have no choice but to step down as judge."

Words from the past tore at his strength, reducing him from the man he'd become to the boy he'd been. He'd never been good enough to please his dad, so he'd gone the other way. Pushed the limits until they'd broken, and his father's life had come crashing down around them.

But he wasn't that rebellious kid anymore. He'd matured, made it to the top in a dog-eat-dog world. He'd just handled and won one of the highest profile criminal cases to hit

Louisiana in many a year. But, back in Natchitoches, he was still Parker Kostner's son.

It shouldn't matter, but it did. The truth was he'd exchange all his *Times Picayune* headlines for one acknowledgment from his dad that he'd been wrong about him. Maybe then he'd believe it himself. Maybe then he'd believe he could handle the role of husband and father without letting everyone who mattered down again.

Strange, but he could see himself in Natchitoches now, working in this very office, going home to Jodie and the boys at night. At a decent hour so he could help bathe them and tell them bedtime stories.

Or maybe his dad was right, had always been right. Maybe he thrived on controversy, gave in to cheap thrills, went for the pleasure of the moment, let people down. Maybe Jodie and his sons would be better off without him.

When this was over, he'd have to make decisions. Right now, the only thing of importance was keeping Jodie safe. He'd talked to Cappan again, and though hundreds of miles apart, they'd reached the same decision.

A stalker who traveled across the country to torment a woman he'd never been involved with was a dangerous psychopath operating on a short fuse. And the next explosion could be at any minute.

That's why Cappan needed Jodie to return to New York. He had to question her further, in person. And she needed to look at mug shots of multiple sex offenders.

Jodie Gahagen, the girl he'd taken to the senior prom, young and innocent, vivacious and witty and one terrific kisser. She'd changed. Now she was one hell of a woman and a fantastic mother. And still a terrific kisser.

Picking up the office phone, he punched in her number. He needed to hear her voice, tell her he was on the way back to her house. Miss Emily answered on the second ring.

"Is Jodie there?"

"No, she's out."

"Where did she go?"

"Let's see. I think she said she was going over to Selda's. No, that wasn't it. I don't remember, but she'll be back."

Leaving Emily and the boys at night didn't sound like Jodie. Apprehension pitted in his stomach. "Do you have the walkie-talkie?"

"It's right here somewhere. Here it is, hanging on my hip."

"Give her a call."

"What do you want me to tell her?"

"Just call her. I want to know where she is."

"Oh, I don't have to do that. I remember now. She was going down to the boathouse to talk to Ben."

"You're sure?"

"Well, of course I'm sure. Now what was it you wanted me to tell her?"

"Nothing, Miss Emily. I'll see her in a few minutes."

He said a quick goodbye and slammed the receiver into the cradle. In two seconds he was heading out the door.

Chapter Eleven

Jodie trod the worn path to the boathouse. The sky was cloudless, the stars so bright she felt she could reach out and touch them for luck. But, as always, the peace and beauty were flawed by the nagging worries that forever preyed in her mind.

She pulled the flannel cape across her chest. The boathouse was in sight, and a beam of light from the unshuttered window told her Ben was still awake. She'd felt bad about cutting him off so quickly the other day. Tonight seemed the perfect time to let him know she appreciated all he was doing for them.

Voices rumbled through the air. She wasn't close enough to make out all of the words, but the tone was unmistakable. Ben was arguing with someone. Her first urge was to turn around and march back to the solace of the house. She didn't give in. Under present circumstances what she didn't know could definitely hurt her.

The voices became more distinct which each step. When she knocked on the door, the loud quarrel quieted instantly.

"Who's there?"

"It's Jodie, Ben."

He jerked the door open. "Is something the matter, Miss Jodie?"

"No, I just walked down to chat for a while. Did I come at a bad time?"

"No. Come on in."

Her gaze swept the room. Grady stood in the corner, taller than she remembered, and muscular like his dad. His hair was cut short, stylish and he was dressed casually in trendy, khaki pants and a collarless shirt.

"Hello, Jodie. Long time, no see."

"It's been a while. You've changed. I almost didn't recognize you."

"Changed for the better, I hope. I'd know you anywhere. Still the prettiest girl in town, just like my dad always says."

A blush heated her cheeks. "Thanks to both of you. If I'm interrupting something, I can come back later."

"An argument," Grady answered honestly, "but it can wait."

"We don't want to bother you with our family squabbles," Ben interjected. "Have a seat, and I'll get you a soda."

"Thanks." She sat on the only decent chair in the place. This was no way for Ben to live, cramped in a spot originally built for housing fishing supplies. Grady propped against the long table where her grandfather had skinned and filleted his catch. Ben dropped to the sagging bed.

She was glad she'd made this visit. At least she could provide a decent mattress for him. She'd see to it first thing tomorrow. Grams would have done it already had she realized the condition of this one.

"You're really going the extra mile, Ben, staying out here when you could be at your own place, sleeping in your own bed."

"But then he'd have to put up with me, or else kick me out. He's loath to do either of those things."

Ben shot his son a look that couldn't be misinterpreted. Grady ignored it and kept talking.

"That's why I have to find a job and get a place of my own. What about around here? The boathouse could use a coat of paint, the gazebo needs power washing, and the fence between here and Miss Selda's needs to be repaired. There's a break down by the water's edge big enough for a grown man to climb through."

"You certainly seem to know a lot about the place."

"I gave it a once-over the other afternoon when I was out here to see my dad. I'm thorough. And I work cheap."

If he worked free, she still wouldn't have wanted him around the place. She hadn't liked him as a teenager when he'd come out in the summer and helped his dad cut grass and weed the garden. He hadn't had much to do with her, but he had hung around when she was outside, appearing from nowhere and scaring the wits out of her more than once.

Now it was his reputation that caused her not to want him around. Troublemaker and loafer, though she had to admit he didn't look the part.

"I could use a little help," Ben said, from his spot near the door. "It's my own fault, but I did let things get ahead of me when I was out of town."

His comment surprised her. She was sure she'd interrupted a heated argument, yet Ben was encouraging her to hire Grady, to make it necessary for them to spend more time together.

She could turn Grady down without hesitation, but it was a lot more difficult to say no to Ben, especially with him living here in one ill-equipped room in order keep her, Grams and the boys safe. He could have stayed in the house, of course. Grams had offered use of one of the guest rooms but he'd refused to even consider it.

Grady leaned against the door frame, studying her reluctance. "Of course, if you don't want me around…"

"That's not it. Look, we'll give it a try. See if it works out."

The smile that crossed his lips seemed genuine, but the taunting look in his eyes made her regret her hasty decision.

Everyone's a suspect. The familiar phrase hammered in her head, tightened the muscles in her throat so that she could barely swallow the soda Ben had given her. How much longer could she go on like this, wary of everyone she ran into, even people she'd known all her life?

One sign of trouble and Grady would be out of here. She couldn't take chances. And she'd make sure Butch had Grady's name on the list of suspects he was checking out.

Eager to leave, she downed a few more swallows of the canned drink and excused herself. The wind had picked up. It wasn't gusty, but strong enough to sway the branches and tease a few of the last leaf holdouts from their stronghold.

Lost in unpleasant thoughts, she walked to the edge of the water.

"A nice night for a walk."

She turned at the voice, her heart racing the way it always did when Ray appeared. "Is that what brought you here?"

"No, I came looking for you." He stepped behind her and wound his arms around her waist, burying his lips in her neck. Tiny shivers of delight feathered her skin. Suddenly she didn't want to go back to the house, didn't want to talk about stalkers or police reports.

"Let's take the boat out, Ray."

"What brought that on?"

"You. The moonlight. The need to feel normal again."

"I'm game. I'm not dressed for it, but I'm game."

"If your shoes get wet, they'll dry. If your clothes get dirty, have them cleaned."

"You have answers for everything."

"That's the problem. I don't have answers, and I'm so tired of searching for them. For a few minutes I'd like to be uninhibited, unafraid, the way I used to be. The way we were when you visited me in New York."

"I'm not sure I have the energy to be the way we were then," he teased.

"Not that. I want to laugh, to act silly, to have fun."

"But not to make love?"

"If it happens."

Ray ran his fingers through her hair, silky curls that tangled his fingers. Leaning closer, he touched his lips to hers and then drew away, sucking in a shaky breath. The taste, the feel, the flowery fragrance. All Jodie. All devastating.

"If I stay with you another minute, it will happen."

"But first the boat ride."

"Won't you mind leaving Grams and the boys alone?"

"Not tonight. Butch talked the chief into assigning a man to watch the house. He's pulling the first shift."

"Then a boat ride it is."

Minutes later he was guiding the small fishing craft down the Cane River, the hum of the motor breaking the silence, the wind in their faces easing but never dissolving the burdens of dealing daily with a killer.

"I feel like the big bad wolf out with Little Red Riding Hood the way that cape's flowing behind you."

"It's russet, not red."

"Moonlight's deceiving."

"Life's deceiving."

He didn't have an argument for that. They rode in silence for fifteen minutes, and for the first time in days, Ray could almost feel his muscles letting go of the tension. He slowed the motor and guided the boat to a small wooden dock that jutted into the river.

"Where are we?"

"A fishing camp. It belongs to a friend of mine, but they don't use it much anymore. It's quiet. We can talk, and laugh and act silly with no one to hear us."

"Don't make fun of me. You have to admit the boat ride was a good idea."

"Great." He killed the motor and stepped out, tying the boat to a post. Jodie joined him on the dock. They walked together, hand in hand, up a grassy hill toward a rustic cabin. An owl hooted, the only sound in their world of isolation.

Jodie stopped and stared up at him, moonlight shimmering in her eyes. "Too bad the world can't always be this peaceful."

"It can. It will be again." He held her close and she cuddled against him, soft where he was hard, curves where he was planes and angles. The ache inside him swelled to strangling proportions. "We just have to keep you safe long enough to see it."

"We're supposed to be laughing and acting silly," she said.

"And making love. But first I have to bring up something serious."

"You are the big, bad wolf," she groaned.

"I talked to Cappan today."

"Can't this wait until tomorrow?"

"No, tomorrow you'll be packing for a trip to New York. The two of us will be leaving the day after that."

"I'm busy, Ray. You know that. I'm still working out the plans for my project. It's Tuesday now. The ad runs Saturday. I have to see Butch again."

"If the trip's successful, you won't have to go through with your plan. Cappan has some ideas."

"I talked to Cappan when I was in New York. Many times. His ideas were useless."

"This time will be different. He has mug shots of everyone in the New York area who's been convicted on multiple sexual offenses in the last decade. He needs you to see if one of them looks familiar. By the time we get there, he'll also have a computer printout of every stalker case that even remotely resembles yours."

"Cappan's been busy."

"He's pulled out all the stops. Even gone so far as pulling up past serial killer data to see if your guy could be a copycat."

"Too bad he wasn't that cooperative before I gave up my job and moved to Natchitoches." She pulled away and walked to a worn hammock that swung between two pines.

"But I was just a woman complaining about some man sending her gifts and breaking into her house without taking anything. We had to wait until the NYPD were convinced the guy had committed a murder before they got serious."

"Cappan's serious now. And so am I."

"Plane reservations to New York are not always easy to come by on short notice."

"We have reservations. We have a direct flight out of Shreveport at eight o'clock Thursday morning. We meet with Cappan right after lunch."

"Why did you wait until now to tell me?"

"Cappan didn't let me know until this afternoon that he could provide everything I asked."

"So this was all your idea?"

"It would have come to this eventually. I just pushed the buttons a little sooner."

"I have the boys, Ray. I can't just up and leave."

He dropped beside her in the hammock. "I've already talked to Selda. She'll stay with your grandmother until we get back. And you said Butch already has cops watching your house.''

''Butch took credit, but that was your doing, too, wasn't it?''

''I talked to the chief of police. He owed my dad a favor.''

''So everything is set.''

''You can say no.''

''And miss the chance to get a real lead? Not on your life. I just wished these actions had come sooner, while Max was still alive. While Gloria Bigger was still alive, even though no one but me is convinced the stalker frightened her into the initial heart attack.''

''I know.'' He traced the lines of her face, trailing a finger down her forehead, over her nose and to her lips. ''I wish a lot of things were different.''

She tipped her head toward him. ''Kiss me, Ray. Make me forget for a few minutes that the world is cursed with people who destroy other people's lives.''

He pressed his lips against hers, and she melted into him, warm and willing. The kiss fed his hunger but didn't begin to satisfy the needs that raged inside him.

''Do you want to go back now?'' he asked, ''while I can still pull myself away from you and walk back to the boat?''

She wrapped herself around him and pulled him down into the roped folds of the oversize hammock. And that was all the answer he needed.

THE HOUSE WAS DARK and locked up tight when they returned. Ray fiddled with key until the back door opened.

Jodie flicked on the light. Her hair was tangled and wild from wind blowing across the water and from making love in a swaying hammock. Her blouse was wrinkled and buttoned crooked, with one side hanging down inches past the other.

She'd never looked more sexy. Ray fought back urges that should have been well satisfied from heaven in the hammock.

"Are you hungry?" she asked, opening the refrigerator and peeking inside.

"Famished."

"How about a BLT on toast?"

"With cheese?"

"Melted and gooey."

"You talked me into it."

Ray peeled the slices of bacon apart and placed them into the frying pan while Jodie sliced a large tomato and a hunk of cheddar cheese.

"We make a good team," she said, slipping a sliver of cheese between his lips.

He let the comment ride. No matter how good things seemed at this minute, he couldn't make promises, not about teams or partnerships or anything that spoke of permanence. Not until he was sure he could make it work. Until he was dead certain he would not fall short again.

His temporary silence did not daunt Jodie. She kept up her cheery chatter while they finished making the sandwiches and then devoured them.

Ray wasn't fooled for a minute. The party atmosphere only covered the surface, like a thin layer of gold over dull, imitation metals. Hopefully their trip to New York would lead to an arrest that could change everything, give her back her life.

And take her back to New York, away from him.

The phone jangled loudly, interrupting his thoughts.

"You answer it, Ray. I hate phone calls this time of night. They're never good news." She picked up the kitchen extension and handed it to him.

"Hello."

The caller was Butch Deaton. "I saw lights on. I thought I'd check and make sure everything's all right."

"Everything's fine. Jodie and I were just grabbing a snack."

"It's a little late for eating, isn't it?"

"Not if you're hungry."

"Tell Jodie I called. If she needs me tonight, I'll be practically within yelling distance."

"I'll let her know."

Ray hung up the phone. "Your Officer Unfriendly seems to be interested in getting more friendly these days, at least with you."

"I know. He has some crazy idea the two of us might have ended up together if he hadn't broken our date for the senior prom."

"Your senior prom." Ray stepped closer. "I remember it well. I had just graduated from LSU. My mom asked me to do a favor for her."

"Take me to the prom?"

"Yeah. It cost her twenty bucks. I needed gasoline to drive to New Orleans that weekend."

"You mean you were paid to date me?" She wadded a napkin and threw it at him.

"Cold, hard cash."

"If I'd known that I would have never let you kiss me good-night."

"Yes, you would have. You initiated the kiss."

"I certainly did not."

He reached over and wrapped an arm around her waist, pulling her to him. "You did. Looking up at me with those big green eyes, tossing that mane of gorgeous wild hair. The same way you're doing now."

And then his lips were on hers. And he was lost in her

again. He lifted her like he might have done Blake or Blair and carried her up the stairs.

He couldn't fight his feelings for her any longer. Not sleeping under the same roof. But when this was over, when the stalker was caught, then he'd have to deal in reality.

The reality that he was not the man she thought he was. The reality was that if he didn't walk away, he would hurt her and the boys, let them down the way he had let down everyone in his life who had ever mattered.

And no matter what leaving did to him, it wouldn't be as bad as watching the love she had for him turn to bitter resentment. It wouldn't be as bad as ruining Jodie's and his sons' lives.

JODIE ROLLED OUT another round of pie dough, flexing her wrists, and laying on the muscle power. Physical activity was great for releasing tension, and after this morning's meeting with Butch, she had more than her share. He'd argued every point, but finally they'd managed to agree on enough of them that everything was set in case the killer really did answer her ad.

"How many more of these rounds do you need?" she asked, turning and spilling a little more flour down the front of her apron in the process.

Selda stopped beside her. "You're just getting started, honey. We're making a hundred meat pies."

"A hundred! Who's going to eat them?"

"A hundred tourists. These are for the church booth. Last year we made enough money the first weekend of the festival to take the golden agers to Branson for five days."

"We're going back next spring," Grams added. "Selda's got a thing for Mel Tillis."

"You should talk. You were drooling over John Davidson."

"I was not. That was my false teeth slipping." Their laughter filled the kitchen.

Selda slammed another package of meat on the table and peeled off a layer of butcher paper. "Do you think this ground beef's too lean, Emily?"

"Way too lean, but the pork's a little fatty. Cooked together we should have enough meat drippings to give the pies a decent flavor."

"I don't believe anyone mentioned we were making a hundred pies when you enlisted my help," Jodie complained good-naturedly.

"You didn't ask." Grams and Selda exchanged sly smiles.

"I've been had."

Blair agreed with her, bouncing a rattling set of plastic keys off the tray of his high chair.

"Did you bring the sage?" Grams asked from her position on her all fours. She was rummaging in the bottom cabinet for her biggest mixing bowl.

"You told me you were going to get the sage and some cayenne pepper."

"The pepper's on the counter. Did you buy sage at the store, Jodie?"

"It wasn't on my list."

"Well, we'll just have to stop cooking and go get some. You can't make Natchitoches Meat Pies if you don't have all the right spices," Selda said.

"I don't know how I forgot to put it on the list."

"No reason to fret," Selda said, wiping her hands on the tail of her apron. "It won't take but a minute to run up to Brookshires."

"I'll tell you what," Jodie said, fitting her fifth circle of pie dough onto a slice of waxed paper. "The boys and I will go to the store and get the sage and anything else you need. They're ready for a break."

"You are such a sweetie," Selda purred. "You're lucky to have her around, Emily."

"That's the truth. I plan to keep her here, too, even if I have to go out and find her a husband to do it."

"The way that Kostner boy's hanging around, I'd say he's sweet enough on her to swing for a diamond."

"Hmmph! That fellow's not her type. The man will talk your ears off, and he's a little too thin," Grams snorted, never tiring of her own version of the matchmaking game.

"Well, a man that handsome could slip his shoes under my bed any night," Selda replied. "Of course, I'd have to double up on my heart pills."

The two women erupted in giggles again.

Jodie unstrapped the safety catches on the boys' high chairs and sat the twins on the floor. Blair crawled toward the table leg and started pulling up. Blake headed for a spot of spilled flour.

She grabbed them both, balancing one on each hip. "I'll be back in a few minutes. Are you sure sage is all you need?"

"That's it." Emily followed her to the door. "Be careful," she said.

"I will. The store will be full of people this time of day." Jodie bent down and kissed her grandmother's cheek. No matter how hard Grams tried to present a calm front, the fear was there, just under the surface of carefree chatter, hiding beneath the thin veil of daily routine. And Jodie had brought the trouble down on all of them. She wasn't sure how, but she had to have done something to cause the stalker to pick her out of all the women in New York City.

The drive to Brookshires was uneventful. She parked near the exit and pulled the double stroller from the trunk before unbuckling the twins' car seats. No use to bother with a cart for one item.

"Mommy's going to make this quick. A can of ground

sage and then home again, home again, clickety clack.'' The phrase was accompanied with one of her silliest faces. Blair giggled; Blake stuck a pudgy hand into her face. He was the doubter. It took a lot more than a silly face to convince him being buckled into a stroller was going to be fun.

Wednesdays were obviously a good day for shopping. Fewer people than usual walked the aisles, most with half-filled baskets, and there were no long checkout lines. Jodie walked straight to the spice aisle. She pushed the stroller to the side while she searched for the sage.

''Jodie Gahagen!'' The greeting was a high-pitched squeal.

She turned to find a statuesque blond standing behind her, a wide smile showing off a row of perfect white teeth.

''Mary Lou Skelton!'' Jodie fell into a bear hug. ''It's been years.''

''Nine. Tommy and I got married the summer after high school graduation and moved to Little Rock. You were the smart one, going to LSU. I was so envious.''

''You were never envious of anyone. How's Tommy?''

''Still sweet as ever. What about you? Did you get married, or are you one of those career women?''

''I'm…unattached now.'' That covered it better than the choices Mary Lou provided. ''How's your family?''

''Daddy retired, just last month. He and Mom are moving up to Hot Springs Village so they can be close to us and the kids. We have two boys and a girl. Do you believe it?''

''I have twins myself.'' She turned back to her sons. ''Oh, my God, my boys.''

''What's the matter?''

''Blake and Blair! They're gone.'' Terror slammed into her, knocking the breath from her lungs. For a second, her body was frozen in fear. The next second adrenaline shot through her in energizing bursts.

She rounded the corner of the aisle. They were there, sitting calmly, each with a sucker, one end clutched in their pudgy hands, the other stuck in their mouths.

She bent down beside them, relief coursing through her in relentless waves. "Where did these come from?" She pulled the candy from their mouths and they wailed in protest. The suckers were red, heart-shaped. She clutched a shelf filled with canned vegetables for support. *He* had been here. In the one split second she had turned her back, he had pushed the boys around the corner and given them the suckers.

She wanted to cry, to scream, to beat her fists against the stacks of cans and send them clattering to the floor.

"Why are you so upset, Jodie? I mean it's just a sucker. They didn't choke or anything."

"It's not the candy. Someone moved them. While we were talking, someone pushed their stroller around the corner."

"Why would they?"

"To drive me crazy. To let me know he was here, watching me. To let me know I can't stop him." Her voice was shaking. So was she, but she couldn't control herself.

Mary Lou backed away, the look on her face proof that she didn't think the drive to crazy would have to be very far. "Maybe you just walked away from them without thinking, you know, while you were looking at groceries."

Jodie struggled for a calming breath. She had to pull herself together for the boys' sake. "No, it's a long story, Mary Lou. But, the boys are fine. That's all that matters."

"Are you sure you don't want me to call someone?"

Like a psychiatrist. Reading Mary Lou's mind was not a challenge. "There's no reason to call anyone." No reason at all. The police hadn't been able to stop him. And in spite of all of his efforts, neither had Ray.

"If you're sure you're all right?" Mary Lou took another step backward, obviously eager to be on her way.

"I'm sure." She waved Mary Lou off and bent again to hug her boys and wipe the tears from their eyes.

"No more candy," she said, giving each tummy a gentle tickle. "We're going home. Mommy will keep you safe."

Her heart was pounding as she paid for the sage and walked to the car. But still she stole furtive glances in every direction. There was a man loading his groceries in the car, a mother trying to keep up with the preschooler who skipped in front of her, a pregnant lady pushing a cart of groceries. Not one person who could possibly be a suspect.

Mommy will keep you safe. The promise echoed in her head as she started the car and drove back to Grams's house. She would keep that promise or die trying.

Chapter Twelve

Jodie rubbed her burning eyes. She'd spent hours staring at countless mug shots that had gotten her the same place every other step in this dance with the devil had. Nowhere.

"Just a few more, Jodie," Ray urged, giving her shoulders a quick massage.

"It's a waste of time. None of these people look familiar. And none of the people I named or described had a record. Cappan even checked out the guy who sells roasted nuts at the corner by my old apartment. He's squeaky clean, at least in this sense."

She vacated the chair next to Ray's, standing and stretching her neck back as far as it would go without making it hurt more than it already did. Every muscle in her body ached, not only from the activities of the afternoon, but from three months of strain, from tension that woke with her in the morning and slept with her at night.

Cappan walked to the open door and peered in. "Any luck?"

"Nothing but dead ends." She walked over and retrieved her raincoat from the back of a chair, folding it over her arm. "I feel like I've looked at snapshots of every psycho in the state of New York except the one tormenting me."

"Who isn't in New York at the time."

"No, the man did what you said he wouldn't, followed me from one end of the country to another."

"Maybe he'd already done that."

"I don't follow you."

"We've been looking for someone who lives, or at least lived, around this area. We could be way off base. Your stalker might be someone from your past, someone from Louisiana who followed you here, or at least came up here looking for you." Cappan propped a hip on the door frame.

"That's impossible. I've lived up here five years, ever since I graduated from LSU."

"What brought you here?"

"I wasn't running from an ex-husband or lover, if that's what you're suggesting. I didn't have one. I came up here with a group of five friends, all women, all of us wanting a taste of big-city life. I'm the only one who lasted."

"But say someone, like Ray here, was so obsessed with you that he couldn't get you out of his mind." Cappan twirled a yellow pencil around his fingers, his gaze moving from first one then to the other of them. "He comes up here to see you and wham!" Cappan popped a fist into his palm to emphasize his point. "The man becomes a full-blown basket case, out of his head crazy for you. He doesn't want to live here, so he tries to frighten you into returning to Louisiana."

"That's absurd."

"Not really." Ray leaned closer, nodding his head in agreement. "Actually, I'd already thought of that, only I can't imagine anyone going so far as to kill a man just to get you to return home. But if the person were from Natchitoches originally or Baton Rouge or anywhere else around there, it would explain how he knew where to find you."

"On the other hand," Cappan said, "in five years you must have broken a few hearts in New York. Your sons' father, for example."

"I told you he isn't a suspect," Jodie answered. "We can leave him out of this."

"Under the circumstances, I can't do that."

"I'm the father, Cappan." Ray glared across the table.

"Sorry, I didn't know. Miss Gahagen refused to divulge that information before she left New York."

"Now you know. So let's get back to finding the killer before he loses it and strikes again. The way I see it, all we really know is that the stalker is obviously obsessed with Jodie."

"And crazy enough to kill because of it."

"But like I told you on the phone," Ray said, "I'm worried about the stalker's reference to 'the others.' In my mind that strengthens the possibility that this man doesn't know Jodie. A serial killer who chooses his victims at random."

"I've been thinking along those same lines. Only not necessarily at random. Maybe the man has criteria. The color of her hair, her southern accent, the way she walks."

"You sound like you might have found something." Ray drew his body to full attention, the muscles in his arms straining against his long-sleeved shirt.

"No, unfortunately. The Serial Killer Task Force has checked the pattern of Jodie's stalker with every open case we have. Only one is close. A couple of women down in the Village, not too far from where Miss Gahagen lived. They complained to neighbors and the police that they were being watched and that someone had been in their houses, going through their things when they weren't home. They turned up dead, about a year apart."

"When was that?" Ray asked, picking up a yellow legal pad.

"In the late eighties. No arrests were ever made. But the pattern was different. There were no notes, no gifts, no contact at all."

"And there's been nothing since then?"

"Not around here. Not that matches the intensity Jodie's dealt with, except, of course when the women knew the suspect. Jilted boyfriends and husbands. That sort of thing."

Cappan tapped the eraser end of the pencil against his chin. "I have heard of something similar recently, but I don't give the tale much credence. The man stalked women he was in love with without letting them know who he was. Eventually, he killed them. He had a foolproof plan that kept the police from catching him. That's all I remember about it."

"Can't you track it down in the police computer or through the FBI?"

"I tried. Couldn't find a thing. That's what makes me think it might have been a made-up scenario. If it was fact, it didn't happen anywhere around here. I can guarantee that."

"How much danger do you think Jodie is in?" Ray asked, "Based on past stalker cases that you can verify."

"A fair amount. I'd say right now you're in more." He pointed his pencil toward Ray. "The man's killed at least once before. According to Jodie, he stabbed Max Roling to death just because he saw him hugging her. You said you're living in her house. I'd say that makes you a prime target."

"And our sons?"

"The way I see it, the risk goes way down there. The man is obsessed with Jodie. He's probably trying to get up the courage to make a bigger move, let her know who he is, maybe abduct her. If he fails, he may lose control and become violent with her, but I don't think he'd touch the kids. The fact that she's a mother may even be a part of what attracts him to her."

"But he has touched them." Jodie insisted. "He moved

Blake from one crib to another when we were still in New York. This week he gave both of them suckers.''

''He's touched them. He hasn't hurt them. He had the opportunity to if that was what he wanted. But nothing is certain with a nut like this.'' Cappan walked over and stopped in front of her chair. ''Promise me something, Ms. Gahagen.''

''What?''

''This man is dangerous. Let the police handle this case. Promise you won't do anything foolish, that you won't go through with the personal ad scheme.''

''How do you know about that? I didn't mention it to you.''

''Ray mentioned it on the phone. I agree with him that it's suicide to play games with a sicko. So for all your sakes, give up playing undercover cop.''

''I'm afraid I can't make that promise.''

Jodie only half listened to the next few minutes of discussion. They were only rehashing anyway, a confirmation that the trip to New York was a waste of time, energy and money. The money, of course, had been Ray's. He seemed to have an endless supply.

By the time they left the office, even the cold November rain was a welcome change from the bombardment of disappointments and foreshadowings of doom the day had brought.

Afternoon traffic was snarled beyond belief, and after five minutes of sitting in one spot, serenaded by blasting car horns, Ray and Jodie gave up the dry taxi in favor of walking the remaining eight blocks back to the hotel.

They shrugged into rain gear and took off at a steady pace, water dancing about their feet as it pooled in the cracks and splashed from the onslaught of an army of homebound workers. A million people, all in a hurry to get somewhere else.

And here in the masses, a killer had picked Jodie out and attached his life to hers. Why? Ray had asked himself that question a hundred times before. If they knew that they might begin to find answers to the question of who.

He took Jodie's arm, guiding her around a major puddle. "We can duck in somewhere for a drink if you like."

"No, thanks. I'd just like to get back to the hotel and into something dry. And I want to call Grams, just to make sure everything's all right."

"How can it not be? Selda's staying over to help with Blair and Blake, and I hired enough off-duty cops to provide round-the-clock protection inside the house."

"I appreciate that."

"They're my sons, too. Besides, I knew you'd never leave them to make this trip if I didn't, not after the lollipop episode at Brookshires."

"I still wish we could have flown back tonight."

"The late flight was booked solid. Besides, the boys are fine, Grams is fine, and you need a night to be wined and dined in style. The stress level in your life is off the charts."

Conversation stopped as they rounded the corner and hurried toward the door of the Waldorf. Ray's thoughts continued. He had more than wining and dining in mind. Hopefully he'd also be able to drill some sense into Jodie. Isolated meetings with someone who could well be a serial killer. The possibility was driving him out of his mind.

But then everything about Jodie Gahagen was driving him out of his mind. Without Jodie his life had been planned, predictable, prosperous. He hadn't had to deal with personal shortcomings. Hadn't had to look inside himself and see the man who lived beneath the trappings of success.

At thirty-one he'd already made a name for himself as a leading defense attorney in Louisiana. After his last case, his stock had climbed even higher. Big-bucks clients from all over the U.S. would be ringing his phone. They'd already started. The work was piling up, and his partners were yelling for his return.

Everything he'd ever thought he'd wanted was falling into his hands.

What Jodie had to offer was marriage, commitment, children. All of the things he'd been sure he never wanted. Even more sure he could never handle.

He could still walk away when this was over. Send a check every month, have the boys visit during the Christmas holidays, a couple of weeks in the summer. Jodie would never cling or beg. She'd be the perfect mother. He'd be the louse of a father.

Nobody would be surprised, least of all dear old grandpa Parker. He'd predicted it years ago.

"You let me down, son. You let your mother down. You let everyone down who loves you. You always do."

Ray pushed the hotel door open, the weight of the past and the worries of the present balanced precariously on his shoulders.

Jodie needed dry clothes. He needed a stiff drink.

"THIS IS THE perfect nightcap." Jodie snuggled beside Ray in the carriage, the hoofs of the horses providing the sound effects, Central Park providing the scenery.

The rain had stopped while they were at dinner, and when they'd exited the restaurant, the air sported a fresh, just-washed feel, too tempting to forsake for the hotel room. Hand in hand, they'd walked down Fifth Avenue.

Jodie had pointed out the sights and Ray had admired them appropriately. Saint Patrick's Cathedral had been his favorite, but he was also duly impressed with a few gems in the window of Tiffany's.

"No wonder you love this city," he said, tucking the blanket around her. "You must miss it terribly."

"I do." She paused, taking a reading on her own feelings. "And I don't."

"I can see how you wouldn't miss some things, like the traffic and lack of sunlight. But you must miss nights like this."

"I didn't have a lot of nights like this. Usually it was work all day, pick up the boys, go home and spend precious little time with them."

"Sounds tough."

"Oh, no. I'm not complaining. I loved my life, at least I did until it was stolen from me. But being with Grams these past few weeks has made me face the fact that she's getting older."

"She's a remarkable woman, feisty as a mother lion."

"Nothing gets by her." Jodie laughed and snuggled closer. "I'm thankful she and the boys have had a chance to get to know each other. I guess I'm not sure I want to leave her again. Or even return to a job that takes so much of my time and energy from Blair and Blake."

"Family." Ray ran his fingers through her hair, his fingers entangling in the curls. "You fit in yours so well."

"You seem to fit in yours just as well."

"Appearances. They're like a good witness. They say the right things, leave the rest unsaid. The jury has to dig beneath the surface to find the truth."

"Like the powerful undercurrent between you and your dad?"

"See, you'd make a good juror."

"Not really. I do better when someone just tells me the truth."

"The truth has two versions."

"I'd like to hear yours."

"I doubt it, but you deserve to know, especially since it

affects you as well now. But not right this minute." He pulled her close and buried his face in her hair. "A carriage ride through Central Park is no time to pull skeletons out and rattle their bones."

"No, it's the time for romance." She caught his lips with hers, nibbling and feathering his mouth with kisses until she felt his muscles relax. Her fingers walked the front of his shirt, down to his belt, and lower still.

"No way, lady." He took her hands in his and pulled them out from under the blanket. "First a desk in a law office and then a hammock," he whispered, his tongue caressing her ear. "But not in a carriage."

"Of course not. I'd never dream of such a thing."

"Yeah, sure, says the insatiable sex goddess."

She poked him in the ribs. "You'll be begging when we get back to the hotel."

"Darn right, I will. Unless you beat me to it."

She snuggled closer, burrowing under his arm and close to his heart and wished the night would never end.

JODIE BRUSHED HER TEETH and washed away the evening's makeup before slipping out of her dress and into a teal teddie with scallops that rode the curves of her breasts. The lacy scrap of satin was a far cry from the oversize nightshirts or simple cotton gowns she usually slept in.

She'd slipped it into her luggage at the last minute, then taken it out, then tucked it back under her underwear and zipped the case shut. Ray had shown up to pick her up just as she was unzipping the suitcase to remove it again. Now she was glad she'd brought it along.

She was in love with Ray Kostner. If she'd ever had any doubts, they had disappeared over the last few days. He was always there, putting her first, never making light of her fears, but doing everything in his power to protect her and the boys.

All the signs were there that he loved her as much as she loved him. Everything except a verbal declaration. He admitted the boys were his, although until he'd mentioned it to Cappan today, it had been their secret. And there had not been a word about what would happen between them when he returned to New Orleans.

Life for her and Ray existed only in the here and now. The future was hazy, a smoky cloud that cast a tint of gray over even their best moments. That was the part of the relationship that worried her, the indication that even if she outsmarted the stalker, their love story was not guaranteed a happy ending.

If she was reading all the signs wrong, if he didn't love her, she could accept that. It would tear the heart right out of her, but she would live with it. If he wanted nothing to do with his sons, she'd grant him that, too. Not so much for him, but for them.

Her position had never waffled. Blake and Blair would be surrounded by love and protected from the type of rejection that could whittle away their self-confidence and destroy their spirit. She'd seen it happen to some of her friends. She wouldn't let it happen to her sons.

Their future as a family lay in Ray's hands. She would fight to the death in a battle she could win, but she would never settle for crumbs. If he wanted to be a father, she expected him to be there for them, dependable, nurturing and loving. If he wanted her, it would be all or nothing. Marriage, commitment and passion ever after.

With steady hands, she raked back the mass of tangled curls that fell over her forehead and dotted a splash of flowery fragrance behind each ear. Satisfied that she looked as good as she could on a minimum of maintenance, she slipped her blue terry robe over everything.

First the terry robe and talk. Then the teal nightie and...whatever the night brought.

RAY STOOD AT the window, staring out at the New York skyline. He wondered how many women out there were suffering the way Jodie had been, alone in a city of teeming millions, stalked by a man who took his pleasure from torment.

Jodie stepped into the room, and his heart took the familiar lurch. He had so little of value to offer to a woman like Jodie, but he would give her what he could. He'd protect her from a killer, with his life if it came to that. Too bad he hadn't protected her from getting involved with himself.

"You look devastating," he said.

"If old terry robes turn you on, you are easy."

"*You* turn me on. In or out of the robe. Preferably out." He tugged at the tie that circled her waist, pulling her toward him.

"I love it when you talk dirty to me."

"Who said anything about talking?"

"Actually, you did." She pulled away. "Earlier tonight, in the carriage."

Ray felt his gut twist painfully. "That talk can wait. It will spoil a perfect night."

"I'd like to hear it."

"Hearing it won't change anything."

"It will help me know you better."

His hands fisted at his side. "It will do that all right, let you know just what kind of man fathered your sons. That will make your day."

"It's night, not day and too late to worry. You've already made several of my days and nights. Besides, you should know what I'm made of by now. I can handle disappointments."

"Then maybe I am the man for you. I can dish them out. But then you know what I'm made of by now, too. You were pregnant with my sons. I ignored your phone calls. You were being followed by a madman, I was in New Orleans defending one of our illustrious senators.''

"You were doing your job.'' She took his arm and led him to the love seat. "And you didn't know about your sons then.''

"You can make excuses all you want, Jodie. But you'll get tired of them eventually. There will finally be one disappointment too many. Ask my dad.''

"No. I'm asking you. What happened between you and Parker?''

Ray got up from the love seat and walked to the stocked bar in the corner of the room. "Can I get you something?''

"No, I'm fine.'' Her voice was soft, reassuring. He wondered if it would be that way after she heard the disgusting truths.

He took out a small bottle of whiskey and poured a shot into a glass, swishing the amber liquid around, buying time. Pulling the memories from the dark crevices of his mind was taking its toll.

"I don't know how well you knew me during my high school years.''

"I knew about you. You were Mr. Cool, the town bad boy.''

"That was me, all right. Charm the girls, skip class, get kicked off the football team when we were headed for state. The team lost the championship game miserably, and my friends hated me for the loss.''

"All of that was a long time ago. Surely you aren't still concerned about what happened when you were a teenager.''

"No. It just establishes the pattern my life has taken. My dad wanted a perfect son. I heard it for as long as I can remember. 'You are the son of a judge. People expect you to be better than the others. *I* expect you to be better.'''

He tilted his head back and took a long swig of the

whiskey, feeling the burn and wishing it were more harsh. Physical pain was a comfort compared to baring his soul.

"That must have been hard on you."

There it was again, the cool voice of reason, spewing from the mouth of a sexy redhead who had been through hell herself. She never ceased to amaze him.

"It was too hard. So I took the path of least resistance. I went the opposite direction, looking for things that would shock, things that would make the citizens' of Natchitoches tongues wag, things that would make my dad lash out at me for being the disappointing son I was."

"But you went to college and turned your life around."

"I went away to college and got Sylvia Stevens pregnant."

"Sylvia Stevens?" Jodie's voice rose an octave or two. Now he had her attention.

"The one and only. Sweet, hometown girl who raced from one beauty title to another. We made love one night after a fraternity party. A month later she showed up at my door and told me she was pregnant with my child."

"Did you love her? Did she love you?"

"No, to both questions. I told her I doubted the baby was mine."

Memories grappled with his self-control, tension turning his stomach into a war zone. He ground his right fist into his left palm, his mouth set so tight he could feel his teeth grinding together.

"She was scared to death, sure her mom was going to go ballistic when she found out her daughter would have to drop out of the Miss Louisiana Pageant. Apparently, the contests were as much for her mom as they were for her. Sylvia begged me to run off with her and get married."

"What did you do?"

"I demanded proof the baby was mine. I should have

been supportive. But, true to form I handled everything all wrong.''

''What happened?''

''Sylvia took an overdose of sleeping pills. She didn't die, but she came close.''

Jodie sat quietly, her gaze penetrating, unreadable.

''Have you heard enough?'' he asked.

''Not until I've heard it all. What happened to the baby?''

''Turns out there wasn't one. It was a missed diagnosis on the doctor's part. But complications resulting from the overdose forced her to withdraw from the Miss Louisiana Pageant. Her chance at becoming Miss America was lost, and once again I was guilty of spoiling someone's dreams. And no one hated me more than I hated myself.''

''You weren't to blame. How could you even think that? You had no way of knowing she'd react so dangerously when you asked for proof of parentage. You couldn't have been more than eighteen at the time.''

Ray poured himself another drink. ''Neither Sylvia nor her mother saw it exactly the way you do. And like all tragedies, there's an epilogue.''

''She can't still blame you.''

''No. Blame wasn't good enough. Sylvia went to my dad and asked for money to start her life over. A lot of money in exchange for keeping quiet about the fact that his son had caused her such pain. She failed to mention to him that although we had made love, there never was a baby. He thought she had lost it when she took the sleeping pills.''

''That's blatantly dishonest. Surely he didn't give her money without asking you.''

''Of course. He would have given her twice that amount to keep her from blabbing the story to his friends. Natchitoches is a small town. They don't forgive too easily, at least that has always been my dad's theory. Not when it's The Judge's son who's involved.''

"Then all of you were wrong."

"No, I was wrong. I've regretted my mistakes every minute of every day since I ruined my dad's and Sylvia's lives, but regrets don't change anything."

"People were disappointed, Ray. Their lives weren't ruined.''

He met Jodie's gaze. Her eyes burned with concern and a depth of understanding that touched his soul. It was as if her compassion released the doors he'd closed on his past and let him explore the disillusionment in a new light.

"My dad and Sylvia wouldn't agree with you. I committed a mistake that made it possible for Sylvia to believe she was pregnant. I let her leave in a state of fury. And, at least in my dad's eyes, I led him into blackmail, caused him to break the law he'd spent his adult life interpreting.''

"But you were only a freshman in college. You panicked and understandably so. Maybe you didn't handle the situation with great empathy, but asking for proof of parentage was sensible. You can't be blamed for the overdose and certainly not for your dad giving in to blackmail threats.''

"Why not? I caused everything else bad that happened in my parents' lives. My parents never forgave me and neither did Sylvia and her family. Apparently the houseful of trophies she'd won meant nothing without the Miss America crown.''

"Even if she'd made it that far, she had only a chance of winning. Your dad is not still paying Sylvia money, is he?''

"No. He stopped after the second payment. That's when some reporter found out that hard-hitting Judge Parker, the man who had no empathy for anyone found guilty of unlawful behavior, was paying a young girl to keep quiet.''

"How would a reporter find out?''

"From Sylvia. My dad quit paying. She followed through on her threat to make us suffer for her pain and disappointment. And she had copies of the checks to back up her story."

"The killing cycle of deceit."

"The only solution in my dad's mind was to step down from the judgeship. He hung up his robes and slipped into a depression that lasted for two years. Being a judge was his life, his symbol that he was what a man should be, better than the best. I took that away from him and nothing I can do now will change that."

Jodie walked over and wrapped her arms about him. The pain in his gut intensified. "I always let the people down who depend on me. If you were smart, you'd be running out the door now," he whispered.

"I'm not running anywhere." She hugged him close, the warmth of her melting the ice that coursed his veins.

"You'll be sorry. You can't count on me. Ask my dad."

"I don't have to ask anyone. I can see for myself who you are—a troubled boy who matured into a wonderful man." A tear trickled down her cheek. He whisked it away with his fingertips.

"Don't you see," she continued, the love in her eyes so tangible, he felt he could hold it in his hands. "In spite of all the conflict between you and your dad, he called, and you put your own career on hold to come running. You moved into my house the second you realized I was in danger, and you've barely left my side since. You've put your own life on the line to keep me and our sons safe."

She stretched on tiptoes and touched her lips to his. "I love you, Ray Kostner. I think I have since the first time you gave me a careless peck on the cheek on my fourteenth birthday."

"You beat me." He kissed her moist eyes and the tip of her nose. "It was the night of your senior prom that did me in. The last kiss, at your front door. I fell so hard my head was still ringing from the blow years later, when I finally looked you up in New York.''

"We saw each other several times when I first got to LSU," she said, her mouth inches from his. "You showed me the ropes, the impressive law student helping out the freshman coed. I never once guessed you cared about me.''

"I didn't have the right. I still don't.''

"I do. I claim the right to love you.''

While he watched, she slipped out of the terry robe and let it slide it to the carpet. "I want you, Ray, all of you. Tonight and forever.''

"I can't promise anything.''

"I didn't ask for promises. I said I love you. Unconditionally. The way you are.''

Emotions exploded inside him. Whether he deserved it or not, Jodie was here, knowing the truth and still loving him. For now, that was all that mattered. He picked her up and carried her to the bed, laying her atop the cool sheets, watching her hair spread like a halo of fire over the pillows.

She pulled him down beside her, running her fingers across his chest, catching the matted dark hairs around her fingers.

"The nightie is exquisite," he whispered, responding to her touch with the primal cravings she always aroused. "But it has to go.''

"You first.''

She ran her finger down his torso, loosening the tie at the waist of his pajamas and scooting them down past his hips. He shed them quickly and then started on her, untying the lacy ribbon, releasing her breasts.

He buried his mouth in one, caressing, sucking, kneading the nipple with his lips and tongue until it stood at rock-hard attention. Only then did he start the exotic journey down the smooth flesh of her belly, his hands sliding over her hips.

Tiny moans escaped her lips, driving him on.

He teased and taunted every soft curve, his fingers and lips seeking the places that gave her the most pleasure. His efforts were rewarded with streams of liquid fire.

"Please, Ray," she begged. "I need you now."

He raised over her and she spread her legs, curling them around him, her body thrusting toward him. He slipped inside her, pushing, throbbing with the need to satisfy her before he lost all control.

She came in an explosion of passion, so intense it sucked her breath away, so perfect he soared with her to the heights before collapsing almost lifeless into the afterglow of fulfillment.

He rolled over, still inside her, her body moist and warm next to his. He didn't know if he was right for her, couldn't believe that joy like this was his for the taking. He only knew that life had never felt so wonderful before.

He closed his eyes and pretended Saturday and her possible date with a killer was only a nightmare that would be gone when he opened them again.

Chapter Thirteen

The sun had just poked its head above the horizon Saturday morning when Jodie crept from the bed, careful not to wake Ray. They had both lain awake until the wee hours this morning, making love, talking about what the day might bring and then holding each other until they fell asleep.

Ray and Butch both saw only the danger in the personal ad. Jodie saw more. It was a chance to draw the stalker out of the shadows and into the light. And if the stalker actually read the ad and called, Butch would be the real undercover cop, following her in secret, watching her from a safe distance, stepping in if the stalker presented any danger. Arresting him when they had the evidence to make murder charges stick.

She had to go through with this. She had everything to gain. She had nothing to lose.

Except her life.

If all went as planned she would be face-to-face with the man who had broken into her apartment, run his hands over her intimate apparel, released his evil all around her like a poisonous gas, deadly yet invisible.

She hugged her arms about her chest and fought the apprehension that rode her nerves like a river of ice.

Ray roused, stretching, one foot escaping the covers. "What time is it?"

"It's early. I woke up and couldn't get back to sleep. I'll go downstairs and start the coffee." She bent over and kissed the top of his head.

"Are you all right?"

"Of course, I'm all right. And don't go around asking me that all day. If you do, Grams will know something is up. As it is, she doesn't suspect a thing."

"You underestimate the lady. She can't remember past her last step, but she's as shrewd as they come at figuring out what you don't want her to know."

"Tell me about it. That's why we have to be extra careful. No one knows about the ad but you, me, Cappan and the local police. We have to make sure it stays that way if this plan has a chance of working."

"Just us and every man, woman and child who reads the personal ads."

"But all they have is a phone number," she assured him.

"Phone numbers can easily be matched to addresses."

"Go back to sleep," she whispered. Sliding into her slippers, she tiptoed down the stairs and into the foyer. Unlatching the dead bolt, she opened the door and scanned the area. No newspaper, and there probably wouldn't be one for another hour. But at some houses in Natchitoches and in the surrounding areas, the paper would have already been delivered, the weekend supplement with the personal ads folded neatly inside.

Seconds later, she had the coffee brewing and a couple of pieces of wheat bread in the toaster. The sun was pouring in the window now, painting the kitchen floor and walls in blinding beams.

Pulling out a tray, Jodie loaded it with two coffee cups, spoons, sugar, cream, toast plates and a crystal bowl of preserves. Not a full breakfast, but a bite. She'd be surprised if either she or Ray managed to get it down.

When the coffee was ready, she filled a silver pitcher

and added it to the tray. The trappings of a holiday for lovers to counteract the ominous cloud that hung over them. Careful not to spill the coffee, she ascended the steep staircase to her bedroom.

"What is this?" she said, pushing through the door. Ray was lying in the middle of the bed and Blake was climbing over him, trying to grasp and pull one of his dad's ears.

"He was awake, rooting around like a hungry armadillo, so I went and got him before he woke Blair. He was wet. I changed him."

Ray held Blake up so Jodie could admire his handiwork. "We didn't bother putting the pajama bottoms back on. He said he needed more freedom to kick."

"Oh, he did, did he?"

"Yeah. It sounded like, 'gibber ga ga gaboo,' but I understood him."

"You are a man of many talents." She sat the tray on the table.

The phone rang, shattering the moment. They both grew silent, listening as the newly installed second line completed its first and second rings. Before it started its third, Jodie picked up the receiver.

"Hello." The word was almost lost, stuck in her throat behind a strangling lump.

"Are you the lady who put the ad in the personal column?" The voice was low and husky, and she could hear deep breathing through the line.

"Yes." She had to push the word out of her clogged throat.

"What do you look like? Are you pretty with long blond hair and big breasts? If you are, I'd like to meet you. Anytime, anywhere. I'd like to..."

Violent shivers shook Jodie's body while the raspy voice on the line told her in painstakingly filthy detail what he'd like to do to her.

Shaking, she slammed the receiver into the cradle.

"It wasn't him," she said. "It was an obscene caller who didn't even know what I look like."

"The kind of low-life pervert that ad of yours is bound to appeal to. Give it up, Jodie, now, while you still can."

She ran a finger down his cheek. "I'd like nothing better. You must know that. But I can't go on living in constant fear for myself and everybody I love."

The red lights on the baby monitor lit up like a Christmas tree, and loud howls blasted forth from the box.

"Looks like your brother's awake, Blake." For once, the howls were a welcome relief. Jodie's nerves were too shot to argue with Ray.

He wrapped an arm around her shoulder. "I didn't mean to get upset with you, Jodie. But when I saw the look on your face while that man poured out his filth, I wanted to climb through the phone and plant a fist upside his head."

"Let's just drop it, Ray. If it takes hearing a few bad words to find Max's killer and stop the assault on my life, I can handle it." With that she was out of the door, hoping she was telling the truth. Caller number one still had her quaking.

THERE WERE A couple of more calls on Saturday morning. The second rivaled the first for indecent proposals. The third was a soft-spoken man who claimed he was looking for a lasting relationship with a good woman.

By the time the boys were down for their afternoon nap, Jodie had stuck the cordless phone in her pocket and retreated to the back porch for a cup of tea. Ray was in the study, typing on his laptop.

She settled in the wooden rocker, letting her heavy eyelids close and her mind wander. Male voices shook her to attention just before sleep claimed her.

Grady and Butch walked up from the back of the property, talking and laughing like old friends. It had been less than an hour since Butch had called for late-breaking information on the success of the ad.

Now he was here, obviously checking on everything for himself. Somehow she was sure the visit was due to a request by Ray. The no-ties man was doing an excellent imitation of a worried husband and father. Had she not been walking on eggshells herself, she could have appreciated the attention a lot more.

"He's been hanging around the boathouse, asking me a bunch of questions," Grady said, his voice carrying from the walk to the porch.

"I want you to keep a close eye on him for me. I don't trust the man as far as I can spit."

"Who is it that you don't trust, Butch?" she asked as he neared the porch.

"Selda's tenant."

"I thought you already checked him out."

"I did. Record's clean, but I've had a man tailing him the past couple of days. He hasn't been near a plantation. Close as we can tell, he's just hanging around town, taking a bunch of pictures of everything and everybody and asking a lot of questions about things that shouldn't concern him." He propped a foot on the bottom step. "How friendly has he been with you?"

"We've talked. Nothing out of line. In fact, he started my car one day when it had stalled in town."

"You didn't mention that to me."

"It had nothing to do with you. He wasn't threatening, just helpful." She stared up at the window to his room. The blinds were closed tight. "He did ask me if I'd have dinner with him sometime."

Butch's eyebrows shot up like question marks.

"It was nothing, Butch, really. I mean he took no for an

answer without getting upset. I think he's just lonely. At first I was a little suspicious, but he seems so…so normal.''

"Depends on how normal you think voyeurism is. Grady tells me he sees him in his window all the time watching you when you're in the yard or on the porch with the boys.''

All of a sudden the air felt heavy and humid, a suffocating blanket that choked her breath away.

"Stay away from him, Jodie.''

"Believe me, I will. Unless the stalker calls—'' She broke off in midsentence. Grady was still in the yard but he watched her like a fox eyeing a chicken nest. One mistake and he'd pick it up, know something was up, figure out that she and Butch were laying a trap. And the more people who knew, the more chance the all-knowing stalker would find out as well.

Everybody's a suspect. The words settled in her stomach like bitter broth.

Butch climbed the steps and sauntered over to the rocker, his voice low, meant only for her ears. "I'll be running errands this afternoon, but I'll have my beeper on every minute.'' His eyes and voice issued a warning. "Call me, at once, if anything changes.''

"I will.''

Butch lingered another second, and she sensed his own nerves were as rattled as hers. One more person she was pulling into danger. She attempted a smile. He tipped his hat and shuffled back down the steps and over to the gate where Grady waited, a foot propped on the wooden post.

They talked a few minutes more, about fishing, the upcoming festival and the problems it created for the local police. Finally Butch glanced her way, tipped his cap again and swung open the gate.

A yellow jacket flew from the creaking wood and into his face. He slapped wildly, flinging his arms, hitting himself on the tip of his crooked nose, backing up so fast he all but fell on his behind.

Grady roared in laughter. "You're not afraid of a little old bee, are you, Officer Deaton?"

Butch shut him up with a look. But Grady was still grinning when Butch marched through the gate. He walked to the edge of the porch.

"I've been meaning to thank you for the job," Grady said, resting his elbows on the planks that extended past the porch railing.

"No need to. The coat of paint on the boathouse spruced it up nicely. You've earned your pay, such as it is. I'm sure you could earn more in town with all the preparations for next weekend."

"The big weekend. Thousands of tourists in town. Not a good time to be checking for strangers, is it?"

"I wouldn't know. That's not my job."

"No, I guess not. You've got bumbling Officer Deaton for that. And, my dad, of course. He pictures himself some big hero, stepping in and catching the crackpot who's been bothering you."

"Just what do you know about my *crackpot?*"

"Just what my dad volunteered when I came to work here. Some nut's following you around, sending you flowers and stuff. I'd hate to be the man if my dad does catch him. He'll leave here in little pieces."

"Gentle Ben. He doesn't have a violent bone in his body."

"Not unless you rile him."

The conversation rolled like thunder in Jodie's head, striking holes in her solution. Grady knew too much about her and the stalker situation. Perhaps the whole town did. Which gave the stalker the advantage and significantly reduced the odds that the trap would work.

Mumbling an excuse, she left Grady standing and went

back inside, creeping into the room where Ray was working. Tucking her feet under her, she curled up in an upholstered reading chair to watch him. As always, his presence eased her fear and doubts and strengthened her resolve.

This time when her eyes closed, they stayed that way until the boys woke up from their naps, demanding her attention.

THE UNBEARABLE TENSION that had hovered over the weekend still pounded in Kostner's head on Monday morning as he drove to the office. Five more calls came in on the second phone line. One had been Butch. The others had been strangers whose conversations had convinced Jodie they were not the man of her nightmares, though judging from her reactions, some certainly had the potential for being dangerous in their own rights. Her ad had played into their hands nicely, providing a phone number for immediate gratification.

Ray massaged his right temple, wishing he'd started the day with a couple of painkillers. Now he'd have to wait until he got to the office and hit the supply in his desk drawer. Only it wasn't his desk drawer today. He'd be moving to the smaller office. Parker was returning to take over his throne.

Ray pulled the car to a stop in front of his dad's house. No need to get out. Parker was at the door, hat on his head, briefcase in one hand, his cane in the other. Punctuality was important. One of his top five sermons.

Ray was always late. This morning was no exception.

"You said you'd be here ten minutes ago," his dad said, scrunching into the front seat, tapping the globe of his watch before buckling in.

"Good morning, Dad," Ray offered. "It's nice to see you, too."

"Well, of course, son. It would have been nicer ten minutes ago. I'm probably sweating in this dadburned overcoat your mother insisted I wear. She thinks I'm going to freeze in forty degree weather."

No use to point out to him that he could have put the coat on after he arrived to pick him up. They both grew silent, and Ray turned on the radio to ease the tension. Parker beat an impatient rhythm with his cane, tapping it against the floorboard.

Ray slowed automatically. Old habits of rebellion died hard. But this time he refused to slide back into the games he'd always played. The accelerator responded instantly to the pressure of his foot, returning the car to its previous speed as his mind went back to Jodie.

If she called, he'd be out of the office like Superman to the rescue. She was not keeping a date with a madman without him, not even if every policeman in the parish were there to watch over her. He had pressured until she promised she would not leave the house without alerting him.

"What do you think about Carl Baker?" Parker asked, bringing up the case Ray had been summoned from New Orleans to handle.

"I think he's innocent. Don't you?"

"That's why I took the case. Do you think we can convince a jury of that?"

"Unless the prosecutor digs up a witness that proves we're wrong. Shreveport murders are a little out of your ballpark, aren't they?"

"A little. Carl's dad's a friend of mine. Besides, it's only an hour's drive to Shreveport, less now that I-49 is finished. The world is shrinking. There's plenty of work in this area for a good defense attorney."

"Too much for you right now, according to your doctors."

"If I listened to them, I'd be an invalid."

"A six-week rehabilitation period after a bypass is not considered excessive for a man your age."

"See, you've been listening to your mother. Age doesn't mean a thing. I've been doing my job in this town ever since I passed the bar exam."

Ray didn't respond. He didn't want to spend the morning arguing, and his father had a way of construing all of his comments as negative. Slowing, he pulled over to the curb and stopped in front of the law office. "Why don't you get out here and open up? I'll park the car in the back."

Parker did, opening the door and getting to his feet a lot more slowly than he had before the surgery. Every movement he made these days was slower than usual. And no matter the friction that met every contact between them, it hurt Ray to see his father weak and struggling.

Ray parked the car and took the back steps to the second-floor office. He usually ran them, hungry for the exercise he missed. In New Orleans, he started each day with an hour workout at the gym, ending with a stint in the steam room and a hot shower.

Today he walked, using the time to work out how he was going to tell his father that Carl Baker had asked him to take over as lead attorney. The case was challenging, but the last thing Ray wanted to do was throw another curve at a man who liked his pitches straight and down the middle. And in his control.

Ray pushed through the door and into the outer office. The room smelled of disinfectant and lemons, the handiwork of the cleaning crew. When Barbara showed up at nine, it would also smell of strong coffee.

A tormented groan rumbled from his dad's office. Ray felt the air sucked out of him. In three steps he was across the room, busting through the door.

His dad lay on the floor, his eyes rolled back in his head,

a straight-backed chair laying across him. Blood dripped from his head and pooled on the carpet.

"A man...in the dark...waiting." Parker closed his eyes and fell silent.

Adrenaline shot through Ray, refueling a body that shock had temporarily drained and rendered useless. He lunged for the phone with one hand and his dad's wrist with the other, checking the pulse as he punched in 911.

Working on automatic, he gave the information to the operator and turned his attention to his father. The bleeding was from a flesh wound, a gash across the top of his eye where the chair had apparently made contact. A knot as big as a baseball had popped up on his forehead, just under the cut. The pulse was weak, the breathing an unsteady rasp that rumbled from his chest.

The next five minutes passed in a murky blur of empty reassurances that didn't lighten when the ambulance arrived and the paramedics lifted Parker onto the stretcher.

"Hold on, Mr. Kostner. We've got you now. We're starting the oxygen and heading out of here."

His dad's hand fell from the stretcher and Ray grabbed it, holding on to it. Every fiber of his body twisted in silent rage as the truth slammed into his brain. Jodie's stalker had struck again.

The attack had been meant for him.

He stooped over to pick up his dad's cane. It was then he noticed the fish fillet knife just under the corner of his desk and bloody footsteps leading to the door of the adjoining office, the one he had taken over.

"Do you think this bird is big enough?" Selda asked, stuffing the turkey with corn bread dressing.

"Unless we're feeding the whole block," Jodie said reassuringly, balancing Blake on one hip so that he could see the Thanksgiving action.

Blair was under the table, looking for the plastic stacking donut that had rolled from his grasp. Already, he hated to be held, wriggling back to freedom as soon as she picked him up.

"It's just us," Selda said, "and Greg's joining us, too. Working in a strange town is no way to spend the holidays."

"What about Ben?" Jodie asked.

"He said he wasn't comfortable at a fancy family dinner, not that this is. But I'm packing a plate for him and one for his son."

"And Eloise Grimes," Grams added, from the far corner of the counter where she was peeling and cubing sweet potatoes. "Her son and his family run off to Lafayette for the holidays every year and just forget she's around. I'm picking her up from the nursing home and bringing her here."

As always, Selda and Grams shared their Thanksgiving bounty with as many as they could and loved every minute of it. Jodie decided her sons could learn a lot from these two selfless women.

"What about the Kostner boy?" Grams asked as if it were an afterthought. "Is he going to come sniffing around when the work's all done?"

Selda called her bluff. "If he didn't, you'd be the disappointed one."

"Ba ga ma um." Blake gave his answer.

"Which means Ray will be here any minute," Jodie translated. "He's at the hospital in Shreveport this morning, visiting with his dad."

"How's Parker doing?" Selda asked.

"Improving steadily. His heart withstood the blood loss without any apparent harm. He still has a bump and nasty bruise on his head, though."

"Do they have any idea who attacked him?" Selda

looked up from her turkey to watch Jodie's face as she answered.

"No. Just a robbery attempt," she answered, following police orders to keep suspicions under wraps. "Apparently, Parker surprised him, and the thief reacted violently."

"I hope they get him. This has always been such a peaceful town. It breaks my heart to see things like this happen."

The telephone in Jodie's apron pocket jangled. For a second, she almost picked it up and answered, but the chill of reality twisted inside her, stopping her.

"It's my business line, I need to take this call where it's quiet," she whispered, trying and failing to keep her voice calm. "Watch Blair for me." She didn't wait for a reply. As soon as she'd stepped into the hall, she punched the button and put the receiver to her ear.

"Hello."

"Hello, Jodie."

Her heart slammed against the wall of her chest.

"Who is this?"

"A friend."

Her heart was racing now, her nerves on edge, her will battling the paralyzing effect of suffocating fear. "Are you the friend who sends me flowers and gifts?"

"I'm the friend who watches over you." The voice was muffled, disguised in some way, impossible to identify even if she'd heard it before.

"I tried to keep you a good girl. But you didn't want to be good, did you?"

She could hear his breathing, heavy with the evil inside him. She hugged Blake so tightly he squealed in protest. Dropping to the couch, she let him wriggle from her lap to the floor.

"I do want to be good. I'm trying to save myself for you. But it's hard when you never let me see you."

"Does the man who sleeps in your house sleep in your bed, Jodie?"

"No. He has his own room."

"You're lying to me. He's been with you. Even in his law office, you let him make love to you. The smell of him is all over you. You are not a good girl, Jodie Gahagen."

Oh, God. This man was sicker than she thought. He had to be stopped now, before he killed again.

"But I want to be good. You could help me. If I could see you, maybe then you could save me."

"Or maybe this is a trick."

"It's not a trick. I just want to meet you, face-to-face. There's a house on the outskirts of town. It's deserted. No one will see us meet there."

"If the police follow you, I'll know it. No matter how clever they are, they are not as clever as I am. You should know that by now."

"I do. I know that better than anyone."

"I won't hurt you, Jodie, not if you're by yourself. But if you lie to me, I can't promise anything. I go crazy sometimes."

"Like when you killed Max Roling?"

"Don't make me do something like that again. Come alone, Jodie. Do you understand?"

"Yes."

She gave him the directions, slowly, her mind in such turmoil she could barely think, her voice so shaky, the words were a muttered garble.

"When shall I meet you?" she asked.

"Now." The disconnecting click of the phone signaled he was through talking.

She reached down and picked up Blake, hugging him close, kissing the top of his head. She'd do the same with Blair. Hold him close. Her sons would give her the courage to do what she had to do to stop a madman.

She punched in Butch's beeper number, putting in her number when the recorded voice gave the instructions. She would tell Butch, but not Ray. He was probably on his way home from Shreveport by now, but she didn't want him to show up at the Coxlin place.

She had to believe she would return safely. But this way, if something should happen to her, Blake and Blair wouldn't be left alone. They would still have a father.

And Ray would not be sucked into her chasm of madness and death.

Chapter Fourteen

Jodie left Highway 119, pulling onto a gravel roadbed that wound through oaks, dogwood and pine on its journey to the old Coxlin place. She was not alone. Rabbits, squirrels, even a doe scurried out of her way, as if sensing she was bringing evil into their hideaway.

The road ended at the house. She killed her engine, lowering the car window and listening. All was quiet, and there was not another car in sight. But Butch should be inside the house by now, hidden in the dark caverns of the attic, waiting for her and the stalker.

Sliding from the car, she stepped off the road, onto what used to be a path to the house. Her feet sank into knee-high grass. Cautiously, she made her way to the old wooden steps leading to the half-rotted front porch.

She slipped her hand to her neck, caressing the small locket Butch had provided, the one that held the tiny microphone that would record the stalker's every word. Take his own testimony and use it to prove his guilt. That was part of the plan she and Butch had worked out down to the last precise detail.

Ray had never approved of the plan. He had refused to listen to reason even though both she and Butch had insisted that an extra person made the setup all the more risky and far less likely to succeed.

Today it would be her, Butch and a madman. Shaking, she gulped in a huge helping of air and took the first step. The rough wood groaned at her weight, and a shudder ran through her. Was Max's killer waiting just inside the door watching her, hidden in dark shadows? The way he had done so many times before.

There was only one way to find out. Nerves riding the edge of control, she crossed the wide porch and pushed through the heavy door before her resolve had time to weaken.

A spiderweb tangled in her hair and eyes. She brushed it away. Silence met her ears. She waited for long seconds and then walked deeper into the interior of a house that had withstood tornadoes and floods only to see its past grandeur dissolve into rot.

She'd been here only twice before. One Halloween on a dare when she was a freshman in high school. The second time had been with Butch Deaton a few days ago.

Today it seemed far more ominous. Dark, crumbling walls, rusted chandeliers that hung at precarious angles, dank, musky odors that choked her breath away. A tomb would be more welcoming.

Bad analogy, she decided, forcing herself to take a deep steadying breath of the stale air. Maybe the stalker wasn't coming. Or maybe he'd beaten her here, parked his car behind dense clusters of trees and undergrowth. Maybe he was waiting for her to find him. More moves in his bizarre game of terror.

"Is anybody here?" Her voice crawled the walls and the rafters, delving into depths of blackness and echoing back like a high-pitched wail.

Even that was welcome relief from the maddening silence. The squeak of the door was not. She jerked around.

"Butch?"

"Who were you expecting?"

"The stalker." Disappointment rushed her senses and sharpened her tone. "You promised you'd stay hidden until the stalker showed up."

"But there's no one here but you and me, Jodie."

"He's coming. He has to be. We had this all worked out, Butch."

"You are so eager to meet the stalker." He stepped closer and snaked an arm around her shoulders, tangling his fingers in her hair. "Are you sure you're ready for him, Jodie? Alone and helpless, the way you are now. Out here where no one can hear your screams?"

His tone grew dark, and icy fingers of fear crawled her skin. But he was frightening her on purpose, trying to dissuade her from doing this again.

She pulled away from him. "I'm not alone, Butch. You're here. But we may as well leave now. Even if the stalker was going to show, he won't with you out in the open. I told you he made me promise not to bring anyone."

"And did you do as he asked, or is Ray with you, hidden in the woods, waiting to rush to your rescue if I don't do the job?"

"I'm alone."

"Perhaps the man who wants you for himself is here with us right now, thinking of how it would feel to crush you against him."

"Cut out the fright tactics, Butch. They won't work with me. I've lived with fear too intimately and far too long to break now."

He reached a hand toward her, then stopped and whirled toward the door as it squeaked open again. This time it was Ray who marched in.

"What in the devil is going on here?"

"Your girlfriend threw a party," Butch answered. "Only the guest of honor didn't show." His voice returned to normal, the Gothic tone discarded like old chewing gum.

Ray unhooked his beeper and threw it in her direction. She caught it one-handed.

"Test it, Jodie. It works fine. So, why didn't it go off before you drove out here? You were not supposed to go through with this unless I was here."

"Just settle down, Ray. I can explain everything."

"Good. I just covered thirty miles in about twenty minutes, panicking every second about what I'd find when I got here. This better be one hell of an explanation."

She didn't have one he'd buy, and she was too frustrated to lie. "Did you ever stop to think that I might know what I'm doing, that I didn't need you to come tearing out here like a macho knight on a quest to save the ignorant maiden?" Without looking back, she marched out of the house and dropped behind the wheel of her car, slamming the door behind her. She left both men standing in a cloud of dust as she spun out.

A few minutes ago she'd been alone, drowning in fear. But at least then there had been a chance that the nightmare she'd been living with for over three months might come to an end. Now there was nothing except the fierce guilt that gripped her heart like ribbons of steel.

Max was dead because of her. Gloria was dead because of her, although no one but Jodie believed the stalker had been in her shop that night. And Parker Kostner was in a hospital, lucky to be alive. Like Russian roulette, the next victim would fall to the luck of the twirl.

Grams, Ray, herself. Even Blair or Blake, totally innocent, totally dependent on her. How had she let this evil creep into their world? She gunned the engine, frustration churning inside her like black coffee left to boil on an open burner.

The stalker had outsmarted them again.

THE PERSONAL AD hot line stayed silent the rest of Thanksgiving Day, giving Jodie time to cool down and all of them time to enjoy a dinner laden with calories and taste and blessed with laughter.

As always, life had gone on. The boys had still entertained with toddler antics, Grams had still told fascinating stories, Selda had still made them laugh. And Ray had glared at her over the top of the turkey, too upset with her to give an inch.

Now dusk was starting to fall on another day. Friday evening and no further attempts at contact by the stalker. Impatience twisted inside Jodie. A dozen times or more, she had checked the phone to make sure it still had a dial tone. But the problems were not with the instrument. They lay with stalker.

Either he had smelled a trap from the start or he had been frightened off by Butch and Ray. But Jodie hadn't given up. The phone was with her now, tucked into the pocket of her green windbreaker. It rested silently while she pushed the boys in baby swings Ray had attached to a low-hanging branch of the centuries-old oak tree.

Grams was inside dozing; Ray was on the porch, spread across the wicker settee, the work he'd brought home from the office moving from one pile to another and back again as he scrutinized page after page. So much for taking the day after Thanksgiving as a holiday.

"That must be pretty interesting fare," she called out. "What are you working on?"

"I'm reviewing cases involving serial killers."

The familiar chill played hopscotch on her nerve endings. "I'm sorry I asked."

"Me, too. And sorrier that I don't have some earth-shattering discoveries to share with you."

"The boys are tired of swinging. I think I'll load them in the wagon and walk down to the river. Do you want to come?"

"I'd love to, but I want to finish this."

"All work and no play…"

"He who finishes his work by sunlight, reaps rewards when the moon shines."

"Who said that?"

"A wise and handsome sage who has plans for playing with you in the moonlight."

A pleasurable warmth spread to her cheeks. Yesterday he had remained a stoic chunk of ice. Finally, he was thawing. She'd assured him she would not meet the stalker again without keeping him fully informed.

"Grams is right," she said, pushing a wind-tossed lock of hair from her eyes. "You do have a twisted lawyer's mind."

"The better to seduce you with, my dear."

She picked up the rubber ball Blair had dropped a minute ago and threw it at him. It missed by a foot.

"And we can only hope you're never elected president. The first pitch of the season might wind up in the stands."

The boys squealed with delight when she piled them into the old wooden wagon. Minutes later, she was moving at a steady clip, down the path that led to the boathouse and the river. Halfway there, she stopped, intrigued by a rendition of an old Elvis Presley song punctuated by rhythmic swishing.

She peeked over a holly hedge. The serenade was courtesy of Grady and an oversize radio. The swishing noise came from a machete. Muscles bulged as a shirtless Grady swung the sharp blade expertly, rhythmically. The machete sliced through a cluster of overgrown berry bushes, leaving the butchered branches to fall where they might.

Blake protested the fact that the wagon was no longer moving with a couple of squeals. Grady looked up and caught her staring. Perspiration dripped from his forehead to be absorbed by the dirty headband that rode the top of his eyebrows.

"Hello, boss lady," he said.

"Jodie will do fine."

"Sorry. Guess my manners aren't good enough for Jodie Gahagen. But you know me, just the son of the white trash gardener trying to get by."

"Ben has never been trash."

"No? You'd never know that by his living arrangements in that old boathouse." He put one hand over his eyes to shade them from the sun. The other still clutched the machete. "Anyway I'm glad you happened along. I appreciate the employment, but this will be my last day to work for you. Next week I'll be heading back to New York."

"I thought Ben said you were living here now."

"I thought I might. It's not working out the way I'd hoped. Natchitoches is just a little too quiet for me. Besides, by next week I'll have taken care of the business I came for."

His gaze raked over her, lingering too long on certain areas. Feelings of uneasiness prickled her skin. "What business might that be?"

"Personal. A woman I wanted to see one last time, to find out if we could make a go of it."

"Could you?"

"No. She's interested in someone else. A bad choice on her part."

Blair fussed and pulled at her skirt. This time she ignored his pleas for attention. "Do you have a job in New York?"

"No, but I'll find something. Of course, I won't be able to live in the Village like you did. I'll move back to the real low-rent district, share my place with a few rats and roaches."

"How do you know where I lived?"

"My dad treated me to dinner one night. Afterward we

walked down to the Village and looked up your place. I suggested we stop in and surprise you. My dad refused. He doesn't go where he's not invited.''

"Jodie!" The piercing yell of her name stopped the conversation cold. Selda was jogging down the path, her short legs going faster than Jodie had ever seen her move.

"Come quick, Jodie. You have to see this." Her breathing was hard and fast.

"Has something happened to Grams? To Ray?"

"No. Just come, Jodie. To my house, upstairs to Greg's room. I think I've found your stalker."

They stopped just long enough to pick up Ray who had disappeared inside for another stack of files. This time Jodie was thankful he was nearby. Selda was not making a lot of sense.

"I don't usually go into rooms I've rented out, not without good reason," Selda explained, leading Jodie and Ray, each holding a child, up the stairs to the second level of her rambling house.

"Why did you go into the room this time?" Ray asked.

"I didn't. I mean the door was ajar. I knocked, and it opened on its own."

"And you found evidence that Greg is the stalker?" The doubt in Ray's voice did nothing to dissuade Selda.

"Just wait. I'm not saying anything. You have to see it for yourself."

Ray reached the door first, but Jodie squeezed past him, stepping inside only to stop cold, her feet nailed to the spot. Greg's bed was neatly made, the white chenille bedspread papered with photographs. Color and black-and-white. All sizes. At least two dozen different poses.

All of Jodie.

"How did he get these?"

"No sweat there." Ray waved his hand toward an assortment of telescopic lenses that lined the top of a walnut armoire. "The question is, why?"

Jodie picked up the pictures, one by one, vertigo gnawing away at her equilibrium. There were shots of her alone. Reading in the back porch rocker, shelling pecans on the back steps, her skirt pulled up to cradle the lapful of nuts. And an enlargement, a color shot of her drying her hair in the sun, her head down, the wet strands shimmering like liquid fire.

The next picture she touched was of her holding Blake and Blair. She shuddered, her breath balled up inside her, struggling for release. He'd said she and the boys would make a great family scene. He'd proved it, over and over.

Picture-perfect images of her playing with the boys on the back porch, pulling them in the wagon, picnicking on a blanket by the river.

She hugged Blair to her, felt his tiny heart beating against her chest. She buried her lips in his wispy red curls, then reached a hand to Blake. Her fingers traced the lines of his baby smooth face, his feathery eyelashes, his perfect nose, his sweet pink lips.

More precious than life, their innocence captured in the camera eye of a killer. Fury took over now, replacing the fear she had lived with for months. This man had taken so much from her, leaving cold, hard emotions in their place.

"Call Butch Deaton, Selda."

Ray slipped an arm around her, but it didn't soothe her. Nothing would ever soothe her until she knew Greg Johnson would never again walk the streets to prey on innocent people.

JODIE DROPPED to the porch swing. The boys were fast asleep and Grams had retired early as well. It had been an eventful day. But tonight, for the first time in months, she would sleep knowing the living nightmare was finally over.

Greg had returned to his apartment at Selda's to find Butch and two other officers waiting for him. According to Butch he was still protesting his innocence loud and long, demanding to see a lawyer. Nonetheless he was behind bars for now, the snapshots confiscated as evidence in the case against him.

And Butch had assured her no judge in the parish would grant parole. Not unless God himself intervened with a miracle. Jodie wasn't worried. She was sure God had not taken league with the devil.

She sipped from the mug of hot chocolate at her fingertips, savoring the warmth as it slid down her throat. All the pieces were falling into place. All but one, and he was standing at the edge of the porch, staring into the darkness.

"I have to go back to New Orleans, Jodie."

The words shattered her newfound peace.

"When?"

"Tomorrow. I'll visit my dad in the hospital and then take a flight from the airport in Shreveport."

"You'll miss the festival."

"I know. At least you and the boys will be able to enjoy it without worry."

She walked over and stood beside him. "We'd enjoy it a lot more if you were there with us."

The muscles in his arms tightened, and his hands gripped the porch railing. "Maybe, for a while."

"No games, Ray. Not after all that's gone between us. Just say what you're thinking." Now she was the one straining for control.

He turned, finally meeting her gaze. "I'm not the man for you, Jodie."

"You're the man I want, the man I love." Moisture burned at the back of her eyes. She fought to keep it at bay.

"No. I'm the man you think you want. But I'd never be

able to live up to your level of perfection. The more you and the boys wanted from me, the less I'd be able to give. I'd disappoint you time and time again, until resentment would be the only emotion we'd feel for each other.''

He turned away again. She moved in front of him, standing on tiptoe, forcing him to look her in the eye. "Do you love me, Ray?"

"Love has nothing to do with this."

"Do you love me? Because if you can look me in the eye and tell me you don't, then I won't say another word. But if you do, then give us a chance."

"A chance to fail?"

"Maybe. Or maybe for more happiness than you ever dreamed possible."

He shook his head. "I can't, Jodie. I can't do this to you or to my sons. I'll send you money, all the money you need. You can stay here in Natchitoches or go back to New York, but you won't have to work unless you want to. You can be a full-time mother to our sons. I'll visit them when I can."

"No."

"It's the best choice for everybody." His voice was heavy with the pain of finality.

Pain gripped her heart, but she held her head high. "I don't want your money, Ray. I don't want visits once a year to dredge up old heartaches. My sons don't need a father who rejects them." She called on every ounce of strength she possessed and forced her ultimatum through clenched teeth. "Either you commit to being a full-time husband and father or you are out of our lives forever."

"Go ahead, push me, Jodie. It's when I buckle. It's time you saw me at my worst. That way you can walk away without looking back."

"I'm not the one walking away, Ray. You will be. All or nothing. It's your call."

He turned away from her and slammed a fist into the porch post. The tears she'd tried so hard to fight broke loose as the only man she'd ever loved took the steps two at a time and disappeared through the back gate.

HE SAT AT an old table in the basement of the house he had grown up in. The house was falling to pieces around him, the way his mother had in the year before her death. The men had quit coming then, quit knocking on her door at all hours to disappear into her bedroom. The laughter and moans of pleasure had stopped. So had the sickening odors of defilement.

It didn't matter anymore. It was time for him to leave Natchitoches and the memories far behind. Maybe if he was out of this house, the urges would die like his mother had or just go away one day and never return the way his wife had deserted him.

But the urges hadn't died yet. Tonight they were stronger than ever. Tonight the basement was filled with Jodie Gahagen. He'd taken out some of the mementos he'd stolen from her apartment in New York and placed them on the table.

A pair of silky panties, a tube of lipstick and one almost empty bottle of body lotion. Items so insignificant to her she'd never missed them. Items that fed him, driving him to do what he had to do.

Painstakingly, he twisted the cap from a glass vial of the liquid that would end Jodie's life. Four vials, saved up from legitimate prescriptions that were meant to save his life.

Jodie could have saved herself. Instead, she'd flaunted her body in front of Ray Kostner, intoxicating him with her sensual ways, making love to him in the law office, even inside her grandmother's house.

Nice women didn't do that.

His hand shook the way it did when the images of the

past merged with those of the present. His mother. His wife. The young blonde in Bossier City, the petite brunette in Ruston. All women who flaunted their bodies in front of unworthy men.

Now Jodie had to die. Saturday night. It would be the high point of the Festival of Lights.

And just like the others, no one would know she had been murdered. He was too smart for all of them.

Chapter Fifteen

Ray was up at sunrise for the drive to Shreveport. The night had been long and sleepless, leaving plenty of time to think of Jodie's ultimatum. To know he would never again wake up to the feel of Jodie cuddled against him. Her hair feathering his shoulders, her face seductive even in sleep, her body warm, waiting to be wakened by the touch of his lips on hers.

To know he would never see his sons grow up, watch them ride their first two-wheeler, play their first game of baseball, catch their first fish. It was like saying he was ready to have his heart ripped from his body while he watched.

He had rights as a father. Jodie knew that as well as he did. She also knew he would never pursue them if it went against her wishes. She wanted a husband to share her life with, a dependable father for her boys.

It was no more than either she or his sons deserved. The question was the same as always: Was he man enough for the task? Or would he fail like he had so many times before when push came to shove?

The drive to Shreveport took an hour. It seemed like ten. The only consolation was that his dad had improved to the point that he was leaving the hospital today.

Ray would go back to New Orleans knowing Parker had

recovered enough to take over his own cases, even handle Carl Baker's defense. And Jodie was safe. Mission accomplished.

Yesterday's events replayed in his mind, the way they had done dozens of times throughout the night and early morning, like a CD that never stopped. Only the CD seemed warped, and the distortions played havoc with the meaning. Ray's fingers tightened on the steering wheel.

Greg Johnson was the type of man Ray would have taken as a client, a man being railroaded by a hungry cop and a frightened woman, the case against him built solely on circumstantial evidence. The snapshots they'd found in his room proved he'd taken pictures of Jodie without her permission. Nothing else.

If the pictures Ray had seen had been the only evidence, he would have attributed them to infatuation. And infatuation with a vivacious, beautiful woman did not make you a criminal. Infatuation with Jodie Gahagen only proved you were human.

But a police search of Greg's room had turned up many more photographs, some showing Jodie in various states of undress, obviously taken without her permission. Shots snapped in New York, inside her apartment, around her office, shopping in the city, playing with the boys in Central Park.

An ironclad case against Greg Johnson. So, why couldn't he accept their good fortune and let it go?

He swerved onto the exit ramp near the hospital, making a few turns and pulling into the covered parking lot. His dad was apparently up and talking. Like his old self, Mom had said.

Parker had requested that Ray stop by this morning. He had a few things he wanted to discuss, but Ray had a few things to say, too. He was a father himself now. It changed the way he looked at his own father, especially when he had come so close to losing his dad in an attack meant for him.

This time he hoped he had the courage to tell his dad what he'd never been able to before. A few minutes later Ray strode into the quiet of the hospital and through the door of room 619.

"Hello, son." Parker's voice was weak but steady. "I was hoping you'd stop by before you flew to New Orleans."

"Mom said you wanted to talk to me."

"I do."

Ray pulled up a chair. "You're looking good."

"I look like a tomato vine in a Louisiana drought."

Ray smiled. His dad's statement was far more accurate than his own.

"But I'm alive. And that's what matters."

"You're right. Look, Dad. I know my apologies don't mean much to you, but I'm sorry about what happened."

"It wasn't your fault. If the swine hadn't attacked me, it would have been you."

Finally, a tragedy his father didn't think was his fault. For a second, Ray was tempted to leave it at that. Conscience forced him to take a deep breath and plow ahead.

"It *was* my fault. The attacker wasn't a chance burglar. I think he was waiting in the office to stab me with a knife we found under your desk. Apparently it slipped out of his hand when he hammered you with the chair. He must have heard me coming and ran before he could find it."

"Why would someone want to kill you?"

"It's a long story. I'll tell it to you some day when you're feeling a lot better."

"Did you catch the attacker?"

"Not then. But he's in jail now. At least the police think they have the right man."

"You don't?"

Ray hesitated. "The evidence looks convincing."

"Good. But that's not why I wanted to see you. I've had time to think while I was in here, about a lot of things. Looking death in the eye makes you do that."

Ray's sentiments exactly. "I've given—"

"Wait. I want to finish what I have to say. Then you can respond or not."

Ray leaned back in the chair, his body tightening into the familiar coils his father's lectures always generated. "I'm listening."

"I've made some mistakes in my life, costly ones. You and your mother have been the ones to pay."

Now Parker had his serious attention. This lecture was significantly skewed, the starting point miles off center from the thousands he'd heard before.

"I wanted everything to be perfect, the opposite of what I grew up with. It's no excuse, but I grew up in hell." Parker's voice grew weaker, and his eyes took on a vacant stare, as if all of him had turned inward.

"My father drank too much," he continued, staring at his hands. "My mother was sick, what they would call manic-depressive now. Then I only knew she was sweet and loving one minute, screaming uncontrollably at me the next."

Ray studied the pain in his dad's face, surprised at the power of memories that had lived inside him for so long. "I always thought your parents had died when you were young."

"No, but by the time Sara and I met and married they had died. My dad wrapped his pickup truck around a tree. My mom died of an overdose of tranquilizers a few months later. End of story. At least it should have been."

Parker stretched to pour himself a glass of water. Ray started to help, but his dad waved him off, fiercely independent as always. Lifting the glass to his lips, he took a long, slow drink before continuing.

"Not a pretty story but it's life. I'm not telling it to you to make excuses, just to help me explain, and hopefully to help you understand why I turned into such a lousy father. I had spent my youth ashamed of my parents, embarrassed by our lives. I was determined to leave that all behind me."

"But I didn't let you."

"I didn't let myself. I pushed you when I should have been clapping you on the back, criticized when I should have been hugging." His fingers tangled in the top sheet. "Turned against you when you needed support."

Ray tried to think of something to say. No words came. Only a dryness in his throat and a stinging at the back of his eyelids.

"I knew I was pushing too hard, but I couldn't stop myself. You and your mom were the best things that had ever happened to me, yet I couldn't do the one thing she wanted most of all. Give you the support you deserved."

Parker pulled himself up and sat on the side of the bed, his thin legs and bare feet dangling from beneath the wrinkled hospital gown.

"I know it's years too late to make up for what we lost. But it's not too late to tell you that I'm damn proud of you, Ray, and always have been." His eyes misted. "And not too late to ask you to forgive me."

"I guess I'd have to ask for the same forgiveness. I cost you the judgeship."

"Did you believe that all these years?"

"Of course, you stepped down rather than face public shame and embarrassment for what I had done."

"No, I stepped down because I wasn't fit to sit in judgment of anyone. I succumbed to blackmail to protect my good name. I told myself that it was for you, but in my heart I knew it was for me. That's why I had to learn again to live with myself."

"I don't know what to say."

"You don't have to say anything. I wouldn't have blamed you a bit if you'd never spoken to me again after I accused you of ruining your mother's and my life. But you were a better man than I ever was. Every time I've ever needed you, you were there. Just the way you are now."

"It looks like a day of confessions. I need to tell you something I should have said a long time ago."

Parker stiffened as if preparing for a blow. "Go ahead. I probably deserve whatever you have to say."

"It has nothing to do with deserving. It's unconditional. I learned that from a very special lady." He got up and stepped to the bed, wrapping his arms about his dad's stooped shoulders.

"I love you, Dad." The words were barely a whisper, but they were out and that was all that mattered.

Sara stepped into the room at that minute, and her gaze darted from her husband to her son, confusion spelled out in the lines of her face and the pull of her lips.

"Are you all right, Parker?" Her voice carried a ring of alarm.

"I'm fine. I was just telling my son that I love him. Now if the both of you would get out of here, I could get some rest."

Neither of them missed the quick swipe of a finger across his eyes. Ray gave his dad's hand a squeeze and backed toward the door, stopping only to give his mom a goodbye peck on the cheek.

"I'm out of here. Take care, Dad. You, too, Mom."

Sara was still staring at them as if they were aliens who'd landed from out of space and taken over her husband's and son's bodies. She wasn't far from wrong, Ray decided, opting for the steps instead of the elevator and taking them two at a time.

JODIE LIFTED BLAIR over the side of the crib rails and handed him his stuffed raccoon, his favorite out of his current menagerie. "You take a good nap, young man. When you wake up you'll be going to your very first Festival of Lights celebration."

Tonight she and the boys would go to the party at Selda's daughter's house. The house downtown, with grassy grounds backing up to the Cane River. From the comfort of Lydia's huge yard, they would have prime seats for the night's events.

They would watch the millions of Christmas lights burst forth in color at the same instant, filling the sky with their glow. Lydia's guests would marvel as shimmering reflections danced over the surface of the river. The boys would delight as the music from dozens of marching bands wafted on the night air. And, finally, the crowning glory. The heavens would blaze with a dazzling fireworks display.

And tonight she and her sons would do it without the risk of danger. They would also do it without Ray Kostner.

"Grams, did I have any phone calls?"

"Phone calls? I don't think so. Well, yes, Selda called to see if you wanted to ride with her to the party."

"I know. I talked to her. I told her I'd take my car in case the boys get fussy and I need to bring them home early. Why don't you go ahead and ride with her so she won't have to go alone? We'll meet you there."

"You can't wait too late, now. The first weekend is the worst. There'll be thousands of people rushing around, all trying to get the best spot on the parade route."

"But we won't be in that crowd. We're watching the lighting display and fireworks from Lydia's backyard."

"You still better get there early. Once that traffic backs

up, it doesn't budge. The whole town is deadlocked until after the fireworks. Even then it moves like molasses. One night Selda and I just gave up and spent the night at Lydia's house. So you can forget any idea of leaving early."

"I'll still take my car. I need to stop at the store for diapers, but we'll leave here as soon as the boys wake up from their nap."

"What about that Kostner boy? Is he going to be tagging after you again?"

"No. He's back in New Orleans." Her heart twisted painfully in her chest. But she refused to give in to gloom. Not when the stalker had been stopped. "Besides, I think it's you he's tagging after, the way you wait on him hand and foot. Could be, it's you he's sweet on."

A tinge of pink lightened Grams's cheeks. "Don't be teasing me like that, Jodie Gahagen." She pushed her wire glasses up a little higher on the bridge of her narrow nose. "Only guy I ever let get close enough to get sweet on me was your grandpa, God rest his soul."

Jodie gave her a warm hug. "My grandpa was a very lucky man."

RAY EYED THE speedometer and cursed the traffic. Both lanes of the interstate were lined with cars, trucks, vans and a fair share of motorbikes, all heading for opening night of the Festival of Lights. And none of them getting there very fast.

The plane he was supposed to be on was probably touching down at the New Orleans airport about now. He'd driven all the way to the airport and then turned around.

Intuition, the sense of survival, too many years of defending men against criminal charges. Probably a little of all of the above. At any rate, in spite of the evidence Butch had collected, he was not convinced Greg Johnson was actually Jodie's stalker.

Which meant he wasn't certain Jodie was safe. Until he was, he could never return to New Orleans. He'd spent the first part of the afternoon talking with an FBI agent. Another wasted effort. North Louisiana had more than its share of murders every year, but there was no record of the type of serial killer he was looking for.

Traffic slowed again, and Ray's speed dropped to a crawling forty miles an hour on a new interstate system meant to go seventy. Three-thirty.

Reaching for the cellular phone, he punched in the Gahagen number. Six rings later he was about to hang up when Miss Emily said hello.

"Is Jodie there?"

"She's upstairs getting ready for the big party at Lydia's. If you were half smart, you'd be here going with her."

"You give good advice. Tell her to wait for me at the house. I may be late, but I'll be there to pick up her and the boys."

The conversation dissolved in a fit of static, and Ray could barely make out Grams's promise to deliver the message. That done, he called his dad's office to retrieve his messages. He had to have something to fill his time while he watched the bumper of the car in front of him crawl down the highway.

The first call was a hang up, the second a woman wanting an appointment. The third was Cappan. Call at once. He even left his home number.

Ray made a mental note of it and then punched it in. Cappan answered immediately.

"Hello, Cappan. Ray Kostner. I got your message. What's up?"

"A couple of things. I'm glad you got my message before you left town. I looked up Greg Johnson like you asked. He doesn't have a record but he has an illustrious background."

"Yeah. What's the story?"

"It appears he's a very aggressive photographer. Once he was arrested for tailing some city councilman in New Orleans. When the story broke that the guy was on the take, your guy Greg was there with a full supply of pictures of the man's rich life-style."

"Anything else?"

"Pretty similar. Only this time it was some big-name football player. He tended to like wild parties. Greg managed to crash them and wound up with the full story in pictures."

"Sounds like a real charmer."

"He has some legitimate credits, too. Some of them very impressive. Apparently he makes pictures talk."

"So, if he expected that a story about a serial killer and his beautiful victim was about to break, he might be snapping pictures like crazy."

"That's what I was thinking, only that wouldn't explain the snapshots of Jodie in New York."

"The ones he claims he didn't take."

"But the police found them in his apartment."

The static started up again. Ray waited until it cleared. "You put some legwork into this. I owe you one."

"You don't owe me. I'd hate to see anything happen to Miss Gahagen. She's some woman, but I guess you know that."

"Yeah. I definitely do."

"Oh, and one more thing. Remember that story I told you about, the one about the psycho who stalked his victims and then killed them?"

"The one who was too smart to get caught?"

"That's the one. I kept asking around. It seems the fellow telling the story was one of the police officers from Louisiana, up here training with our community policing program."

Static rumbled like thunder over the wires. Ray gritted his teeth and swallowed a curse. "Keep talking. I'm still here."

"Well, one of our guys, a fellow named Lando, was out with a bunch of the trainees after a session. They started drinking. He said this guy told a bizarre tale about some man following women, sending them gifts and flowers. He claimed he was only trying to keep them pure. When he caught them with another man, he killed them."

"Where was this?"

"The man didn't say. According to the story, the killer was supposed to be too smart to get caught. But he must have slipped up somewhere if the cop knew about him."

"What was the name of the man who told the stories?"

"Lando doesn't remember. The only thing he knows for sure is he was with the bunch from Louisiana. They've been up here a half dozen times or more during the past few months. The training's finished now, though."

"Did Lando give you a description of him?"

"Tall, a little overweight, brown hair. Said his nose was a little crooked like it had been broken before. So if this killer was so smart he never left a clue, how do you think they caught him?"

Ray beat a fist against the steering wheel. "He made the oldest mistake in the book, Cappan. He couldn't resist telling someone what he'd gotten away with."

The phone connection faltered again, the static now overtaking the line. Ray hung up the phone. He'd heard enough. Now he just needed to get to Natchitoches. He glanced at the speedometer and cursed the snail's pace he was traveling.

He punched in Jodie's number again. This time the phone rang a dozen times but there was no answer. Apparently she hadn't gotten his message to wait on him or else ignored it. Good.

She would be much safer at a party surrounded by friends. He dialed Lydia's number. A busy signal droned in his car. He'd try it again in the next few minutes. He needed to warn Jodie that her stalker was still on the loose.

A stalker whom Jodie would trust with her life.

"THESE PECAN PRALINES all but melt in your mouth, Selda. I'd love to have the recipe."

"It's easy as making candy." She laughed at her own joke. So did everyone else within hearing distance.

Jodie leaned back on the quilt she'd spread in the yard. Blake and Blair were right beside her, in their double stroller munching on slices of banana. Lydia's school-age youngsters had served as entertainment committee, pushing them around the yard and pointing out each design in the spectacular light display.

The first weekend in December had arrived and the weather was perfect. Light sweaters were the uniform of the evening and there wasn't a cloud in the sky. Lydia's guests had feasted on home-cooked specialities, brought to the party in stuffed picnic baskets and casserole dishes.

Fried chicken, smoked hams, potato salad, baked beans, yams, fall squash and even a pot of chicken and dumplings. All washed down with pitchers of iced tea and pots of strong coffee and followed by banana pudding and chocolate cake. And of course, Selda's pecan pralines.

The leftovers would have fed another group of the same size. Home cooking and plenty of it. It was the way of the south. Even Butch had shown up a few minutes ago, leaving his duties long enough to stop by for a bite of food. Hyped as he was, he'd only eaten a bite or two. It was Natchitoches's big night. The local police surely had their hands full.

But things were quieting at Lydia's. Everyone had gathered into clusters of friends and families, waiting for the fireworks to start. The only thing missing was Ray. Jodie's heart settled like lead in her chest.

"Jodie, telephone," Lydia called from the distance, just as she started to put the boys on the quilt beside her. "You'll have to take it in the house. No telling where the cordless phone ended up with this bunch of people. I think it's been off the hook half the evening. My husband said he tried to get us for hours."

"Can you keep an eye on the boys, Grams?"

"We'll watch them, Miss Jodie," Selda's grandkids chimed in before she had a chance to answer.

"And I'll help them," Selda assured.

Jodie hurried to the phone, her traitorous heart racing. Maybe it was Ray, calling to say he missed her already, as much as she missed him. Calling to say he didn't want to live without her.

"Hello."

Her greeting was met with silence.

"Hello. Ray, is it you? Hello."

Nothing. The caller hadn't hung up. There was no dial tone. She waited, then tried again. "If someone is there, say something."

Apprehension crawled her skin. She counted to ten, forcing her breathing to steady and her pulse to slow. The stalker was in jail. She was safe. She couldn't let the past torment her this way.

Finally, she pasted a smile on her face and walked outside, down the back steps, over the grassy yard that sloped toward the river.

The first fireworks of the night took to the sky, crashing above her in fiery splendor. Reds and greens and touches of gold. She made her way through the guests, all with their heads back, their gazes glued to the sky.

Finally she saw Grams. Selda was right behind her. So were Lydia's two children.

"Where are the boys?"

Another crash, another spray of colorful stars in the sky.

"Where are the boys?" Her voice rose with the panic that twisted inside her.

"They were right here a minute ago." Selda jumped up from her quilt and ran over to Jodie.

Jodie's gaze swept the area, cold fear strangling her breath from her body, clawing at her insides, tearing through her mind in waves of horror.

The stroller was down the hill, at the edge of the river. For a second her legs were watery worthless limbs, too numb to move. Then she ran, her feet flying, her lungs burning.

She fell to the ground beside the stroller, tears stinging her eyelids. The boys sat calmly, still buckled into place. She picked up one and then the other, holding them to her chest, rocking them in her arms.

Selda and Grams stopped beside her, panting from the fastest they'd walked in years. "Is everything all right?"

"Yes, the boys are fine."

"I guess one of the kids around here gave them a ride while I was staring at the fireworks. I'm sorry, Jodie. I should have been watching closer."

"It's okay. No harm done."

The two women started back up the hill. Jodie bent down to fit Blake back into his seat. Something was stuck to the back of the stroller. She hadn't noticed it in her initial excitement over finding the boys, but it was there, shining in the glow of the fireworks that were building to a crescendo in the sky over their heads.

A note.

No. It just couldn't be. Her brain screamed the denial, but even as she lifted the note closer to her eyes, she knew the nightmare had returned. Shaking, she read the words inside the red heart.

I'll be waiting for you at the Coxlin place. Come alone.

MORE THAN AN HOUR had passed by the time Jodie maneuvered through the traffic and reached the drive that ran from the highway down to the old Coxlin place. She slowed, driving through dark shadows and whispering pines to her rendezvous with a killer.

Somewhere in the blackness that surrounded her Butch Deaton's car should already be parked. He had responded to her call to his beeper number immediately, trying to persuade her not to come here tonight and then finally agreeing to carry through on their previous plan. He had called her back on her car phone just minutes ago, assuring her the plan was in place.

The house was in front of her now, the steep pitch of the roof silhouetted against the moon, like it had been that Halloween night so long ago. Haunted, her friends had said. That night they had been wrong. Tonight they would have been right. Haunted by a madman.

She pulled the car to a stop. No sign of anyone, but that didn't mean the killer wasn't inside waiting for her to enter. Trembling, she opened the car door and stepped onto the soft earth. She forced her lungs to breathe, forced one foot in front of the other as she crossed the overgrown path that led to the house.

The bottom step creaked at her weight, and her heart slammed against her chest. He was here, like he said. The door was open, and a figure stood just inside, his large frame backlit by a flickering glow.

As she watched he stepped back into the shadows.

She gulped in a ragged breath and took the last few steps to the open door.

"Come in, Jodie. I've been waiting for you."

Chapter Sixteen

"Butch." A quick surge of relief crashed into a shudder of disappointment. "Why are you in here?"

"I came to meet you, Jodie, the way you wanted me to."

The dark tone of his voice drew gooseflesh to her skin. She looked past him. Logs in the fireplace were beginning to blaze and flickering light from a dozen candles danced along the shadowed walls and crept into the far recesses of the room.

Evil accosted her senses. Thick and tangible, dark and choking. "He's somewhere near, Butch. I can feel him." Her voice was a raspy whisper.

"Very near."

"You have to hide quickly. If he sees you he'll run like he did before."

"Not this time." He stepped closer, out of the shadows and into full candlelight.

"Come upstairs with me, Jodie." He extended a hand.

But something was wrong, dreadfully wrong. Butch's dark eyes were glazed over, his voice a hoarse slur.

"You've been drinking, Butch."

"No, Jodie. I'm perfectly sober. Completely in control." She backed toward the door.

"I asked you to come upstairs with me, Jodie."

"No. You're drunk. I'm getting out of here."

He grabbed her arm and twisted it behind her. Pain shot through her in mind-numbing stabs. She struggled to break away. His arm flew up, and the blow struck her across the side of the head.

"Don't fight me, Jodie. Just do what I say so I don't have to hurt you again. I don't like to hurt people, not even bad girls like you. I'm a gentleman."

She stared at him, her brain slowly absorbing the unflinching truth. "You, Butch. You're the stalker, the man who murdered Max."

"Does that surprise you? It shouldn't. I've always liked you, Jodie. Even in high school, you were the prettiest girl in the class. Thin and lithe, your skin smooth as silk. And you always smelled so clean and wholesome. You were a good girl then." His finger traced a shaky line from her forehead to her lips and then slid down her neck to the rise of her breasts.

"Why are you doing this?"

"You made me do it." He shoved her toward the stairs. "That's why I have a surprise waiting upstairs for you."

"Don't do this, Butch," she pleaded, her voice scratching against the dryness of her throat. "I'm a good girl. I saved myself for you, just like you said."

"No. I thought you were different, but you're like the others." His voice rose, the accusing tone of a mother scolding a child. "You were with Ray Kostner. You let him touch you. His smell is all over you, defiling you."

He shoved her again, pushing her up the rickety stair steps. She tried to think. This was not the Butch she knew. His mind had slipped into a black chasm, his body following its dictates as if in a trance. Somehow she had to get to the man beneath the veil of insanity.

"I'm your friend, Butch. I can help you."

"You were never my friend. You used me. That was all.

Even in high school you thought you were too good for me. You let me take you out, but it was Ray you let kiss you on the lips. You broke a date with me so that you could go to the prom with him.''

''That's not true, Butch. You broke the date. You'd been in a fight. Your nose had been broken. It was swollen and bruised.''

''It doesn't matter. One kiss from Ray Kostner and you dumped me. You're like the other women. I should have known it last year when I visited you in New York. You flaunted your body in front of me, a hussy in a little black dress that was made to drive men wild.''

''It was just a dinner dress, Butch. People dress up more in New York.''

''Don't beg now, Jodie. It's too late. You knew I wanted you, but you pushed me out the door. But I couldn't quit thinking about you. I wanted you so badly. That's why I looked you up again. All alone with your babies. I wanted to save you. You wouldn't heed my warnings.''

''No.'' Her voice wavered. She bit her lip hard, determined not to give in to tears or weakness. But how could she reason with a madman?

One by one, he forced her up the stairs, his mouth at her ear. ''You only want a man for one thing. You and the others. All beautiful, all bad. That's why you have to die the same way they did.''

''What others?''

''The other women like you. Flaunting themselves like cheap whores. But they didn't want a decent man. They pushed me away just like you did. So I watched them and waited, until the time was right.''

''And did you send them gifts, too, and write them notes?''

''A few, not as many as I did you. You were special. I gave you chance after chance, but you kept going to Ray instead of me. I tried to stop you. I told you that you were making a mistake. You wouldn't listen.''

They reached the top of the steps. He took her arm and pulled her down the narrow hallway.

''Where are you taking me?''

''You'll see.'' He stopped at a half-open door that hung precariously from broken hinges. ''Close your eyes, Jodie. That way you can enjoy the surprise.''

His rough hand swept over her face, covering her eyes for her when she didn't do it on her own. A final shove and she was inside. He dropped his hand, brushing it across the front of her body.

''All for you, Jodie.''

She gasped and stumbled backward. The room was filled with red roses, their fragrance gaggingly sweet. Nausea welled up inside her.

''For your funeral.''

Her funeral. The thought melted the shock that was destroying her will. Her gaze spanned the room, searching for anything that might serve as a weapon. Reason was out of the question. She had to fight for her life.

And she damn well would. Blake and Blair depended on her. She would not let a madman take her away from them. She would not let a murderer win.

''If you kill me, you will go to jail. Ray will not rest until you do.''

''But Ray won't know I killed you. You made it so easy for me, Jodie. The personal ad, the place, the timing.''

She stiffened. A minute ago, she'd almost felt sorry for Butch, felt as if some demon had taken over his body. But he knew exactly what he was doing, had orchestrated this whole encounter with the skill of an artist.

Butch was not possessed. The evil was all his own. She knew now he was capable of anything.

"Why did you kill Gloria Bigger? You did kill her, didn't you?"

"So you finally figured that out. I killed her because I had to. She saw me that night when I went to the florist shop. I made a mistake. A bad mistake. I should never have used Max Roling's credit card in Natchitoches. But I did it without thinking. The training in New York was over, and I was so desperate to contact you, to let you know I was on my way back to you."

"So you went to the florist shop that night to steal her copy of the ticket. But all it took was one phone call from Ray to find who had sent the flowers."

"I didn't count on Ray. I thought you would call the police. I would have handled everything myself. That's why I didn't send you anything in Natchitoches until I was on my way back from the final training session. I had to be sure no one else was assigned to your case."

"You planned everything so well." She took a step closer to a glass container of roses. A second is all it would take to lift it over her head and bring it smashing down on his. But she'd have to find a way to divert his attention elsewhere. She needed to keep him talking while she thought of a foolproof plan.

"You even attacked Parker Kostner without getting caught."

"I didn't mean to hurt *him*. It was his son I meant to kill."

"Then why did you hurt him?"

"It happened so fast. I was waiting in the dark. When the door opened, I swung the chair. I didn't kill him. He didn't deserve to die."

"You didn't kill him because you heard Ray coming. And you had lost the knife."

"You're wrong. I didn't even realize I had dropped the

knife until after I'd left the building. I never kill without reason.''

"You are a very smart gentleman," she said, inching still closer to the heavy crystal container.

"Very, very smart. That's why no one will ever catch me. I walk into hospitals, apartment buildings, even business offices without anyone objecting. Just a policeman doing his duty. No use to kick doors down like they do in the movies. We have tools that open doors faster than you can with a key."

"So that's how you got inside my New York apartment?"

"Of course. Your neighbors saw me and smiled. So nice to have a policeman checking on you and keeping you safe from your stalker."

He laughed, low and mocking, and the sound echoed through the cold room, chilling her to the bone. "Even your grandmother was cooperative, inviting me in for tea and leaving me alone to pay visits to your bedroom. The bedroom where you entertained Ray Kostner."

"Greg Johnson didn't take the pictures of me, did he, Butch? You took the pictures."

"He took the ones that were on his bed. The others were mine. I watched you from an empty apartment just across from yours. Watched you through a lens that magnified every curve of your body. Watched you rub lotion into your skin, smooth, sensuous strokes up and down your legs, between your thighs. You did it to torment me."

"No." She eased backward, slowly. "You know I'm a good girl, Butch. And it's late. I need to go home now and check on my sons. You need to go home, too. You're a *policeman.*"

She stressed the word, praying to get through to the man who had sworn to protect.

"Policemen protect the world from women like you. I'm

doing my job." He grabbed her arm and pulled her toward him.

"Policemen don't kill."

"Of course, they do. They kill the people who deserve it. That's why we have guns. But we've talked enough, Jodie. Now I have my last gift for you."

One arm wrapped around her, his fingers digging into her shoulder. With the other hand he reached into his pocket and fished out a plastic bag. His gaze remained fastened on her as he slipped a syringe from the wrinkled plastic. "Just a shot, Jodie, quick and simple. Your heart will speed up, faster and faster until it bursts from the pressure. Then it will all be over."

"You won't get away with this."

"Ah, but I will. I always do. Time and time again. The autopsy will show a heart attack. You came here and found this roomful of flowers and it frightened you so badly you went into cardiac arrest.

"Some people will even wonder if you put the flowers here yourself. You thought someone was stalking you, and you let it drive you crazy."

Jodie trembled. Her last chances were slipping away. A few more moments and the needle in his hand would be plunged into her flesh. If she was going to die anyway, she would go down fighting.

In one jerking movement, she lowered her head and buried her teeth into the hand that dug into her shoulder. Butch yelped in pain, but his grip tightened. She struggled, heaving her body toward the vase.

She never reached it. Instead his hand wrapped around her throat. She gasped, fighting for air as life ebbed away. Finally, she collapsed against him. Only then did he release his hand on her throat and push her onto the floor.

A noise rumbled in her head, like a door slamming shut.

Butch stiffened. Balancing the needle on his leg, he reached into the holster at his side and hoisted his revolver.

"Jodie!" The voice boomed through the house.

Ray. But it couldn't be. He was in New Orleans, running away from her, from his sons.

He called her name again, and then she heard his footsteps on the stairs. The gun in Butch's hand was pointed toward the door.

She forced air into her burning lungs and screamed. "He has a gun! Don't come up here!"

She felt Butch's hand before she saw it, slamming her against the wall. And then she felt the needle, piercing the skin, stinging. She fought to push it away. Strength surged inside her, an explosion in her chest.

She jerked her knee, hard, landing a blow into Butch's crotch just as a fireplace log came flying through the open door. Butch fell backward, firing the gun as he did. Bullets sprayed the room, ricocheting like marbles.

But she was free. With one hand she jerked the needle from her arm, hurling it towards Butch as he reloaded. It missed its mark, crashing against the wall. The glass splintered and the remaining drug seeped onto the floor.

Her chest was caving in from pressure now, but she forced her body to move. Grabbing the vase, she lifted it high above her head and brought it down with killing force.

Water and shards of broken glass sprayed the room as Butch sank to the floor. She fell on top of him, pounding her fists into his chest.

"How could you kill Max? How could you kill Gloria? How could you? How could you?"

Tears fell like rain from her eyes, and her heart beat so fast she thought it would burst from her chest, but she couldn't stop.

Her heart was still racing when Ray gathered her in his arms and held her close. It was still racing when he rocked her to him, his voice so shaky that for a minute she thought one of the bullets had found its target.

It was still racing when he wiped the tears from her eyes and placed a long, warm kiss on her lips.

It was then that she noticed they were not alone. Two policemen stood in the door, guns drawn, staring at them.

"Did you shoot him?"

"No, I didn't have to," Ray answered. "Jodie knocked him out cold."

"Looks like your suspicions were right," the other officer said, his gaze taking in the sight of vases of roses and half-burned candles.

"Looks like it." Ray led Jodie past the body and the officer who was leaning over it. "Now, it's in your hands. I'm getting the bravest little mother in the parish out of here."

JODIE SAT on the back porch, leafing through the information from the advertising firm where she had worked in New York. One of her clients had a debut product he wanted to introduce to the world of consumers. He'd liked her work in the past and he'd asked for her specifically this time, even if it meant conducting business via electronic means.

It was the perfect opportunity. She could be here with Grams and work her schedule around Blake and Blair. Surround herself with their love while she worked through a heartache that might never heal.

Ray had walked out of her life, the same way he had done before. Completely. No thanks for the memories. Not even a proper farewell between him and his sons.

He'd stayed with her all night after the fateful meeting that led to Butch's arrest. He'd taken her to the hospital and then held her while the epinephrine Butch had injected into her veins ran its course. Cradled her body against his while her heart rate had slowed to normal.

The next afternoon, he'd left for New Orleans to take care of an emergency he said he had to deal with personally. He'd promised to call.

That had been seven long nights ago.

At first she'd taken him at his word, the same way she'd done when he walked out of her apartment two years ago in New York City.

Once again she'd jumped at every ring of the phone, run to the window whenever a car stopped outside, waited up every night for some word. Only this time she didn't phone him. He knew what she wanted. He knew she loved him. It was his call.

If he chose to have no part of her and their sons, she'd swallow the pain, cry her tears in the loneliness of night, heal the jagged edges of her broken heart with love for her boys.

She'd be mother and father to them, surround them with so much love they'd never miss having a father. And she wouldn't miss him, either.

A tear stung at the back of her eye. She fought but couldn't stop it from escaping to roll down her cheek. One day she wouldn't miss Ray Kostner. Maybe, if she lived long enough, but who lived to be a thousand?

Grams opened the back door and joined her on the back porch. Selda followed a step behind, a plate of cookies warm from the oven in hand.

"I hope we're not interrupting anything," Selda said.

"Not a thing."

"Good. Greg filled me in on some details, especially the ones concerning how Butch tried to frame him. I thought he'd leave town as soon as he got out of jail, but he's still here and he's still snapping pictures. Now I'd like to hear the rest of the story, if you feel like talking about it. Like how Ray Kostner ended up at the Coxlin place at just the right time."

"Apparently he changed his mind about flying to New Orleans that day," Jodie said, retelling the story she'd already shared several times with Grams. "He talked to the detective from the NYPD while he was driving back to Natchitoches for the Festival of Lights. That's when he got the idea that Butch was my stalker. Another call, this one to the local chief of police convinced him his hunch was right. Butch was one of the officers who had been in New York this summer for some special training."

"Then Ray Kostner went right straight to Butch's house," Grams added. "He lives on an acre or so just north of Highway 6, so he could get there even with the parades going on and traffic blocked all over town."

"But obviously Butch wasn't there. I saw him at Lydia's not long before that," Selda said.

"No, but Ray took a page from Butch's handbook," Jodie said. "He let himself in. There were a number of prescription drugs in the house, enough to ride an emotional roller-coaster wave for days. Evidently, Butch kept his problems a secret around Natchitoches. He saw doctors in Shreveport, Alexandria and even Longview, Texas to get the drugs that either kept him sane or drove him crazy. The jury is still out on that."

"I didn't know it was that easy to get drugs."

"I don't think it is, Selda, at least not around here where people know him. But he had found ways. Apparently he's had psychological problems ever since high school. They escalated when his mother died and again when his wife ran off with another man. That was the year he killed the first woman."

"And he confessed all of this?"

"No. Most of it the local police have discovered since

his arrest. He has admitted to killing six people in all, though.''

"Most of them with medicine from the insect bite kits Ray found in his house," Grams added, her memory doing an amazing job of remembering the details.

"I'm still not sure how the insect bite kits fit in with all of this." Selda passed the plate of cookies around and took one herself, biting into it and wiping away the crumbs that fell into her lap.

"The kits contain small amounts of epinephrine. That's the medical term for adrenaline in drug form. Butch took the medication from several kits, until he had enough in the syringe to cause a heart attack."

"You are lucky to be alive."

"I am. I wouldn't be if Ray hadn't shown up when he did."

"Ray?" Grams scratched her head. "Did I tell you he called yesterday while you and the boys were at the park?"

Her heart did a flip-flop. "No. What did he say?"

"That he'd be picking you up this afternoon at three. Said he had something to show you."

"Probably a ring," Selda mused. "That boy's so sweet on you, he lights up like one of those Christmas light displays every time you walk into the room."

Warmth spread through Jodie like wildfire. Ray had called. He was coming back to her. She glanced at her watch. Five before three. She ran trembling fingers through her hair, a useless attempt to tame it.

Punctual for the first time Jodie could remember, he rounded the corner of the porch at precisely three o'clock, as always opting for the back door. He hugged Grams and Selda and stopped beside her. She was already on her feet, but he pulled her into his arms, holding her extra tight and kissing her full on the mouth. Not overly passionate, not in front of company, but enough to know that she sure had been kissed.

"Did you miss me?" he asked, his lips curled in a devastating smile.

"Have you been gone?"

He faked a wince of pain and turned to Grams and Selda. "May I steal my woman away? I promise to have her back in an hour."

My woman. The words danced inside her. "I can't leave now. The boys are asleep."

"We'll watch them," Selda said, winking at Ray. "Even if you're gone more than an hour."

Ray led her to the Porsche, opening the door for her, bending to kiss her again.

"Where are we going?"

"It's a surprise."

"I don't like surprises."

"You'll like this one. At least I hope you do."

He drove a few blocks east and then cut back toward the river, turning down a street shaded by towering oaks. It was an older section of town, with big houses, neatly groomed with wraparound porches and charming gables.

He pulled up and parked in the winding drive of one that sported a new coat of paint.

"Who lives here?" Jodie asked, lowering the car window.

"That's what I want to talk to you about. I'm not good at this, Jodie. I've never done it before. But I think beneath that magnolia tree would be a good spot."

He climbed from under the steering wheel and darted around the car and to her door. Hand in hand he led her to a spongy carpet of damp leaves.

"Jodie Gahagen." His voice was husky with emotion. "I love you. I want to spend the rest of my live with you and with our sons."

Tears filled her eyes.

"You don't have to answer this second."

"Yes."

"I know my track record isn't too good."

"Yes, Ray."

"But I'll work on improving it."

She put her finger over his lips. "I said, yes, Ray. I'll marry you."

He swept her into his arms, twirling her around and around until they were both drunk with movement and love. Leaning against the tree for support, he fished in his pocket. "It's here somewhere." A second later he came up with a jewelry box. He lifted the lid and pulled out a ring, a band of gold with one twinkling diamond in the center. Holding her hand, he slipped the ring on her finger.

"It's beautiful."

"Is that why you're crying?"

"I'm not crying."

He took a handkerchief from his pocket and dabbed at the tears running down her cheeks. "One more thing," he said, swinging his hand in the direction of the house. "What do you think?"

"About what?"

"The house. It has a perfect tree in the backyard for hanging swings, and there's lots of room for sandboxes and playing catch. I could put a basketball goal over the garage. When the boys are older, I mean."

Jodie put a hand to her temples to stop the whirling in her brain. "You're going too fast."

"I know. You said all or nothing. I want it all. I've already put a down payment on the house, but I can get out of it if you don't like it."

"But your job is in New Orleans."

"Not anymore. I gave notice today. I'm going into practice with my dad. Maybe not forever, but for now. I'd like to get to know him while I still can. I'd like our sons to know their grandparents and their Grams.''

''You don't have to do this, Ray. I love you. I'd live with you in New Orleans. As long as we love each other, any place we live will be home.''

''I know. And I may want to move back to New Orleans some day, but, for now, I'd like to be here in Natchitoches. I want to have time to spend watching my sons grow. Maybe a daughter or two as well. I want to be a real husband and father. I wouldn't be able to do that in the demanding position I just left.''

''I love you,'' she said, her voice catching on the words that sprang from her heart.

He leaned close, touching his lips to hers. He kissed her long and hard, their breaths mingling, the passion inside her bubbling like champagne.

''Now, would you like to look at the house?''

''Yes.'' She left him behind, running up the walk.

''Wait, I have to carry you over the threshold.''

He did, kissing her again in the process.

''I already love it,'' she said. ''Where's the bedroom?''

''Since when did you ever need a bedroom?''

She stuck out her tongue and took off at a run, taking the steps two at a time. He caught up with her at the top of the landing, wrapping his arms around her.

They dissolved in a flurry of laughter and a wellspring of love. It was a long time later before they continued the tour and finally made it to the bedroom of a house they'd already christened with their love.

Head Down Under for twelve tales of heated romance in beautiful and untamed Australia!

Here's a sneak preview of the first novel in THE AUSTRALIANS

Outback Heat **by Emma Darcy available July 1998**

'HAVE I DONE something wrong?' Angie persisted, wishing Taylor would emit a sense of camaraderie instead of holding an impenetrable reserve.

'Not at all,' he assured her. 'I would say a lot of things right. You seem to be fitting into our little Outback community very well. I've heard only good things about you.'

'They're nice people,' she said sincerely. Only the Maguire family kept her shut out of their hearts.

'Yes,' he agreed. 'Though I appreciate it's taken considerable effort from you. It is a world away from what you're used to.'

The control Angie had been exerting over her feelings snapped. He wasn't as blatant as his aunt in his prejudice against her but she'd felt it coming through every word he'd spoken and she didn't deserve any of it.

'Don't judge me by your wife!'

His jaw jerked. A flicker of some dark emotion destroyed the steady power of his probing gaze.

'No two people are the same. If you don't know that, you're a man of very limited vision. So I come from the city as your wife did! That doesn't stop me from being an individual in my own right.'

She straightened up, proudly defiant, furiously angry with the situation. 'I'm *me*. Angie Cordell. And it's time you took the blinkers off your eyes, Taylor Maguire.'

Then she whirled away from him, too agitated by the explosive expulsion of her emotion to keep facing him.

The storm outside hadn't yet eased. There was nowhere to go. She stopped at the window, staring blindly at the torrential rain. The thundering on the roof was almost deafening but it wasn't as loud as the silence behind her.

'You want me to go, don't you? You've given me a month's respite and now you want me to leave and channel my energies somewhere else.'

'I didn't say that, Angie.'

'You were working your way around it.' Bitterness at his tactics spewed the suspicion. 'Do you have your first choice of governess waiting in the wings?'

'No. I said I'd give you a chance.'

'Have you?' She swung around to face him. 'Have you really, Taylor?'

He hadn't moved. He didn't move now except to make a gesture of appeasement. 'Angie, I was merely trying to ascertain how you felt.'

'Then let me tell you your cynicism was shining through every word.'

He frowned, shook his head. 'I didn't mean to hurt you.' The blue eyes fastened on hers with devastating sincerity. 'I truly did not come in here to take you down or suggest you leave.'

Her heart jiggled painfully. He might be speaking the truth but the judgements were still there, the judgements that ruled his attitude towards her, that kept her shut out of his life, denied any real sharing with him, denied his confidence and trust. She didn't know why it meant so much to her but it did. It did. And the need to fight for justice from him was as much a raging torrent inside her as the rain outside.

MEN at WORK

All work and no play? Not these men!

April 1998

KNIGHT SPARKS by Mary Lynn Baxter

Sexy lawman Rance Knight made a career of arresting the bad guys. Somehow, though, he thought policewoman Carly Mitchum was framed. Once they'd uncovered the truth, could Rance let Carly go...or would he make a citizen's arrest?

May 1998

HOODWINKED by Diana Palmer

CEO Jake Edwards donned coveralls and went undercover as a mechanic to find the saboteur in his company. Nothing— or no one—would distract him, not even beautiful secretary Maureen Harris. Jake had to catch the thief—*and* the woman who'd stolen his heart!

June 1998

DEFYING GRAVITY by Rachel Lee

Tim O'Shaughnessy and his business partner, Liz Pennington, had always been close—but never *this* close. As the danger of their assignment escalated, so did their passion. When the job was over, could they ever go back to business as usual?

MEN AT WORK™

Available at your favorite retail outlet!

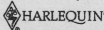 

Look us up on-line at: http://www.romance.net

PMAW1

Take 2 bestselling love stories FREE

Plus get a FREE surprise gift!

Heat up your summer this July with

Summer Lovers

This July, bestselling authors Barbara Delinsky,
Elizabeth Lowell and Anne Stuart present three
couples with pasts that threaten their future happiness.
Can they play with fire without being burned?

FIRST, BEST AND ONLY
by Barbara Delinsky

GRANITE MAN
by Elizabeth Lowell

CHAIN OF LOVE
by Anne Stuart

Available wherever Harlequin and Silhouette books
are sold.

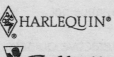

HARLEQUIN®

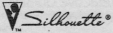

Silhouette®

DEBBIE MACOMBER

invites you to the

★ ★ ★ HEART OF TEXAS ★ ★ ★

Join Debbie Macomber as she brings you the lives and loves of the folks in the ranching community of Promise, Texas.

If you loved Midnight Sons—don't miss Heart of Texas! A brand-new six-book series from Debbie Macomber.

Available in February 1998 at your favorite retail store.

Heart of Texas by Debbie Macomber

Lonesome Cowboy	February '98
Texas Two-Step	March '98
Caroline's Child	April '98
Dr. Texas	May '98
Nell's Cowboy	June '98
Lone Star Baby	July '98

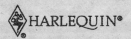

HARLEQUIN®